I was escorted back to the front of the house by Captain Verlak, Doom striding off down that never-ending hallway toward – well, it wasn't for me to think about. Just as my foot hit the top step, she called out to me.

"Silvija Sablinova."

I turned to look at her. "What is it?"

"You're not one of us, so this might not mean very much to you," she said, and there was an intensity in her voice that was almost as powerful as Doom's. "But you should understand that you've been given a very special opportunity, one that Doctor Doom offers to very few people. Getting the chance to serve him was the most challenging thing I ever decided to do, and it proved the mettle of my character to me."

I shook my head. "I'm not serving him. This is a job, just like any other."

"Not like any other," she replied. "Not even close. And I think you know that, Silvija. Just… tread carefully, and whatever you do? Don't fail him."

MORE MARVEL HEROINES

Elsa Bloodstone: Bequest by Cath Lauria
Black Cat: Discord by Cath Lauria

Rogue: Untouched by Alisa Kwitney

Domino: Strays by Tristan Palmgren
Outlaw: Relentless by Tristan Palmgren
Squirrel Girl: Universe by Tristan Palmgren

MARVEL HEROINES

SILVER SABLE
PAYBACK

CATH LAURIA

ACONYTE

FOR MARVEL PUBLISHING

VP Production & Special Projects: Jeff Youngquist
Associate Editor, Special Projects: Sarah Singer
Manager, Licensed Publishing: Jeremy West
VP, Licensed Publishing: Sven Larsen
SVP Print, Sales & Marketing: David Gabriel
Editor in Chief: C B Cebulski

MARVEL

© 2023 MARVEL

First published by Aconyte Books in 2023

ISBN 978 1 83908 219 1

Ebook ISBN 978 1 83908 220 7

Cover art by Bastien Jez

Distributed in North America by Simon & Schuster Inc, New York, USA
Printed in the United States of America
9 8 7 6 5 4 3 2 1

ACONYTE BOOKS

An imprint of Asmodee Entertainment Ltd

Mercury House, Shipstones Business Centre

North Gate, Nottingham NG7 7FN, UK

aconytebooks.com // twitter.com/aconytebooks

There are Silver Sable fans out there who've been eager for new content and who welcomed me into their fold as soon as they knew her book was coming. I hope this one makes you as happy as it does me!

CHAPTER ONE

What do you think of when you hear the name "Silver Sable"?

Do you picture the mercenary? The freedom fighter? The woman who's made some regrettable decisions when it comes to her personal life?

All of these impressions are valid. So all-encompassing that sometimes, I can't see beyond them myself.

Tonight, though, I *needed* to see past them. I needed to go all the way back, to ground myself with the very earliest tendrils of my memory, because given the meeting I was about to walk into, I couldn't afford not to be ready for anything that might be brought up.

When you've been invited to a talk with Victor von Doom, it always pays to be prepared. Even when your preparations hurt.

It's difficult for me to remember my own past. Not *all* of it, of course – as a mercenary, I need to be able to put names to faces fast, memorize and retain the layouts of buildings and cities, anything that makes taking down my target easier. Every job I take leaves an impression, whether it's hunting down Nazis, fomenting revolution against tyrants, or underwater battles with benthic beasts.

But the early years, those are so much harder. To recall the person I so briefly was, the child who didn't even know what to fear beyond spiders and dark places and unquiet dreams… it's almost impossible to get a clear mental image of what I experienced so long ago. However, to properly move forward sometimes requires a hard look back, and so… let me see, how do these stories start?

Ah, yes. Once upon a time.

Once upon a time, there was a little girl named Silvija who lived with her parents in a small but beautiful home in the country of Symkaria. They loved her very much, and she was so happy with them. Her parents hoped their daughter would grow up in a peaceful land, with the freedom to live any sort of life she chose for herself.

Then one day, her mother was murdered in front of her. Her father's enemies gloated in the light of the terrible fire that consumed Anastasia Sablinova, and little Silvija screamed and begged and wept for the impossible – for her mother to be returned to her. It couldn't happen, of course. Not even her father's vengeance could turn back time and heal that first deep, terrible wound.

Silvija's hair went from gold to silver, and after that day, she never cried again. Not from pain, not from heartbreak, not even from joy. She learned to fight from her father, pushed herself to train until she couldn't be broken, hardened her heart and gathered allies and set herself one great, overarching goal: to serve her home nation of Symkaria to the best of her ability, for as long as she was able to. After all, families could be taken away but nations, those were permanent… weren't they?

Silvija learned the hard way just how wrong she was. Wars could be fought, leaders could be overthrown, nations and their people could be conquered. The fate of Symkaria seemed to be one of subjugation, over and over again, by a string of dictators with more will than wisdom, more cruelty than compassion. And so Silvija Sablinova became Silver Sable, and she fought the same battle, over and over, and each time it destroyed her a bit more, until she became the woman she was now.

A woman willing to consider another path. A woman *desperate* for a different choice. A woman capable of putting even the depredations of Doom into the dark places in her memory, so that she could try to make a brighter future for her country. A country that was currently under the rule of none other than Victor von Doom himself.

All of which leads me to tonight, with me standing in the boarded-up remains of the old Symkarian embassy in New York City and staring at myself in a full-length mirror in what used to be the Symkarian ambassador's bedroom as I prepare for dinner with Doctor Doom.

"Oh no," Juliet said abruptly as she reentered the room, her head shaking a negative as she looked at me. "No, you're not going to dinner with one of the most powerful men on the planet wearing a pantsuit that makes you look like you just stepped out of the eighties. *Shoulder pads*, Silver, really?"

I frowned at her. "The saleswoman said they were making a comeback."

"She was a lying liar who lies," my coworker – and fashion consultant, apparently – said flatly. "They're not making a comeback – at least not that *wide* of a comeback. What are you, a linebacker?"

"A what?"

Juliet waved her hand dismissively. "It's an American football term, don't worry about it. Truly, though, Silver... no. Tell me you brought something else to wear."

I reached into my bag at the foot of the bed and pulled out an outfit that I would be far more at ease in. "How about this?"

"Your body armor?" Juliet brushed a shock of short purple hair out of her face and crossed her arms as she considered it. "I mean, it's very 'you.' I guess it wouldn't be out of character, but... is that the tone you're going for?"

Tone? My armor was flexible, comfortable, and effective. Did all of that constitute a "tone"? "What do you mean?"

"I mean, you're going to dinner, not heading into a fight. Wearing armor might send the wrong message."

Ah. I hadn't considered it from that angle. While nothing would make me feel better than punching Doom in the face before sticking one of my throwing knives up his nose, that would be taking things in the wrong direction.

"Besides, that's the set that's still all messed up from the shark bite," Juliet added, pointing at the mended section on the left thigh of the suit. My own thigh twitched with reluctant muscle memory at the reminder of that little incident. "Wearing half-assed armor would be even worse than a pristine set."

"I don't have anything better," I confessed. "The pantsuit

was the only thing I bought when I went shopping earlier today." I had some lounging clothes, a few pairs of jeans and shirts to help me blend in if I was out walking around the city, but those wouldn't work for this.

"Not a problem." Juliet checked the phone on her wrist. "When's the dinner? Maybe we have time to sneak in a quick trip to a department store."

"In half an hour."

"Oh." She looked at the pantsuit and sighed heavily. "Well, if we rip the shoulder pads out and pair it with a really nice blouse, maybe there's still hope."

I didn't have a really nice blouse with me. I had three fitted T-shirts and a men's gray Henley, a leftover from one of those "regrettable life decisions" that I'd kept because it was so darn comfortable. "Um…"

"Silver." Juliet shook her head. "Tell me you have another shirt to wear under that jacket. The one you're in is so wrinkled!"

It was, wasn't it? "I just bought this thing," I muttered, pulling at the base of the shirt irritably. It was pink. *Pink*. Pink was not my color – it showed blood abominably, for starters – but the color was the least of my worries right now.

"Didn't they fold it before they put it in the bag?"

I frowned. "Why bother?" Buy, shove, leave. That was the most efficient way to shop.

"*Silver!* This is linen, you can't treat linen like that!" Juliet looked at me like I was a particularly slow puppy who still hadn't learned not to scratch at the door. "Shoot, OK. We need to iron it, at least. Let me check around to see where they keep it…" She began opening doors – there were a surprising number of them, for a single room. A *large* room, but a single one. I tugged in frustration at the shirt again, smoothing all the wrinkles out – then watching them reappear.

Like magic. Ha.

I didn't like magic, not of any kind. I was going to have to keep that sentiment to myself tonight, though. Victor von Doom was one of the greatest sorcerers the world had ever known, a man who kept his home country of Latveria safe – and subdued – as much with spellcraft as with more typical armaments. Guns I could deal with, robots I could handle – heck, until recently I'd been using an android avatar myself to do my work, to help conceal the fact that I was still alive. But magic?

No, thank you.

"Um... Silver?"

I glanced over at Juliet, who was standing in front of the opened closet, her eyebrows so high they were nearly touching her hairline. That was uncommon enough as to be alarming. I immediately went into professional mode.

"Is it a bomb? What sort, can you tell? Can you see a trigger mechanism? Let me–"

"It's... not a bomb," she interjected, her voice still a little stunned but her surprise diminishing. "Just, um. Well. Look."

I joined her in front of the closet, which was – oh.

Oh.

"That's a lot of dresses," Juliet said carefully. "I thought the last ambassador of Symkaria to the States was a man."

"He was," I confirmed. "And he was unmarried, but he did love to, ah... be *generous* to his guests, from what I hear."

He had abandoned the embassy in a very big hurry after the scandal had come out about him facilitating illegal weapons dealing on embassy grounds. That had been years ago, but these dresses still looked nice. Fashionable. Expensive. A little dusty, but you couldn't have everything.

"Pick one," I said, pulling my jacket off and throwing it onto the bed. "I've got five minutes before I have to leave."

"You don't just throw clothes around like that," Juliet muttered, pawing through the dresses even as she shot me an exasperated look. "This is why your shirt is a mess."

"*You* wear nothing but tank tops and yoga pants."

"That doesn't mean I don't know how to treat nice clothes!"

"I thought you hated that jacket anyway."

"You–" She rolled her eyes, pulled a sparkly pouf of silvery fabric out of the closet, and threw it at me. "Put that on."

"Yes, ma'am." I ignored her sotto voce diatribe about how I didn't appreciate her and pulled the dress free from the hanger, then stepped into it. It was… oh, huh, surprisingly comfortable. Snug but not too tight around my chest, didn't have a terribly deep neckline, left my shoulders free for ease of movement, and the bottom half might cling to my hips a bit more than I liked, but then it opened up into a… what were the things called… fish style? Yes, fish style.

"Mermaid cut for the win," Juliet said, moving in to zip up the final inches of the back. "This looks good. Like you want to look nice, but you're not trying too hard." She sniffed and winced. "Smells a little like mothballs, but we don't have time to screw around with it. Get your shoes on."

"I already have them on."

Juliet sighed. "No, I mean your high heels."

"Yes… I have those on," I said slowly, like *she* was the cute but dim puppy now. "You saw them just a moment ago, on my feet."

"Oh. Huh." She looked down at the hem of the dress, which trailed a good two inches of fabric onto the floor. "Dang, you're short."

I smacked her on the shoulder. "Shut up, I'm the perfect height."

"For climbing through tunnels and crawling between walls and fitting into other tight spaces, yeah. Not for this dress. And I didn't bring any heels with me." She turned slightly. "Maybe X-Ray has some—"

"Her feet are twice as big as mine!" I protested. "And she's no more likely to wear high heels than you or I. No. I'll just have to… um."

Juliet snapped her fingers suddenly. "I've got it! Hang on, let me grab something out of the ops center, don't move!" She ran out of the room, leaving me standing there in a dress that would try to trip me the second I took my eyes off my feet, with my silver hair tied up in a simple bun at the back of my head, without jewelry, without makeup, and without anything that made me feel like *me*.

I glanced at the bed. Well, *that*, at least, I could take care of.

Twenty minutes later I stood in front of Doctor Doom's Manhattan brownstone with the hem of my dress only a bit uneven, thanks to Juliet's hasty stapling job, and my katana strapped across my back. I had my derringer at my hip as well, but I'd left the chais back at the embassy. There was such a thing as over-armed, after all.

I took a deep breath, steeling myself for what was about

to come. *No way out but through. He can't say yes unless you give him the chance.* Slightly fortified, I reached out to ring the bell.

The door began to open just before my hand touched the button.

CHAPTER TWO

Even if I hadn't known ahead of time that this unexpectedly modest – for New York City, at least – home belonged to Doctor Doom, I would have been suspicious that it was more than it appeared. There were a plethora of security cameras on it, as well as numerous cameras on *other* homes and across the street that were directed here, rather than at their own front porches. The bay window facing the street looked normal, but I knew deceptive architecture when I saw it. Whatever that "glass" was made of, it was heavy enough to warrant extra support beneath it. And if I looked carefully, I could just make out the hair-thin crack in the porch that ran lengthwise beneath the kitschy welcome mat beneath my feet.

If I so much as looked at this door the wrong way, I had no doubt that the ground would open up beneath me and send me down into some dark, inescapable laboratory in the depths of Doom's home. Or maybe it would just deposit me straight into the sewers. Either way, I didn't care to test it.

The biggest clue that this home belonged to Doom was the woman who opened the door. She loomed over me, and not simply because she had six inches on me. Looming was probably part of the job description for the head of Doctor Doom's personal guard, and Kariana Verlak was as expert at that as she was at everything.

I had never met her before, but I knew her by reputation. A Latverian patriot and a true believer in Victor von Doom and all that he stood for, if Captain Verlak got the slightest inkling that I meant her boss any harm, he wouldn't need to use his magic to incinerate me or throw me to a Doom bot. She would shoot me through the eyes without blinking.

Or, well, she would try.

I kept my hands away from my weapons and tried for a nonchalant expression. The last thing I needed was to get into a staring match with this patrician-looking woman right now. I was a guest here, and a supplicant; as much as I hated it, I needed to act like it. "Captain Verlak."

"Ms Sablinova." She looked me over, then smirked. "Nice dress."

"Thank you." *You jerk.* Captain Verlak was wearing a set of fitted black fatigues with Latverian-green accents on the shoulders and lapels. She looked disgustingly comfortable in them, too. I counted up to three weapons on her, then stopped. *No sizing her up. You're not here to pick a fight.*

"Please come in." She stepped aside, and I felt a brief wash of relief as I stepped off the unreliable front step.

My relief vanished as a matrix of red laser light suddenly appeared over my body. I couldn't help it – I pulled my katana, holding the blade out in front of me as I searched for the origin of the light.

"*Scan complete,*" a pleasant robotic voice said in Latverian. "*Visible armaments only. Threat assessment level – two.*"

Oh. This was just the next layer of Doom's personal security. I felt slightly embarrassed as I slid my sword back into the sheath.

"Feeling a bit jumpy?" Captain Verlak asked. There was absolutely no effort to hide her smug smile this time around.

I forced a return smile. "Perhaps. After all, you never know what lurks in the shadows behind a laser targeting system, do you?"

"This is the house of Doom. You doubt his ability to rule within it?"

"Only in New York City," I replied without thinking.

Captain Verlak narrowed her eyes as her smile became a scowl. "What exactly do you mean by *that*?"

Fabulous. All I had to do was rule my own tongue for one night, and I had already let it run a bit too free. There was no getting around it now, though. Best to be honest. "Well, this city is home to the one group of superhumans who consistently overcome Doctor Doom's schemes. If there were any place where he was at a disadvantage, it would be here."

The captain's expression darkened further. "You have the audacity to stand here and criticize Victor von Doom in his own home? You–"

"Now, now, captain." The voice was deep, sepulchral almost, and sent a shiver of completely warranted terror down my spine. I fought to conceal it – I had met with Doom before enough times that I was fairly certain of my reception. If he wanted to kill me, he wouldn't go to the trouble of inviting me here. He'd wait for a convenient moment when I was nearby and simply do it. *Perhaps he'd just grab me out of the air and break my neck, like he did with—*

No. I couldn't think about that right now. I *couldn't*, not if I was going to keep my head. Unburying every wrong Doom had ever done me would get us nowhere right now, and I had places to be.

"There is freedom to be found in the truth," he went on. "I would no more deny my defeats than I would ignore my successes." Doom stepped forward into the light of the crystal chandelier that hung fifteen feet above our heads. "There are very few people who would ever say as much to my face, though."

I didn't know I *had* said it to his face, but I should have figured as much. I was in his territory, and Doom was nothing if not thorough when it came to protecting what was his. "My apologies." I inclined my head to him. "I meant no disrespect." It was true, and not just because every inch of him was intimidating.

Victor von Doom was tall and broad-shouldered, that breadth only emphasized by the dark green cloak he wore over his armor. His face, hidden as it was behind his iron mask, shouldn't be as affecting as it was, and yet I didn't even need to make eye contact with him to feel pinned as he focused his attention on me. The will of Doom was a palpable thing, something those of us who were Latveria's neighbors knew well.

His enemies knew that very well, too.

"I know," he said, picking up the conversation that I'd

nearly forgotten about already, weighed down as I was by his regard. I straightened my back and focused my gaze on his chin. *Better.* "And that is why you are still invited to dinner and not battling alligators in the sewers twenty feet down. Come." He turned and moved deeper into the brownstone, cloak billowing out behind him in a way that shouldn't be possible without wind.

Now it was my turn to hide a smirk. It was a little reassuring to know that my host wasn't without his own subtle sense of vanity.

I followed in his footsteps, and Captain Verlak fell in behind me. We walked… and walked… and walked, marching along a hall more reminiscent of Versailles than the strictures of the New York real estate market. There were doors on both sides, some of them open, and a quick glance inside showed expansive rooms that were far, far larger than ought to be possible. Had Doom actually built extra dimensions into his house? Or was this nothing more than advanced holographic projections designed to discomfit and confuse a visitor?

Either way, it wasn't for me to be concerned with. I followed, and soon enough we were turning and stepping into a small – by comparison – room with dark wood walls, a polished marble floor, and a table set with a white cloth, two crystal wine glasses, and an extensive dinner spread. To my surprise, Doom sat at the chair that had no place setting, while Captain Verlak sat down to his right, leaving the chair straight across from him for me.

Great.

Well, dinner *was* part of the deal. I sat, taking my katana off and setting it to the side of my chair, and the captain poured the wine, then dished up the first course, a creamy kohlrabi soup. I inhaled the warm, familiar scent and smiled slightly. This wasn't a dish I'd ever readily found in the States, and neither I nor anyone on my team was much of a cook. I reached for my spoon, then paused.

"It's not poisoned," Captain Verlak said lightly before taking a spoonful for herself.

"I…" Honestly, I felt awkward eating without my host joining in. To my surprise, it was Doom himself who allayed my concern.

"There will be a time for speaking of serious things," he intoned, "but first I invite you to partake of my hospitality without reserve."

"Thank you." Thus encouraged – or commanded, really – to dig in, I ate through the soup, then a plate of piping hot cabbage rolls with polenta, sour cream, and sausages on the side, and finally finished the meal with a small serving of thick, blood-red, sour cherry varenye. I resisted the urge to scrape the side of the crystal bowl with my spoon once I was done, and instead set it down on the edge of the plate. The captain, who'd easily kept pace with me while I was eating, stood up, cleared the dishes, and stepped out of the room.

Interesting. There was no other staff member present, not even a robotic one. This more than anything informed me that our conversation was being treated with the utmost secrecy. I supposed I should be grateful he wasn't spreading Symkaria's misfortune around any more than he had to.

This was the moment that Doom finally chose to get down to business. "Tell me what you're here for tonight, Silver Sable."

Interesting. While Captain Verlak had gone out of her way to use my original name, Doom was going by my professional moniker. *Time to get down to business, then.* "I'm here to discuss the future of Symkaria with you."

"Your embattled home country, of course. You're welcome."

I frowned. "I'm sorry?"

"Surely you know that without our annexation of Symkaria, your country would be in a state of mass exodus, its people abandoning it and restarting their lives far from the land of their ancestors. Under Latverian leadership, that abandonment has been delayed."

It was hard to tell if he was being sarcastic or earnest as he said this. Either way, I didn't like it. *Gratitude* wasn't my foremost reaction to seeing my country subsumed to the will of yet another dictator.

"But at what cost?" I asked. "You've been selling off our assets at a breakneck pace. Before long, Symkaria won't have a single functional museum or working factory."

"Your country has debts," Doom replied simply. "They must be paid. I assure you, the terms I obtained from the World Bank are far more favorable than any you would have gotten otherwise."

"They're still ruinous!" I threw my napkin onto the table in frustration. "You're stealing all Symkarians' hope for an independent future by getting rid of our cultural treasures and the machines that would make independence possible! You–"

"Symkaria has no functional government." Doom's voice cut through my diatribe like a bolt of lightning, silencing me in an instant. "Symkaria *has* had no functional government for years. It has careened from the control of petty tyrant to petty tyrant, and they have done far more damage to your country's future than I ever could. *You* yourself refuse to step into a position of true power in your own homeland, despite your royal lineage."

"It's because of that lineage that I *can't* simply step into power," I said, desperate for him to understand. "I'm not going to be another Countess Karkov, telling people that I should rule over them simply because of who I happened to be born as."

"Your people adore you. Surely they would vote you into power."

I sighed. "What body would organize and oversee the elections? How would we pay them? How would they be certified? Who would I even run against? I've considered all these possibilities, but the truth of the matter is that Symkaria has become *too* used to tyrants. They've lost confidence in democracy. I would be a tyrant by default." That was something I had never aspired to. The people of Symkaria already felt voiceless. I wasn't going to add to that subjugation, even unintentionally.

"So, you do not wish to be a tyrant, yet you acknowledge there is no other way for you to take power. You would work to do right by your people, but you see that once you were *in* power, you would be regarded as something you despise." Doom shook his head. "You carry a head full of contradictions and a heart full of frustrated yearning, and yet you would still petition me for... what, exactly? Can you even articulate it? Or are these merely the outbursts of an angry child?"

Don't stab Doctor Doom. Stabbing Doctor Doom would be bad... no matter how satisfying you'd find it.

Get it together, Silver.

"Perhaps my country isn't quite ready for total independence," I said. "But there must be another way to pay off our creditors. If Symkaria is to recover, it needs to be free of *all* sorts of tyrants, monetary included."

"What solution are you suggesting?"

I took a deep breath. "Allow me to take on Symkaria's debts. Sable International is highly profitable, and I've got interested investors who can help me take my work to the next level. I'll be able to hire more people, complete more jobs, and earn more profit than ever before. I've already got ten times our annual operating expenses in the bank. That should be enough to pay off at least a *few* of the–" I stopped, because I was being treated to a sound I never thought I'd hear. It wasn't a pleasant one.

Victor von Doom was laughing. At *me*. He was full-on *laughing* at me, the sort of low-chest laugh that would have made any voice boom, but with him made it sound as though his voice was echoing with its own chuckles and chortles. It was humiliating to be the focus of such a laugh, and I felt my cheeks flush hot even as my palms burned to grab at my blade or unholster my derringer here and now. Whether to shoot Doom or myself I didn't know. I felt brutally humiliated.

His laughter finally rolled to a stop, and he steepled his fingers together as he looked at me. "Ah, Ms Sable. You are correct. You would make a terrible politician. A good leader," he clarified, and the slightest hint of my mortification faded, "but a bad decision-maker. Do you have any idea what the debt of Symkaria is currently?"

A chill gripped my throat and clamped down. I forced out a hoarse, "No."

Doom named a number, and I just about fell out of my chair. Holy... I would have to work for a hundred years nonstop to pay off that amount of money, and that wasn't even considering how much interest it would undoubtedly accrue as time went on.

"Ah," I managed after a few more seconds of internal writhing. "I see. Yes, that's... untenable."

"Untenable indeed." The tenor of his voice changed again, becoming a trifle softer, almost... kind? How strange. I wasn't even sure he was *capable* of kindness. "Your notion is a noble one, but you simply do not have the means to pay off this debt on your own. It may be hard to believe, but auctioning the items in your museums and selling machinery to interested companies is one of the least destructive ways to handle this, and in all likelihood it *still* will not completely discharge Symkaria's debt.

"Companies have already come to me asking permission to mine your mountains and cut down your forests. Our neighboring countries want to divert your rivers and lakes to fuel their agriculture, and offer your people visas to come and work for them – but never allow them to attain citizen status there."

It was worse than I imagined. So much worse. Without our natural resources, Symkaria wouldn't be able to feed its own people. Once we lost our people, our nation would be nothing but a land of dust and memories, and even those memories would fade with time. I clenched my hands around the chair's armrests. "There must be something I can do." An uncomfortable note of pleading had entered my voice, one I despised but couldn't quite do away with. Doom respected honesty, and I was honestly desperate right now. "Some way to make this better. If I can't take on all the debt, there must at least be a way that I discharge *part* of it, or–"

"You may be able to discharge all of it."

I was so startled that for a moment, I couldn't even speak. "But…" I shook my head slightly in an effort to clear it. "But you said that there was no way I could pay off my nation's debts."

"You yourself cannot, that much is true," Doom said. "But *I* could."

I took a second to parse what he was saying. "You mean you would repay Symkaria's creditors on… my behalf."

"Precisely."

Well, if this didn't sound like a deal with the devil, I didn't know what did. Unfortunately, I was out of options. All my life, I had tried to put the needs of my country ahead of my own. It seemed like every time I tried to focus on myself, every time I did something just because I wanted a diversion, it went badly for me. I'd nearly died the last time I was in New York thanks to one of those "diversions," and my brief marriage hadn't ended on a much happier note.

I was at my best when I put the needs of the many ahead of my own. I was a symbol of Symkaria. It was time I started acting like one. "What is it you want in return?" I asked as evenly as I could.

"I want you to hunt down an item that could potentially

reshape my own life as much as I have the potential to reshape Symkaria's future," Doom said. He leaned forward, and his eyes, that were so hard to see in the low light, glinted intently. "I need you and your Wild Pack to find the Clairvoyant."

CHAPTER THREE

The Clairvoyant... Obviously it was a reference to an ability to see into the future, and one that was oddly familiar, but I couldn't place it off the top of my head. I didn't know if it was a person, a place, or a thing. "What exactly is the Clairvoyant?"

"A device that can see into infinite futures and show the user a host of potential solutions for them."

That sounded... well, it sounded self-defeating, honestly. Anyone could imagine infinite futures – what did it matter if a device did the same thing? Unless Doom was looking for a *specific* future – maybe one he wanted to avoid, or purposely bring about. If this device could show not only a potential outcome but the arc of how the person using it got there, then *that* might be very interesting indeed. Especially for someone who craved control as much as Doom did.

Clairvoyant, Clairvoyant, who had I heard talking about that... ah, yes. Spider-Man. It had come up in a random bit of conversation when we were flying to Symkaria to take on the Green Goblin and Countess Karkov. He'd mentioned something an old friend of his had built, and then–

"Wasn't the Clairvoyant destroyed?" I asked. I was sure Spider-Man had said that the device had been destroyed.

"One of them was, yes."

"One of the– how many are there?"

"The device's creator, James Tolentino, built two of them," Doom said. "He did indeed turn one over to be destroyed by Spider-Man, but he was unable to resist the lure of making another. As far as I know, he is using it even as we speak, and evading apprehension with great facility."

Well, sure. If you had a device that could look into the future and foresee all the different ways you could be captured, it couldn't be that hard to look for the best way to escape as well. I imagined that peering into the future all the time could get dizzying for the user after a while, but that wasn't my concern. "Is pursuing this man going to cause a problem with Spider-Man?"

"Mr Tolentino is hardly careening around the world like a cannonball with Spider-Man's blessing, if that is what you are imagining."

That *wasn't* what I was imagining, exactly, but it was tough to believe that Spidey would sign on to letting a friend of his run around with a piece of technology that was rare enough – and powerful enough – to keep the interest of someone like Victor von Doom. Heck, Spider-Man had destroyed the last Clairvoyant, if I recalled correctly. They must have had a falling out.

"If you think that Spider-Man would never let something like this happen, think again," Doom advised me. "I have it on good authority that while he is a soft touch for an old friend, he's also a very busy young man. He cannot keep track of everyone who crosses his path, and it seems that Mr Tolentino is heavily invested in wanting to stay out of sight and ahead of capture right now."

I could hardly blame him. Being captured by Doctor Doom was very low on absolutely everyone's list of things to aspire to. "What is *he* getting out of the Clairvoyant?" I asked.

"Does it matter?"

That... was a very good question. In all honesty, it *should* matter. After all, Jamie Tolentino built the thing. If anyone had reason to use it however he wanted to, it was him. On the other hand, how safe was it to go around with a device that could literally see into the future? How *sane* was it? How long could he stare into the abyss, so to speak, before it finally stared back at him, and he lost himself to it?

I wondered if Doom had considered these outcomes for himself as well. Knowing him, he had, but had dismissed them just as fast. Doom was many things, but lacking in confidence wasn't one of them. Besides, I'd taken worse contracts for *much* less on the line.

This job was the key to a brighter future for Symkaria. If I could pull this off, I would put my country onto a better path. Yes, we would still be under the rule of Doom and Latveria, but we would have the means of production to build a better future as well as the historical artifacts to remind ourselves of our rich and prosperous heritage. All of that, and the only thing I needed to do for it was to hunt down one man, one man who had to sleep *sometime* and couldn't always be watching his back, and get the Clairvoyant from him?

There had to be a catch. "Why haven't you gone after it yourself?" I asked, cleansing my palate with a sip of water. I shivered – it was surprisingly cold in here. Or perhaps it was the way the room seemed to chill as I questioned Doom's ability to get what he wanted.

"Consider, for a moment, the difference between me and you," he said. "Not simply in a physical sense, but on a cosmic, metaphysical scale. Consider the impact our actions are likely to have throughout the multitude of universes that our choices move us into. Imagine them as ripples in a pond, and then tell me: which of us would it be easier to see coming?"

I'd gone from mildly offended at the beginning of that explanation to... still mildly offended, but at least understanding where he was coming from. On the grand scale, Doctor Doom had a much larger presence than I did. "You're telling me he's finding it easier to evade you than he probably would me."

"Indeed. Mr Tolentino has evaded either myself or teams I directly sent after him three times now." And didn't he just sound *thrilled* about that. Not. "My powers are myriad, but even an intellect like mine can't foresee every eventuality, and that includes finding ways *not* to be seen by the Clairvoyant."

And here *I* was, seriously considering getting him a way to foresee every eventuality. I didn't know yet what Jamie Tolentino was doing with the Clairvoyant, but I could imagine a heck of a lot of things that Doom might do with it. Very few of them were benevolent.

If I got this device for him, would he never again lose to the Fantastic Four? Would he find new ways to impose his will on other neighboring nations and incorporate them into his sphere of political influence, or expand Latveria outright? If I did this, would I really be handing over any hope of a free future for Symkaria by giving one of our oppressors the very tool he needed to ensure we never slipped away?

"I can tell you're thinking hard about this," Doom intoned. "Rather too hard. You fear what I might do with the Clairvoyant, but let me assure you – there is no future I cannot bring about if I focus all my will upon it. None." His voice was as hard as his armor. "You think I could not make something of this sort for myself if I truly desired to? Or use my darker arts to produce a prophecy, to lay out a glorious path into the future? The only thing that the Clairvoyant will afford me is a certain *ease*, Ms Sable. It will not tell me anything I couldn't eventually figure out for myself."

It would be very easy to believe him right now. Doom had a quality of... call it conviction, call it self-aggrandizement, call it *destiny*, about him. It all came back to his unshakable belief in himself, the way he could set a goal and fight for it against hell, alien invasion, super-powered evildoers, and everything in between. What he decreed would come to pass almost always did.

But maybe it only did because he played too many people like me for patsies, bending us to his will and getting him what he needed to play his epic-level games without even realizing we were being made fools of.

Either way, it didn't matter. I had already decided to do this. The potential reward was just as concrete as the potential downside was abstract.

"I want a contract," I said at last. "Laying out all the terms of our agreement."

"Agreed."

"And, in the interest of honesty, I want you to know that I'm going to have a copy of it held in trust to be sent to the Fantastic Four in the event of my untimely death or Latveria's subjugation of Symkaria." I held my breath. This would be an understandable place to balk, if he so chose; I was *explicitly* stating I didn't trust him right now. That was the sort of thing that got some men rather... what was the word... spicy? Salty? Upset, anyhow.

"I accept your addendum. Now, here is mine." He leaned forward, and I found myself unable to look away from those eyes once more. "I will give you one month beginning from tonight to get this work done. After that month, our deal is over, the contract moot. I won't punish Symkaria for your failings, but I will not give you the chance to make a deal like this with me again. If you fail now, you fail forever, and your future as the savior of your nation fails along with you."

I swallowed hard. I hadn't been expecting this, although I should have. Almost every client set a time limit for how long they'd give me to complete a job, but this... this was no ordinary job. This was the difference between a future with the promise of independence, and one with the threat of lifetimes of indentured servitude. One month.

I would have to make it count.

"Agreed."

"Very good, Ms Sable." He sat back, steepling his fingers again. "Captain Verlak, bring the contract."

I whirled toward the door, but no one entered. Doom shook his head. "She wasn't crouched in the hallway peeping through the keyhole," he said in a tone of mild amusement.

"That would imply her listening in was unwelcome. She has been monitoring our conversation remotely from the moment she left the room."

I wasn't entirely comfortable with being spied on like that, but… it wasn't my house. "Why not let her stay, then?" I asked.

"So that you could be assured you had my entire focus, of course. Something I do not offer to many people."

I was hoping to avoid having quite this much of Doom's focus ever again. It was too tempting to break open the dark parts of my mind and demand answers to questions that I already knew he would never answer to my satisfaction. Better to let old pains lie, and focus on the future. Not *my* future, but Symkaria's future.

The contract – which had somehow been produced in seconds and contained every clause I could think of adding and more, including information on all of Doom's previous attempts to lasso James Tolentino – was read through and signed by both parties in short order. Then it was just a matter of getting out of there and bringing our new job back to the Wild Pack.

I was escorted back to the front of the house by Captain Verlak, Doom striding off down that never-ending hallway toward – well, it wasn't for me to think about. She opened the front door for me, and as I stepped through, I felt fortunate she didn't try to kick me on the way out. I fully expected to hear it slam shut a second later. Instead, just as my foot hit the top step, she called out to me.

"Silvija Sablinova."

I turned to look at her. "What is it?"

"You're not one of us, so this might not mean very much to you," she said, and there was an intensity in her voice that was almost as powerful as Doom's. "But you should understand that you've been given a very special opportunity, one that Doctor Doom offers to very few people. Getting the chance to serve him was the most challenging thing I ever decided to do, and it proved the mettle of my character to me."

I shook my head. "I'm not *serving* him. This is a job, just like any other."

"Not like any other," she replied. "Not even close. And I think you know that, Silvija. Just… tread carefully, and whatever you do? Don't fail him."

On that surprising note, she *did* shut the door. I watched it close, then picked up my skirts and walked swiftly down the rest of the stairs.

I had the job of my life to start planning.

CHAPTER FOUR

No matter what stage I got to in life, no matter how great – or how poor – my reputation was, I always worked with a team. As a mercenary, it was a necessity. When you were selling your services to the highest bidder, you needed extra insurance to make sure the person hiring you wasn't going to try to do away with you once the job was done. Not to mention, using a team increased the odds of success of any job.

Going it alone... the last time I attempted it, I almost died. If it hadn't been for the quick actions of my ex-husband, I *would* have died. I had too much to do now to take my life for granted, so if that meant dragging the entire Wild Pack into a deal with Doctor Doom, then that was what was going to happen.

That certainly didn't mean they were going to be happy about it, as none of them were fans of Latveria *or* its tyrant-for-life. I'd do my best to butter them up in the morning, though.

Unless we were actively working a job, evenings were time

off for my team, so it was hardly surprising to get back to the embassy and find that the only person still there was Juliet, who preferred late-night video game sessions to hitting the bar scene. I was effectively alone for now, which was fine.

I got past the basic security measures I'd set on the embassy since we came here – an off-the-shelf but decent video surveillance system, facial recognition software at all entrances, and a tripwire setup that would set off an alarm loud enough to wake the dead. Then I headed up to the former ambassador's room, eager to get out of this borrowed dress and back into something that didn't make the first two cab drivers refuse to let me into their cars.

Or possibly that was the sword I was carrying.

I took off my sword and gun, unzipped the dress and let it fall to the floor in a heap, then kicked the shoes off. They landed in the corner and ricocheted off the wall with a *bang*, tilted against each other like a pair of pointy-toed drunks. I pulled some comfortable sweatpants and a T-shirt out of my bag and slid into them, then sighed and grabbed the dress and shoes and put them away neatly, in the closet. *There. Now Juliet can't yell at me.*

I cleaned up – the other thing I'd taken care of as soon as we got to New York was getting the water turned back on here – and got into bed, then pulled up the files Captain Verlak had sent to me. It was time to get a better idea of what we were going to be dealing with.

James "Jamie" Tolentino, graduated from Empire State University a few years back, had a mother and a younger sister, father deceased… He was brilliant but erratic, with a compulsive gambling problem. Hmm. That would explain why he was hitting so many casinos. I was surprised they hadn't banded together to keep him out at this point – he had to have made over a million dollars in just the past week given how rapidly he was making money. It was honestly a little odd. There had to be an easier way to make cash by seeing into the future. Casinos had security, they had software to help them recognize cheaters, they had rules about who could and couldn't come in... so why did he keep frequenting them?

Maybe I would ask him when I caught him. In the meantime, I needed to get a feel for what Doom's people had done wrong. It wasn't like he *himself* was going after Tolentino. How big a shadow could his influence cast, when it was just a group of minions?

Some of the nervous ache in my chest began to recede as I reviewed the documentation of Doom's attempts. His teams were pretty good, but they'd made some very obvious mistakes. Too many people converging from one direction, no one on backup in another case, ignoring exits they thought were too unlikely for Tolentino to access... I could see a dozen ways to improve on these extraction attempts. And improve I would. If I didn't get Jamie Tolentino by the third try, I would go dancing at a club wearing those ridiculous shoes, just like Tango had tried to convince me to tonight.

"Come join us after your meeting," he'd urged as he and the others got ready for their night on the town. Why did going out require that everyone *smell* so strange? Body spray, perfume, cologne, deodorant – the four of them together were an assault to the nose. "It'll be a good way to let off some steam! Text us when you're done and we'll–"

"No," I said, holding up a hand. The smile fell off his face, and I immediately felt bad. Tango was my longest-serving teammate after Juliet. I needed to do better. "I mean, no thank you. I don't think I'd be interested in that, especially not after spending an evening with Victor von Doom." It was a thin excuse, and from the look on his face, he knew it.

Tango – he had another name, of course, but I tried to stick to everyone's code names, it made it simpler – kept trying to draw me into team-building and/or bonding experiences, which I just couldn't make myself be excited about. We were a team, yes… we were a team because they had the expertise I needed, and I paid them very well for it. We weren't a *family* or some other nonsense like that. They didn't really want me with them when they were trying to have fun, and I didn't want to intrude on their night out when I could spend it better on work.

"Also, nobody needs to see or hear another rendition of your version of '…Baby One More Time' at a karaoke bar," Juliet had put in lightly, coming to my rescue. "Last time you hit yourself so hard you literally almost knocked yourself out."

"It was a funny interpretation of the lyrics!" Tango protested, his smile back even as Foxtrot, Romeo, and X-Ray started ribbing him mercilessly. "I just kind of, y'know… had a little too much to drink and…"

"And cold-cocked yourself on the jaw. We know. Get out, you bunch of disgraces. And no karaoke!" Juliet had yelled after them as they left. She turned to me once they were gone. "Don't worry, Silver. I've got your back."

I'd forced a smile for her. "I know." I wasn't sure *why* she had my back, but I was grateful for it. Juliet was definitely the closest thing I had to a friend among my... among my everything, it seemed.

That was... a little sad. Just a little, though. You don't need friends. You need to be strong, independent. You need to be a symbol of what Symkaria can become.

I dreamt that night. It wasn't pleasant. Not as bad as the nightmares I got sometimes – usually after talking to my sometimes helpful, always pigheaded ex – but not fun either. I was being pursued by something that growled and snapped at my heels, and everywhere I tried to hide fell apart. Each time I abandoned a hideout for the next, whatever was chasing me grew larger, and got closer. By the time I finally snapped out of my dream, it had filled all the space around me, like a fog made of teeth and snarls, closing in on me from everywhere except exactly where I was looking.

That's what you get for drinking Latverian wine. I should have declined, but that was easier said than done when you were dealing with Doctor Doom.

I got up at five AM, put on my shark-bitten uniform – you really had to squint to see the repairs, Juliet had exaggerated to get me into that dang dress – and began making a series of calls. By the time the first of my people were stirring two hours later, I had an extensive spread on the table: bagels and cream cheese with lox from a spot Spider-Man had recommended the last time we talked; pancakes, bacon, and scrambled eggs from a restaurant two blocks away; and even a bag with fresh croissants in it. I'd also ordered everyone's favorite drinks from the nearest coffee shop. I might not be their "friend," but I tried to be a good boss, at least.

"Hgggn..." X-Ray was the first one into the dining room,

scrubbing both hands over her face as she stumbled forward like something out of a zombie movie. She was the tallest person in our group, with long blonde hair and biceps the size of my head. She was brutally proficient at hand-to-hand fighting, and she also had a debilitating caffeine addiction. "Coffee. Is there… yeah?"

"Yes," I said, pointing at the cardboard tray containing all twenty-four-ounce containers. The sheer American excess of it all made me wince, but seeing X-Ray latch onto hers and down half of it in one long gulp made me wonder if I shouldn't have ordered her another. "Did you have a good night?" I asked, because I knew she would expect it.

"Um." X-Ray flopped into the chair next to me and pinched the bridge of her nose for a second. "I… think so? I don't really remember; after the fifth bar, I started getting a little… out of it. I had to be carried back here by–"

"Romeo," I cut in, sensing she'd been about to use his real name. *Code names only.* Letting yourself get sloppy and begin using someone's actual name would inevitably lead to a mistake in the field. She'd been with me for three years now, since before the last Symkarian revolution. She knew the rules.

She rolled her eyes, then grimaced. "Ow. Fine, yeah, *Romeo* had to carry me back here. But hey, I got to drink something that literally glowed in the dark, so that was cool. The bartender called it the Lightning Bolt." She grinned. "They had a bunch of Avengers-themed drinks. The Smash was neon green. I think it's a kind of liquor only made by monks or something like that, and the Repulsor was just a double shot of the most expensive whiskey they had in the place."

"I got that one," Romeo volunteered from the door. He looked like he was in a little better shape than X-Ray – lighter bags under his eyes, for one – but he also homed in on the coffee like it was a lifeline. Sunlight glinted off his bald head as he swallowed down his oat milk, half-caff, sugar free... honestly, I couldn't remember everything that he'd asked to be in there, but the combination smelled dubious. He seemed to like it, though. "Then I got it again, then again, then again–"

"Blowing the entire night's budget–" X-Ray interjected irritably.

"–and having a good time doing it," he finished with a smile that I could tell was smug even behind the beard. "Ooh, bagels, lemme at 'em."

"Help yourself."

Tango was next, fresh from a shower and smiling broadly. "Is that my tea?" he asked, pointing at the tall cup of oolong in the container.

"It is."

"Because you're the only one who drinks that crap other than Sable," X-Ray said, giving a little groan of discontentment as she finished off the last of her coffee.

"It's good for you," Tango said between sips of his tea. "It's full of antioxidants, decreases inflammation, helps with stress reduction..."

I chuckled. "You're going to be drinking a lot of that in the coming weeks."

"Oh yeah?" He looked at me with interest. "You got a job from the big bad doc?"

"I did. One that could change the future of Symkaria for the better if we get it right."

"Do tell."

"Once Foxtrot and Juliet get here," I said. I didn't want to have to explain this more than once. I sat back and watched them eat, sipping at my own tea – decaffeinated, because I didn't like the idea of being reliant on a stimulant to get through the day – and eventually we were joined by the last two members of our team, who were arguing over… something. I heard the words VPN, opportunistic encryption, and split tunneling, and then I tuned out and let them get their food, arguing the whole time.

They were the most technically proficient people on the team and worked together to provide oversight and backup on missions. Foxtrot worked with the team at large, while Juliet was the equivalent of my handler, since I usually took point in our work on the ground. Foxtrot was the oldest member of the team, and his hair was almost as pale as mine, but he had the manners of a little boy who didn't know how to chew with his mouth shut as he argued his point.

"Nothing you're saying is so important that I need to see the inside of your mouth," X-Ray snapped at him.

He smirked at her. "That's not what you said last night."

"Ugh, don't be gross," she scoffed. I noticed Romeo's eyes narrow a little bit as he looked between the two of them. Hmm… trouble brewing? I hoped not – the last thing my team needed were intimate personal entanglements. Not that I could do anything about it if they *were* getting entangled, but it never ended well.

A few more minutes of eating, drinking, and gentle ribbing over what had happened the night before – and I didn't need to *know* that about the rats of New York City, my god – and my crew was finally ready to focus, all eyes on me. I leaned forward, folded my hands in front of me on the table, and smiled. "So, here's the good news. Doctor Doom has agreed to pay off all of Symkaria's outstanding international debts in exchange for doing one relatively straightforward job for him."

There was a long moment of silence. Hmm, I'd expected a little more enthusiasm than that. After all, we were all Symkarian. Paying off our country's debts would be a profound relief. Juliet finally spoke up. "Aaaand… what's the bad news?"

"The bad news is that 'relatively straightforward' is *very* relative," I replied. "Because our target happens to possess a device that allows him to see a huge number of possibilities in the future and respond to them accordingly."

This time, the silence was deafening.

CHAPTER FIVE

It took a lot to surprise my team. You couldn't be a member of the Wild Pack if you weren't fairly unflappable. Over the past few years we had careened from emergency to disaster, terrorist takedown to super villain face-off, Nazi dismantlement – it should have been *dismemberment* as far as I was concerned – to liberating an entire nation. It was challenging work, requiring everyone to be on point for days or weeks at a time, but by now we were a smoothly oiled machine. So, to see my machine grinding to a halt, so to speak, was… concerning.

"You want us…" Foxtrot began slowly.

"To sneak up on a guy," Romeo continued.

"Who can't be snuck up on," X-Ray finished. She was looking a bit ashen. "And you made this deal with Doom. *The* Doom. Doctor Dictator-von-Badass-von-Mystical Super-power-von–"

"Yes," I interjected before she could add any more descriptors. I got the point. "I'm not saying it isn't going to be a challenge."

"Fighting the Green Goblin was a challenge," Tango said. "Finding a guy who can literally see us coming… Look, Sable, you know we've got nothing but respect for you. However, and with respect… this sounds insane."

"It's not." No one seemed to agree with me, not even Juliet. I sighed. "I understand that this job seems daunting at first glance. However, I'm confident there's a way for us to figure this out. The man with this device, James Tolentino – he's not super-powered. He's a regular person who happens to have invented something miraculous. He still needs to eat, to sleep, to recuperate. He can't be on guard all the time, and he's traveling alone with no one to watch his back. He's got vulnerabilities."

"But he's a genius," Juliet said with a frown. "So he's undoubtedly considered all his weaknesses and goes out of his way to mitigate them."

"Yes, that's probably true. But I'm sure we can find ways around that."

Foxtrot was still frowning. "And Doom wants us to do this because…"

I shrugged. "He wants the device."

Romeo snorted. "Then why doesn't he just go and get it for himself?"

"He's too big a fish in too small a pond," I said. "Too easy to see coming. His people didn't fare much better."

"Wait." X-Ray held up a hand. "Wait. So, Doctor von Big Brain himself couldn't apprehend this guy, so he decided to get *you* to do it? By offering you literally the one thing you couldn't refuse?" She leaned over and banged her forehead on the table. "We're screwed. Oh my god, we're so dead."

I resisted the urge to roll my eyes. There was enough childishness happening right now without me adding to it. "We're not going to be dead."

"Doom is going to *kill* us when he figures out we can't get this done."

"We have an entire month to do it," I said reasonably. That was plenty of time to work out a strategy, a proper plan of attack.

"A *month?* That's it?" X-Ray exclaimed. The conversation devolved into a chorus of groans, complaints, and general grousing that did very little to elevate the discourse into the realm of the useful. I let it go on for a few more seconds before I cleared my throat.

"I would never take a job that I didn't feel we could complete," I said seriously, looking each one of my people in the eyes. "I value our lives and our reputations too much to do that. I've already been over the information Doom shared about his attempts, and I can see a lot of places for improvement. I believe that we can do this, and if we do, our actions will have positive consequences for the entire nation of Symkaria. Our *home.*" I could see a few faces soften and was relieved I was getting through. I paid well, of course, but people always worked a little harder when they were working in service of something they believed in.

Doom knew that. Strange to think that he and I could agree about something.

"Also," I added, "I made it clear in the contract I signed that the only person to be held responsible for any failure is me. Your names aren't even specified. If things go badly, I'll be the only one to suffer for it."

Tango shook his head. "That doesn't seem right. We're your

team. It's our job to make this happen just as much as it is yours."

"But I'm the one who decides which jobs we take," I pointed out. "And in this case, my decision is final. Foxtrot." He perked up as I handed over a thumb drive. "This has all the personal information on James Tolentino that I received from Doom, including his last confirmed sightings. He's been staying in the United States for the most part, and focusing his scam on casinos – big ones, generally. I need you to find him. As soon as you do, we're out of here."

"Got it," he grunted, holding the thumb drive like it was a scorpion just waiting to sting him. I couldn't fault him for being cautious – it *did* come from Doom, after all. You never knew what might spring out of his tech.

I stood up from the table. "I suggest you all pack up. I want to be under way by the end of the day at the latest." Then I smiled. "Thanks for joining me for breakfast."

"Thanks for giving me indigestion," Romeo muttered. X-Ray hit him on the shoulder, and he winced.

Time for me to make my exit. They probably had plenty to talk about amongst themselves, and it would be easier without their boss breathing down their necks. Besides, I had some calls to make. I hadn't brought all of our equipment with us from the home base in Symkaria, but I rented space in several storage facilities across the US for this exact reason. As soon as I knew where we were heading, I'd arrange to have our gear dropped off there. Let me see, we'd probably need an armored vehicle, plenty of weapons – not that those were ever hard to find in America – some top-of-the-line observation and evasion equipment, a few–

"Hey, Sable?"

I turned around in surprise to see that Tango had followed me into the hallway. He looked uncharacteristically serious. Rain or shine, bullets or frag grenades, Tango almost always had a smile on his face. He was our getaway guy, the man who could drive or pilot anything, and he was usually as fast with his words as he was with his feet. Not this morning, apparently. I felt a little bad for bringing his mood down so low. "Yes?" I asked.

"I'm sorry, but I have to ask... are you sure about this?"

I sighed internally. Just what I didn't need this morning – one of my people doubting my authority. Was I perfectly sure we could pull this off? No, but that was *my* problem to deal with. The last thing I needed right now was to cast doubt on my team's ability to get the job done. "I wouldn't have signed on the dotted line if I wasn't sure."

"It's just–" He scratched at the back of his neck, fingers catching in the wisps of black hair that had fallen out of his short ponytail. "We're not super heroes. And I know you said Tolentino isn't either, but he's got something on his side that gives him a heck of an edge. Basically a super-power, y'know? How are a bunch of regular people – and I know that we're highly skilled, I'm not talking us down," he said as I opened my mouth to object. "But you have to admit that we're not packing the same kind of heat a guy like Doom can bring to the table, so... How can we possibly expect to improve where he's already come up short?"

"It's because Doom is such a colossus that he's unable to get close to Tolentino," I said. I felt pretty sure about this part – I don't think Victor von Doom would have confessed such a weakness to me unless it was a genuine one. He was a lot of things, including massively overconfident, but not the kind of person who hid from their own flaws. "This is one of those times when having no special powers is going to play in our favor." Tango still looked doubtful. I stepped a little closer to him.

"Listen. We didn't have to be Spider-Man to save our country from the Green Goblin and Countess Karkov, did we?"

"It didn't hurt to have him there," Tango pointed out.

"No, but in the end, who rallied the people themselves to fight back against the invaders? *We* did." It was one of my proudest moments, and one of the things that had driven me to take this contract. The people of Symkaria had responded to my call for help; now I would do my utmost to help them in return.

"Everywhere, every day, all over the world, regular people are changing the future," I went on. "They're taking care of themselves and their neighbors, they're saving lives, they're building communities that will last. This kind of change and support is the true heart of civilization: not what showboating super-powered people do in the limelight, but what everyday people do for themselves. It's not flashy or newsworthy, but it accomplishes more for mankind every day than super heroes or their nemeses ever could. That's what *we're* bringing to this job. We're capable of doing great thing without having to scream to the heavens about it, and that includes bringing in James Tolentino."

He met my eyes for a long moment before he finally nodded. "All right. You say it can be done, we'll get it done.

Plus." His mien brightened a little bit. "How many people can say they made it work where Doctor Doom himself failed? Not that many."

"Definitely not many who want to live," I agreed, and his smile dropped again. "I'm just kidding," I added. "He won't kill us." *As long as we don't give him a reason to.*

I headed up to my room to pack after that. It was pretty easy – I was a one-bag kind of traveler with the exception of ensuring I had enough weapons and ammunition. Fortunately transporting those wasn't a problem right now, since we had our own plane courtesy of a friend-only deal from Parker Industries, whose CEO was close to Spider-Man. It wasn't the fastest thing out there, but it was more than enough for the Wild Pack to fly in and out of danger all over the world. Although given the price of fueling it up these days, I wasn't crazy about flying *all* over the world right now, but certainly we could manage a few cross-country jaunts if we needed to.

"Hey, Sable?" Juliet poked her head into my room. "Foxtrot's come up with something. Looks like we're off to Oklahoma."

Dang, Foxtrot was good. "Oklahoma?" I raised an eyebrow as I considered it. "Do they even allow gambling there?"

Juliet nodded. "The casino is on First Nation lands, and it's one of the biggest in the world."

"Hmm. Well." Big or not, I doubted it was as tough to crack as the Palace or Mercury Rising. "I guess we'd better get going, then."

"Hey." She glanced at the massive closet with a smile on her face. "Are you going to bring the dress along?"

I scoffed. "It didn't even fit me."

"You could get a tailor to shorten it! It looked *really* good on you, and it's just going to molder away here otherwise." She must have seen that I was running out of patience, because she shrugged and ducked out again with a shouted, "Think about it!"

Think about it? There was nothing to think about. I wouldn't be wearing that dress again, ever, and that was final.

Besides, I didn't even have shoes that matched it.

CHAPTER SIX

I refused to court failure. Although I fully expected our first attempt to be a learning experience for my team instead of an unmitigated success, I wanted to be as thorough with it as possible. That meant that after arriving in Thackerville, Oklahoma and getting rooms at the hotel that was a part of the massive gaming and entertainment complex there, we didn't make a move on Tolentino. Not yet. Instead, we tailed him for three days, getting a feel for how he liked to pass the time (gambling in the high-stakes rooms), when he paused to eat and drink (meals were inconsistent and drinking was near-constant), and where he slept (one of the smaller rooms on the first floor, close to the exit. Smart.)

The more I watched him, the less I was able to figure out how this man had stymied Doom and his minions. He seemed to move through the day like a zombie, shuffling from room to room, always with a drink in his hand, never really bothering to look up. He wore mirrored sunglasses *inside* – a true jerk move, or so Romeo informed all of us. He was so stooped he hardly looked like he could be the contemporary of Spider-Man. What was happening to this man? How had he fallen so low?

This was the point where I made a fatal mistake – overconfidence. After reviewing the data from Doom for the tenth time, I concluded that the best way to go about this would be to corner Tolentino in a place he couldn't readily escape from, one of the high-roller rooms most likely, and confront him directly. Doom and his people, for all their efficacy, were the opposite of subtle, while my people had made an art of blending in. Ability to look into the future or not, Tolentino couldn't smash his way through walls or vanish into thin air. I would give him the chance to come with us willingly, and if he refused, well… then I would take away the chance to come with us willingly and do things the hard way.

I sent Romeo into the high-roller room that night, disguised as a Russian oligarch looking for a place to play in between making deals with local oil companies. X-Ray kept a watch on the door from a bar down the hall, where she pretended to drink with great facility. Foxtrot and Juliet were holed up in one of our suites, with Juliet tapped into the casino's internal security cameras while Foxtrot kept an eye on all the outward-facing ones. I was the rover, flitting from table to table, machine to machine with an idle step and a drink in my hand. It was cold enough in the casino that no one questioned why I was wearing long sleeves in Oklahoma in the summer, which gave me the excuse of hiding the body armor I was wearing beneath my convenient sweater as well.

We were ready. Romeo would play a few rounds with the group at the table, then at the next break he would approach Tolentino to talk – just to talk. He wouldn't be able to carry any conventional weapons into the high-stakes room, after all. If Mr Tolentino resisted Romeo's friendly advice, then X-Ray and I would move to assist in securing him. Meanwhile, Tango was staged outside, ready to drive us out of here for a quick exit if we needed one. It was a good first effort – perhaps not foolproof, but certainly not foolish.

Or so I thought before we were all made fools of.

There were five players at the table, six people including the dealer. The room had a private bar as well, with a watchful bartender who continually refilled people's drinks. Romeo had to drink *some* to keep up pretenses, but he was good at holding his liquor. He played the part of the overly merry, money-to-burn oligarch like a pro, sloppy with his playing but just serious enough so that he wasn't completely discounted by the other players. Not that it mattered – an hour in, and Tolentino was up by almost a quarter of a million dollars, having only lost a few hands here and there. I could tell from the looks the dealer was giving him that she was thinking of calling in hotel security, but first Romeo called for a break.

"I need a moment, eh? Give my wallet time to stop smoking." He smirked and reached for the cigarettes he carried in his jacket. "Speaking of…"

"No smoking inside, sir," the dealer snapped before getting up and walking out the door. We watched as Tolentino, still seemingly in a daze, shuffled his chips into a neat pile before heading over to the bar. Romeo got up to join him, and a moment later the bartender was presenting both of them with shots.

"To your health," Romeo said, throwing his back before leaning in a little closer to Tolentino. "Listen, my friend… you should know that–"

"I know who you are."

Romeo, to his credit, didn't startle. The rest of us immediately tensed up, though. "X-Ray, stand by to intervene," I said, putting my drink down and heading for the high-roller room. Traffic had picked up massively on the casino floor, though. Why were there so many people here now? "Juliet, where are all these people coming from?"

"A fight just let out," she said grimly. "The casino was hosting an MMA event tonight. It was supposed to go for another half an hour, but the last three fights were all TKOs. It wrapped up early."

Shoot. I kept pushing my way through, but it wasn't easy. People were hooting and hollering, some of them reenacting parts of the fights. A few of them were arguing, getting louder and louder the closer I got to them.

"I know why you're here," Tolentino went on, his voice low but calm as he spoke to Romeo. "And I'm telling you right now, it's not going to happen. Tell your boss not to bother trying, because your chances are next to zilch."

Romeo scoffed. "You have a lot to say for someone with no way out of here."

"Oh, I have a way out." I heard the thunk of a shot glass hitting the bar top. "Whereas you are going to sleep for a while. Goodnight."

"You – hey, youuu…" Romeo's voice trailed off, tone

slurred but still projecting indignation, before he collapsed. Drugged, *shoot,* his drink had to have been drugged. We'd all gotten overconfident.

"X-Ray, get in there, now!" I snapped over the line as I tried to skirt around a group of drunken idiots fighting about whether a ref's call had been fair. One of them disagreed with the other badly enough that he threw a punch. It went right past the other man, who staggered to the side–

And then the punch came right at me instead.

I caught it, of course. I wasn't about to get hit in the face by some random civilian, even if he was twice my size. I twisted his wrist, got his arm over my shoulder, bent just enough to get one of his feet off the floor and – *flip.* A second later he was flat on his back, staring up at me in pure, drunken befuddlement.

"What the– hey!" The guy who'd avoided his punch looked from the man on his back to me in burgeoning dislike. "You don't get to treat my bro like that!"

I didn't say anything – I didn't have time for petty arguments with incidental annoyances. I kept moving, still having to fight my way through the crowd, when all of a sudden, my feet were off the ground.

That jerk had *picked me up.*

X-Ray was having her own difficulties, I could hear it over the line, and Foxtrot was saying something, but my focus had completely narrowed down to the person who'd made the mistake of treating me like I was some little doll. I had trained my whole life in combat, and there was nothing more infuriating than someone looking at me and seeing a petite woman who could be picked up and thrown around like she was nothing. Like *I* was nothing.

Absolutely not.

I slammed my head back into the man's nose even as I brought my right heel up into his crotch. The angle wasn't perfect, but I traumatized him enough to make him drop me with a screech as he doubled over. I scraped the edge of my shoe down his shin as I fell, then turned around, grabbed him by the hair, and kneed him in the face. He fell straight onto the last man I dropped, out cold. Lucky for them, none of the other gentlemen in their party thought it would be smart to continue to mess with me.

"X-Ray, status report," I said as I continued toward the hallway. I was almost there.

"My status is *screwed!*" she snapped. "Where the he– *ow!*"

A second later I rounded the corner and watched as four men in black suits – casino security – dogpiled her two feet from the door into the high-roller room. A moment after that, James Tolentino came out, whistling a merry tune while cradling his chips in his hand. He lifted his sunglasses just long enough to meet my eyes, then winked.

Winked. The arrogance, the casual dismissal, they piled onto my already angry psyche and made me furious. I surged forward, determined to reach him before he walked away, but then–

"I'm onnit!" A second after this announcement, Romeo came stumbling through the door after Tolentino. "M'okay, I got 'im, I'm–" He immediately tripped over the pile of people in the hall, going down like a sack of potatoes. His head hit the wall, and he cursed as he started to bleed.

Of course I went to his aid. Nothing was more important to me than the wellbeing of my team, even if it meant I had to watch that smug, winking piece of work walk away from me with a quarter of a million dollars in his hands, whistling the whole way down the hall.

But it wasn't too late. He still had to cash the chips out, and I had three people left.

"Juliet, Foxtrot, time to mobilize," I said. "You should be able to corner him at the cashiers. Do *not* let him go without–"

"Um."

That was not a good "um." I never heard "um" from Foxtrot. He was too precise to use language like that. "What?" I asked apprehensively as I ripped a sleeve off one of the security guard's shirts and pressed it to Romeo's head. Not the cleanest bandage, but I didn't have a lot of options right now. X-Ray was still cursing, trying to get out from under them, and they were all shouting. I could barely hear Foxtrot over the noise. "*What?*" I repeated.

"Uh... the Human Torch is here."

What the heck? What was a New York City super hero doing in Oklahoma?

"And he's got Wyatt Wingfoot with him."

Wingfoot... I'd heard of him before, a Native American tribal chief and medicine man. He wasn't a member of the tribe that owned this casino, but I could see them calling on someone local in an emergency. He was friends with the Fantastic Four and She-Hulk, and apparently he had one of the Four on speed dial. "And they're backing up the reservation cops and casino security," Foxtrot went on. "I think there's a SWAT armored car incoming as well. In fact–"

"Hey, hey, no problem, no worries!" That was Tango,

speaking up for the first time and sounding forcibly cheerful. "No problems here, officer, I'm just chillin'!"

"Get out of the vehicle and onto the ground, now!" someone shouted. "Out of the van, now! Show us your hands, show us your hands!"

Oh, that didn't sound good. How did they home in on him so quickly? Tango had literally done nothing this entire evening except sit there in the van we'd rented.

"Sure, you got it, just let me – ow, no need to rough a guy up, I'm just–"

"Sable, duck!" Juliet shouted. I threw myself over Romeo and covered the back of my head with my hands, and a second later the Human Torch smashed through the wall right above my head. Heat from his flame filled the hallway, and I wondered for a second if he was going to be able to rein himself in when–

"Felicia?" The flame abruptly went out. "What are you doing *here*?"

I turned my head to look at Johnny Storm, wearing his team colors and a look of mild surprise, like a golden retriever who'd just been told to chase a ball you hadn't really thrown.

"Wrong woman," I said, almost choking on a cough. I was *not* Black Cat, aka Felicia Hardy, aka a sneaky thief who wouldn't be caught dead in a casino dogpile.

The confusion cleared from Johnny's face, and he scratched the back of his neck sheepishly. "Sorry, you just – not so much in the face, but with the hair, it's kind of a unique color, y'know? I bet you get that all the time, huh?"

"No," I said coldly, getting to my feet and helping Romeo up as well. "I don't."

Johnny Storm looked at me for a moment, then smirked. "Yeah, on second thought I guess not. You're, like, five inches shorter than she is."

You will not hit the Human Torch in the face, you will not hit the Human Torch in the face…

"Get these people off me," X-Ray grunted from where she was still being squashed by three of the security staff.

"Not a chance," the man whose sleeve I'd ripped off barked at her. "You think we're going to let a bunch of terrorists go free? I've already called the FBI; they're on their way."

Terrorists? FBI?

A tall man with long, dark hair and broad features poked his head through the hole in the wall. "C'mon man," he said with a sigh. "Less destruction of private property, remember?"

"Wyatt, you told me to get here fast!"

"And now you've made a brand new hallway in my friend's casino!"

"She can spruce it up, redo the floors and the electrical, and nobody will ever know," Johnny said with the easy assurance of a guy who didn't understand the actual cost of a regular person's labor. He looked back at me. "So, lady who isn't Black Cat – who are you?"

"My name is–"

"Silver Sable." Wyatt Wingfoot was looking at me now, with surprise but not suspicion. That was an improvement, at least. "Last I heard, you were off fighting for Symkaria."

"My crew and I came here on a job," I said quickly. "We're tracking a man traveling all over the country, mostly to casinos, and ripping them off for millions of dollars." Time to be judicious about what we were *actually* doing. The world and Johnny Storm didn't need to know our business. "He's got the ability to see a short way into the future. This was our first attempt to apprehend him, and as you can see..." I gestured at the chaos we were mired in. "It didn't go well."

Bang bang bang! "Open up the door!" Over the comm, I heard someone hammering on the door to our suite. Foxtrot and Juliet had been caught in the net now, too.

"Let them in and cooperate," I told my team with a sigh. "We've got a lot of explaining to do."

CHAPTER SEVEN

Explanations took the better part of the rest of the night. From what I could put together, apparently Tolentino had called in a bomb threat to the casino naming my crew as suspects, detailing everything from what we were wearing to the license plate number on Tango's van, then bribed the bartender to drug Romeo's drink halfway through the night before their game even started. The owner of the casino *was* in fact a friend of Wyatt's, and when she called Wyatt for help, Johnny Storm – who was visiting his friend for the weekend – decided to come with him and help shut the threat down.

Of course, by the time *we* were shut down, the actual threat had cashed in his chips and walked out the door with a spring in his step and a smile on his face. Foxtrot had left the cameras rolling, so the last we saw of Tolentino he was stepping into a rideshare and heading for the airport.

"Which is where we need to be," I finished wearily at – god, was it really five in the morning? At least my team had gotten excused to go and sleep. Most of the casino's people had tapped out as well. "As soon as possible. The longer he has time to put miles between us, the harder it's going to be to hunt him down again."

"You didn't do such a great job 'hunting' him this time," Johnny said, actually doing the air quotes thing. How obnoxious.

"It could have gone better," I agreed coolly. "Especially at the end, when we were buried under plaster dust and nearly 'cooked to death.'" *Yeah, you don't like it either, do you?*

"It wasn't that hot."

"Hot enough to–"

"All right, all right." Wyatt held up a hand. "You were trying to take out a threat, and the casino has insurance to cover superhuman damages like this."

That was a little unusual outside of a big city like New York, where this kind of collateral damage was way more common. "Really?"

"Yeah." He glanced at Johnny, who went red.

"It was one time," he muttered. "I was *barely* drunk."

"Drunk enough to set the roof ablaze while you were singing pop songs. How does that one go? 'Something something firework, something something–'"

"Hey! I'm sorry for the roof thing, but I refuse to be ashamed for showing my love for pop songs! They're *good!*"

If I didn't step in, I had the feeling we'd be here for another seven hours. I turned to the casino's owner, a tall, stout Chickasaw woman with long gray braids that complemented the silver color of her very expensive suit. *She* was wearing shoulder pads and pulling it off, darn it. "Mrs Colbert, I'm very sorry for the trouble we caused, but you can see why we couldn't inform you in advance, can't you? The more people who are in on our attempts, the easier it will be for Mr Tolentino to foresee them."

"It seems to me that he foresaw them very easily anyway," she replied dryly. "But I'm willing to give you the benefit of the doubt, as long as *you* promise not to return to my casino. Ever."

"Agreed." I was certain we wouldn't need to – Tolentino hadn't hit the same place twice so far. "Thank you," I said before I stood up from the table and turned to go.

"Hey, where are our thanks?" Johnny asked.

It took everything I had not to reach for one of my chais. "Why would I thank you?" I demanded.

"For not beating the snot out of you, obviously. Trust me, I could have brought a *lot* more heat than I did."

"So could we." I leaned in a little toward him. "And we don't even need to light ourselves and everything around us on fire to do it. Count yourself fortunate." I turned on my heel and walked out of the conference room to the sound of Wyatt chuckling.

As soon as the door shut, though, my shoulders slumped and my head drooped. My team and I were exhausted, we'd barely escaped serious legal action, and Tolentino hadn't just evaded us – he'd run circles around us. That was three days gone from our month – ten percent down.

I'd expected us to fail, but… part of me had held out hope that this really would go as well as I'd planned. That we'd covered every angle, looked at every option. The truth was, we'd been staring into a funhouse mirror, given the illusion of control without even realizing everything was backward and upside down. We'd been played.

Trounced.

Humiliated. And oh, how it burned.

We'll do better next time. I tried to believe that as I headed for our suite. We had our baseline now, and we wouldn't be caught off guard again. This was going to get complicated, but we could handle that. We *would* handle that… and speaking of handles, why – wasn't – this – one – *turning–*

Juliet opened the door a second later. "You could have just knocked," she joked.

Ugh, I really *was* tired. "Thank you," I said softly as I stepped into the room. I was met with a chorus of snores, some soft, some very much not soft – X-Ray had clearly broken her nose and not had it set correctly at some point, because that resonance was otherworldly. "How did you know I was coming?"

"Internal surveillance, remember?" Juliet gestured toward her tablet, which was still hooked in to hotel security. "I was waiting up for you. It's fine," she added, "it's dinnertime in Tokyo, so I got to hang out with my raiding group for a while."

"When do you sleep?" I asked, shrugging out of my jacket with a sigh.

"I catnap. It works for me. I saved you the single bed." She pointed toward it. "I'll do some poking around and figure out where Tolentino is headed next while you get some sleep. We can–"

The quiet was broken by the sound of a cell phone ringing. Actually, *all* our cell phones were ringing, all at once. Was I the only person who'd bothered to silence mine? I reached into my pocket, ignoring the groans and complaints of my rousing team, and checked the screen. No number.

Not that I needed a number to know who was on the other end of this call. I steeled myself, then answered the call. "Hello."

"Quite a dramatic first effort, Sable, I must say. Not a very good one, though."

I relaxed a little when I realized I was talking to Captain Verlak, not Doom himself. "It was only our initial assay. We'll get him next time."

"Will you? In my experience, Tolentino only got better at evading our efforts to capture him, not worse."

I was not about to be browbeaten by Kariana Verlak over the phone where my entire team could hear. "Your personal experiences with failure in this matter are just that, yours. We *will* get him."

Romeo hissed a breath between his teeth, his face going almost as white as the bandage on his head. Everyone in the room seemed to hold their breath for a moment.

"At least you're determined. I've been instructed to tell you that your target is on the way to Monaco."

I glanced at Foxtrot, who was already heading over to his computer to verify the information. "How can you be sure?"

"Few things are hidden from Doom."

"And he's exerting himself on our behalf? How *kind* of him."

Captain Verlak actually laughed. "I think you better than most know not to make the mistake of thinking of him as kind. He's not the sort to throw an investment away, though. You've interested him, Silvija. Don't waste that." She ended the call, and I immediately turned to my team.

"Foxtrot, is she on the level?"

"Still working on getting the passenger list from the airline," he said, "but there *was* a flight to Nice that left six hours ago. Should be arriving there soon. I've got contacts who'll send me security footage so we can get visual verification."

"Perfect." Monaco. City of millionaires, tax dodgers, gamblers, and mad scientists. I was already starting to feel better about this. There were so many big names floating around Monaco at any one time, we would be small fish in a very big pond. It had to be easier to sneak up on Tolentino there, and if we changed our approach enough this next time… yes, we could do it. I was certain of it. "All right. As soon as we get verification, Foxtrot, get someone to put a discreet tail on him. Don't associate us with it at all," I added.

"Got it, Sable."

"Everybody else, pack up. We're leaving. We'll come up with a new plan on the plane."

My team hustled to follow my orders… except for Tango, who glanced at the unused bed, then at me. He sidled over and whispered, "Sure you don't want to take the time for a quick nap?"

His concern was touching, but his voicing it right now was not. I couldn't afford to look weak in front of my team. "I can sleep on the plane. Right now, we need to get going." I slipped into one of the bathrooms – the suite had two, thank goodness – and began to pack up my toiletries, resolutely avoiding looking at my face in the mirror. I knew what I would see – dark circles, terse lines, lips thinned from annoyance and fatigue. The usual, these days.

I was doing what I had to do – what I *wanted* to do – but

there were times I wished I could just ... take a break. Not just for an hour or even a day, but a *real* break where I did nothing but lie on one of the beautiful beaches we were about to be adjacent to, with a drink in one hand and an unrealistic but delightful romance novel in the other, reading about people overcoming simple obstacles and being happy.

I silently promised myself that when this was over, I'd do it. When we'd caught Tolentino and given his device to Doom, when he'd paid off Symkaria's debts and the country was on the right path again, when I'd made sure we had a functioning government and restored the faith of our people in their leadership, I'd take a vacation.

So, in about twenty years then.

I sighed and shoved my toothbrush into my bag. My personal pity party could wait until after we'd secured Jamie Tolentino.

Monaco. We'd get him in Monaco. I felt certain of it.

CHAPTER EIGHT

Four days and twenty hours later I was dangling from the skid of a helicopter a hundred feet over the Mediterranean Sea, just beyond Monaco's yacht-filled Port Hercules. I'd lost my gun and my sword, was completely disconnected from my team, and was doing my best to hang on despite the way the pilot was flying us in ever-tighter circles. If I fell from this height I would probably break every bone in my body.

It would have been easier to hold on if Tolentino weren't laughing at me from the passenger seat. "I only saw three futures where you made it all this way!" he exclaimed, grinning broadly. This close to him, I could see the pearly gleam of his teeth – they were almost too bright, as though they were lit by some sort of inner light. "Well done! That's narrowed your paths down to one where you die, one where you *wish* you'd died, and one where you don't lose anything but your dignity."

"I won't stop coming after you!" I shouted at him. If I could just shift my grip a little bit higher, I might get the leverage to throw my leg up over the skid and climb into the cabin. "You might as well give me the Clairvoyant now and save yourself the trouble!"

"Who's troubled? I think the only person who's going to be in trouble is you, Silver Sable." The copter spun again, and I nearly lost my grip. All right, that plan was shot. I glanced down at the glassy, smooth sheen of the water and grimaced. It was an unusually clear, windless day, with no waves to break the surface tension below. A hundred-foot fall wasn't necessarily fatal, but–

From the corner of my eye, I saw a motorboat cutting a line through the dark blue water below. It was towing a parasailer who was floating a good five hundred feet above me – too far up for me to break my fall on their chute. But maybe…

"You're going to go for it, aren't you?" Tolentino laughed again. "Good luck!" The helicopter suddenly bucked like a wild horse, throwing me upward, then swinging me around again. I grimaced against the stab of pain in my shoulders and turned my head to keep the incoming parasailer in view. A few more seconds… just a few more…

My right hand slipped, throwing off my trajectory. That was it, I was going to fall and – no, there was still a chance if I hit things *just* right. I waited for the copter to spin one more time, then let go with my right hand and dropped–

Then fell into the skid on the other side. I hit it too hard to get an actual hold on it, but was able to use it to redirect my fall so that my wild career sent me straight toward the rope connecting the parasailer to the boat. I missed grabbing it with my painful, stinging hands, but managed to wrap a knee around it. I clenched down hard with my thighs as I began to spiral downward, the rope staying admirably taut – although I could hear the guy sailing above me shouting curses at me in both French and Ligurian.

Gradually I slowed down, and by the time I landed on my butt in the boat I was actually upright, clinging to the rope with my elbows as well as my legs. The woman driving the boat, a busty brunette in a string bikini, stared at me in stupefaction.

"I apologize for dropping in like this," I said in French, picking myself painfully up off the carpeted floor – carpet, who put carpet in a *boat*? At least it was soft. In the distance, I could see a pair of jet skis hurtling toward us in a hurry. My team. *Better late than never.* "I'll be out of your way in just a moment."

"Pas de problème," she murmured, then finally heard the shouts coming from up above and, with a squeak, went back to driving the boat so her passenger didn't end up joining us on the water.

It took all of my focus and my last shreds of dignity to make it onto Tango's jet ski when he and X-Ray got to me. Everything hurt. At least one of my shoulders was dislocated, my hands were swollen from exertion and smacking against the skid, and my legs had just done the equivalent of a hundred-foot pole slide. Now that the adrenaline was wearing off, I felt each and every inch of it, too.

"Sable, are you OK?" Tango asked anxiously as we headed back for shore.

"I'll be fine after I get some first aid and rest for a while," I replied. He glanced back at me with wide eyes – I must not have sounded as confident as I'd been trying for.

"When we lost contact with you, Foxtrot started checking every video feed he could hack into, but we never thought Tolentino would have a helicopter on standby. Then Juliet saw some clips of you being shared on social media, and we figured out what had happened."

Social media? I was on social media? I would rather have shattered every bone in my body than end up plastered across the internet. God forbid I ever became a *meme*.

Doom wasn't going to like this. Not at all.

An hour later I was cleaned up, covered in ointment, pumped full of painkillers, and doing my best to drown my sorrows in my third beer. I usually never drank on a job, but I was making an exception this time, because an earful of angry Captain Verlak compounded with the knowledge that, yep, I'd become a meme – so fast! Why didn't people have better things to do with their lives? – meant that my usual coping strategies weren't working.

"It could be worse," Juliet tried from where she was sitting, tablet in her lap, the video of me pinwheeling through the air still repeating on her screen. At least she'd silenced the irritating falsetto "Wheeeeeeeee!" that had been dubbed over it. "At least Verlak gave us Tolentino's next likely location. It's not that bad a flight to Macao from here."

"We don't have many contacts in Macao," Romeo said, tipping back his own beer. "It's going to be a tougher site to work."

"This one was tough enough," X-Ray said with a sigh. "I didn't know there *were* any badgers in Monaco, much less that many of them."

"I'm sure they were shipped in for the occasion." Which must have taken quite a lot of forward planning. Just how far into the future was he looking?

Far enough that I was worried nothing I did might be enough.

Nope, not going to go there, not even in the silence of my own mind. The rest of my team wasn't so reticent. "Sable…" Foxtrot began tentatively. "Maybe it's time to try to renegotiate terms with Doom. See if we can get an extension, or–"

"No." There could be no renegotiating. It was all or nothing. "No, it's just time to try something new. We'll trade places." I pointed at Foxtrot with my beer. "I'll be on lookout, and you'll take point next time. Juliet can be your backup."

"Um." Juliet raised a hand. "I'm not so sure that I–"

"You'll have your own backup, of course," I assured her. "But we need to change the people who get close to him. We'll come up with something new to try, different faces, and see how we fare next time. We still have three weeks." A day over, actually, but it was safer to underestimate than overestimate. I needed the sense of urgency to keep me sharp. "We won't dive right into our next attempt, I promise. I'm not going to risk your safety."

"Thanks, but… maybe you should be a little more careful about risking your own, too."

I waved her concern away. "I told you, I'm fine."

"Stay that way," Tango said intently. "I was worried we'd be fishing pieces of you out of the sea an hour ago."

I forced a smile. "It will take more than a little helicopter ride to break me."

CHAPTER NINE

In fact, it took a boat ride, a rooftop chase through downtown Shanghai, *another* helicopter ride, and a very uncomfortable few minutes on the back of an angry camel to break me.

It wasn't that we didn't come close. We did; so close I could almost taste victory a time or two. There was a moment in Atlantic City where we boxed Tolentino in completely. I'd heard him swearing as I closed in, my fingers flexing with anticipation at getting my hands on this man at last. I would truss him up like a roast pig and deliver him to Doom with a flourish – but no. He'd managed to put a group of chatty octogenarians between us, and by the time the elderly cadre had cleared the way, he was gone. It took hours of reviewing the footage to realize that he'd been carrying a wig in his jacket and had slipped out with the rest of the blue-hairs.

It was even worse in Montreal. We'd followed him from the tables to a magic show, thinking he was going to try to blend in with the crowd again – easy enough to do in the dark. To keep from giving ourselves away, we'd gone in quietly, expecting to have to search every corner for him.

Instead, he ran up onto the stage, interrupting the magician who was about to lock his "beautiful assistant" in a box. He grabbed the short, horn-headed wand the guy was holding, said "Sorry about this," and then–

He was gone. At first, I thought it was a ruse – this was a *magic* show after all, he'd probably fallen through a hidden trapdoor or something like that. But the way the magician started screaming bloody murder and scrabbling across the stage looking for the wand, I appeared to be underestimating Tolentino's vanishing act.

"That was the Wand of Watoomb!" the magician shrieked as he crawled around on hands and knees, throwing props aside in his desperate search. "I spent my entire life savings on it! That was my ticket to the big time! *Bring it back!*"

This little episode turned into a federal investigation into Canada's black market for magical devices, jail time for the magician, a huge fine for the casino, and another strike on bringing in Tolentino for us. Once the Wild Pack was finally out of the interrogation room – again, this was the third time we'd been questioned by the authorities since this job began – Captain Verlak called. I waved my people off and took it by myself.

The last thing I needed was for them to hear me being chewed out yet again.

Only the lecture was different this time, insofar as it wasn't a lecture at all. "Our sources are currently unable to locate Mr Tolentino," she said without preamble. "Can you tell me why?"

"He used an unregulated magical object to make himself disappear," I said tiredly as I walked along the green space beside the massive casino. I found a tall, shady tree and leaned against it, exhausted.

"Hmm. And what did you do to try to prevent that?"

"What?" Where was *this* coming from? "How was this *my* fau–"

"Your objective is to obtain the Clairvoyant for Doom. You can't do that if Tolentino loses himself between dimensions with it. Did you even think to try and stop him?"

"We had no idea it was a genuine magical artifact," I snapped, straightening out of my slump through the power of indignation. "Obviously I didn't want him to vanish, I wanted to take him into custody!"

"Really? Because it's been weeks now of attempting just that, and none of your efforts have worked out for you yet. You have a *reputation* for being the best, regardless of the abilities of your target. It makes me wonder whether or not you were perhaps paid to look the other way in this case, maybe by Mr Tolentino himself, in order to facilitate his escape."

"I would never do that," I said coldly. "Once I take a contract, I'm true to it. You must have seen plenty of evidence of *that* in my record as well. Plus, it doesn't make sense – no one can offer me what Doom can. I wouldn't jeopardize my country's future by going back on an agreement with him."

"Perhaps. But–" She paused as someone began speaking to her in the background. A minute later she returned to the line. "Our sources say he's finally reappeared, in Tokyo."

I felt weak with relief. "You see?" I said with confidence I didn't quite feel. "I told you we weren't playing both sides." This was good, this was very–

"The method we were using to track him previously has failed, however. We'd homed in on the energy signature of the Clairvoyant, but it seems he discovered our tactic and countered it. It's sheer luck we were able to locate him this time around."

Oh. "I'm sure you've got other methods at your disposal for finding him, don't you?"

"We do, but they require more manpower than Doom is willing to allocate for you." I opened my mouth to object, but she cut me off. "Giving you Tolentino's location was a courtesy, not a requirement of the contract. You have no cause for complaint."

That was, unfortunately, true. "I understand," I said stiffly. "If you'd be kind enough to share the specifics of his last known location, we'll take it from here on out."

"Hmm." The subsequent silence made my toes curl up in my boots and my free hand tighten around one of my chais. "I'm going to be honest with you, Silver Sable. I'm not sure you and your crew are up to this task."

No. Oh, no. "That's not your decision to make."

"It's certainly one I have a say in. Doom wants to give you the benefit of the doubt, but I don't know that you and your team have the… *flexibility* required to pull this off."

I took a deep breath and fought my racing heart back down to something reasonable. "We still have time. You made the contract for one month, and I want every day of that."

"If you're sure that's what you want." Captain Verlak hesitated for a moment, then added in a softer voice, "There are many worse things than fealty to Doom, you know. Symkaria would not suffer under his reign. The people of Latveria have one of the highest qualities of life in the entire world."

"They also have to put up with things like periodic eldritch invasions," I said, because Doom might be one of the most powerful people on Earth, but even he couldn't avoid social media capturing Hell's incursion into Doomstadt on Walpurgis Night. "I'd rather avoid that for my people, if possible."

"Suit yourself. You're right when you say I don't have the authority to pull you off this job. But… Doom may grant you leniency if you come to him honestly and tell him you can't do it. He won't be so inclined if you get to the end of the month with nothing to show for it but wasted time."

I knew that, in her own way, Captain Verlak was trying to do me a kindness, but I didn't appreciate or need it. "Thank you for letting me know where Tolentino is. I'll be in touch soon." I ended the call and indulged in a silent scream for a moment as I pressed the phone to my forehead. This wasn't good, wasn't what I needed right now. I needed to think. I needed a plan that would *work*. I needed to make my next effort our final one, because my people were on the verge of collapse. Their motivation was sapped, their energy was low, and all of us were exhausted from running around the globe after a man who was always five steps ahead. It was exhausting to weather things going wrong over and over, but I had no choice. I had to be strong for the sake of my crew, even if I was starting to think I'd made a promise to Doom I might not be able to keep.

Verlak was right – we'd botched every attempt so far. Utterly and completely failed, and that was unacceptable. It was time to start thinking beyond our usual tactics, time to do something truly unexpected. But what? We'd exhausted our arsenal of tricks. We were good, the best, but we weren't super heroes. None of us had magical powers or brilliant inventions or mutations to help us bend reality to our will.

So… then we had to find someone who *did* have that kind of power and bring them onto the job.

I was probably going to do permanent damage to my corporate bank account at this rate, but the more I thought about it, the more I seriously considered the idea of outside help. It wasn't like I'd never worked with contractors before – I teamed up with Spider-Man frequently, and he'd almost always proven a boon to whatever job was at hand. Of course, he was also annoyingly chirpy and ridiculously optimistic, but no one was perfect.

Although he came pretty close.

Hey, you could…

No. No, I wasn't going to ask Spidey to join the hunt for Tolentino – at least, not yet. Apart from Tolentino being an old friend of his, I really didn't want to answer the questions Spidey would inevitably ask about who this job was for. He tended to be a little… black and white in his thinking when it came to working for parties like Doom, and I didn't want to deal with moralizing on top of everything else.

All right then, not Spider-Man. But who? It had to be someone who wasn't a major power to keep from drawing too much attention, someone who was willing to work for money – or whatever else I could come up with to offer them –

and someone who had that element of unpredictability I was looking for.

Tough but not too tough, wasn't so busy saving the world to forget they needed cash to eat, flexible...

One name popped into my head, and I groaned out loud. Oh please, no. Not her. Anyone but her... but even as I complained to myself, the back of my mind was already running with the idea.

She was ideal in so many ways. Capable and quick, versatile in her choice of "work" – and I used that word lightly, since she was a professional thief – smart enough to get away with most things, and unpredictable thanks to the probability manipulator that was implanted in her. Ha, she was downright *volatile.* I didn't like her, not in the slightest, and she didn't care for me either – probably because we shared an ex – but if anyone could help us get this done, it was her. The realization was both bitter and freeing. I didn't make a habit of lying to myself, and I wasn't going to start now.

I had my target. Now I just needed to convince her to sign on.

No... first I needed to convince my team to give her a try. And that wasn't going to be easy, but then, nothing about the Black Cat ever was. She was a consummate liar, a narcissist, a troublemaker, and did I mention she was a professional thief? This might take a *lot* of convincing.

It did.

"You can't be serious," Juliet snapped the second after I brought it up that night in our hotel room. "Felicia Hardy is the worst possible choice for a job of this importance. She turns everything into a con. There's no way we could trust her with an item like the Clairvoyant."

"If all goes well, we won't have it in our possession for long," I reminded her. "And I think even Miss Hardy would think twice about stealing something out from under the nose of Doom."

Romeo and X-Ray looked uneasily at each other, as if they were imagining it.

"It's not just her we'd have to worry about," Foxtrot added. "She runs with a two-man crew. We'd have to bring them on the job as well, or risk them crashing it at the worst time."

"Right." Ah yes, Boris Korpse and Bruno Grainger, the Black Cat's nimble henchmen. A scientist and a hitter, if I remembered correctly. Also expert conmen, because who else would Felicia hire? "I don't see a problem with bringing them in as well. I'd rather have them where we can keep an eye on them than let them help her from afar."

Tango made a face. "That's three extra people, Sable, half of what we're fielding. We don't have the manpower to babysit them."

"I'm not suggesting we babysit anyone." He was right, that would be untenable. Instead... "We need to trust them to work with us."

"That's an internationally renowned thief we're talking about," Juliet reminded me with a scowl. "She's conned everyone from the Thieves' Guild to the Sorcerer Supreme. How can we possibly trust her and her people with any part of this?"

Luckily, I had an answer ready to go. Props to myself for spending five hours brainstorming approaches earlier in the day. "We have to tempt them with something they want, of course."

X-Ray raised an eyebrow. "Something they'd want more than the Clairvoyant? Something they couldn't, like, find for themselves?"

"Exactly." I crossed my legs, feeling a little smug.

"And you *have* something like that?"

"As a matter of fact, I do." I had certain packrat tendencies that a former therapist attributed to the loss of every physical touchstone I'd had as a child when my home – and my mother – were burned. Whether they were right or not, I kept everything I'd ever found on my previous jobs in a very carefully hidden warehouse back in Symkaria.

Good thing, too. I was pretty sure I had the perfect thing to tempt Black Cat into helping us capture Tolentino. I just had to get it, then bait the trap so she'd actually show up. I couldn't just request a meeting with her – Felicia and I stayed out of each other's ways. She'd love nothing more than to stand me up… but I was going to make her *want* to meet with me.

"Pack up, everyone. We're going to make a quick trip to Symkaria before heading on to New York City."

And I was going to need to make a quick call to Doom. I'd need his permission to borrow something if this was going to work. Which it would.

It had to.

CHAPTER TEN

One hideously uncomfortable phone call, a solo trip to my warehouse to take a few pictures, and a visit to Symkaria's national museum later, and we were back in New York readying a trap for a cat. One I hoped wouldn't turn out to be a rat.

I didn't like to work with people I couldn't completely trust, but in this case, I thought the benefit outweighed the risk. After all, I was baiting the trap with something I knew that Felicia Hardy would want, and once she found out what I was *really* offering for her help, well...

Hopefully that would clinch the deal. You could never be entirely sure about a person's reaction when you delved into their past, but I'd yet to meet a person in her line of business who was completely without daddy issues. I could give Black Cat a key to unlocking her former mentor's psyche, as well as the chance at a fabulous secret fortune.

While rumors abounded that Felicia was the one who'd ensured the Black Fox vanished from the face of the earth, I knew it had to be more complicated than that. They'd been close; they'd been family. Rare was the person who could throw family away without any emotional repercussions, whether they were worthy of that stain in your heart or not.

Not that *I'd* know anything about that.

I put aside my angst and focused on the matter at hand. Over the past three days, we had managed to put together what seemed like a legitimate exhibit here in New York: a special viewing of the crown jewels of Symkaria. Thought lost during the tumult of the Second World War, they'd resurfaced in the fifties on the black market, apparently sold by one of the king's former ministers. They'd passed hands from collector to collector until one of Symkaria's prime ministers, one with a mind toward resurrecting the monarchy in *his* image, got his hands on them in order to lend his claims credence.

He'd been overthrown a few years later, and the jewels had been transported to the National Museum, where they were forgotten as Symkaria descended into chaos once more. They'd been collecting dust in the basement there for over thirty years and were only seeing the light of day now thanks to Doom's agreement to my request.

You might not think three days was enough time to prepare for an exhibit – where to have it? How to advertise? Who to invite? How to secure it? But it was amazing what you could get done when you had the authority of Doom working on your behalf. A few calls and he'd arranged everything, including a viewing space at the Latverian embassy and invitations for all the most glamorous people in New York City. He'd even formally arranged for myself and the Wild Pack to be the contractors tasked with bringing the jewels to him, so that we could easily explain our presence there.

I hadn't been sure Doom would go for it. I *really* hadn't wanted to talk to him about bringing in Black Cat – it felt like highlighting me and my team's inadequacy, and I was sure Captain Verlak was doing plenty of that for us behind the scenes. But I also didn't want to steal from my own national museum when I knew full well that all the treasures in it were considered "collateral" for Symkaria's outstanding debt. So, talking with Doom it was.

He'd been surprisingly amenable.

"Get them. Bring them here. They will serve your purpose well." He'd paused, then said, "As long as you don't let Black Cat *actually* steal them."

"I won't," I'd said grimly. I would literally stick myself to her with webbing if I had to, but there was no way she was getting away with our bait when it was only meant to lure her into helping on the *other* job.

I wasn't sure of a lot of things these days – my confidence had taken a beating along with all the rest of me these past three weeks – but I *was* sure that Black Cat would try to make her move before the jewels actually made it to the embassy. She was good, but nobody wanted to risk stealing from Doom. That meant she would have to try to take them once we touched down in JFK, before we reached the embassy. It narrowed her potential moves considerably, enough that nothing was going to surprise us.

How could I be so sure she was coming for the crown jewels? History and gut instinct. Symkaria's crown and scepter weren't particularly exceptional, as jewelry went – all of the pieces had been mined in Symkaria, not stolen from elsewhere, so there was a lot of lapis lazuli and topaz, with a few diamonds and emeralds as accents. They were singular pieces, though, interesting because they were so unique, and the Black Cat loved to sparkle.

I'd decided on a versatile approach to this job. Everybody had their skillsets, everybody knew how to work as a team. I let Foxtrot and Juliet coordinate things from a hotel room near the airport, gave X-Ray and Romeo their legs so they could respond as needed, and only kept Tango with me for retrieval and return, to pilot the plane. Tango had been with me almost as long as Juliet, and I knew I could rely on him to do what needed to be done without question. He'd do it while poking fun at me or making jokes, sure, but I could handle that. I liked it, actually. Nobody else bothered to joke with me these days.

I tried to catch a few winks on a pulldown bunk in the storage compartment on our way back to New York – I was exhausted and needed to be in top form coming up against Black Cat. I did sleep, but my rest was uneasy, plagued with the intractable feeling of failure, like I was missing something big. When a bit of turbulence woke me up, I didn't bother trying to sleep again, just wiped my eyes and headed into the small cabin, making strong black tea for myself and Tango as I went.

"Here." I passed him the travel mug – tea sweetened with far too much honey – and sat down in the copilot's chair, sipping at my own bitter brew.

"I didn't mean to wake you up," he apologized as he accepted the tea.

"It's fine. I wasn't getting much rest anyway." I stared out the dark window. We'd left the dawn behind, heading back into the early morning darkness of the East Coast as we crossed the Atlantic.

"Yeah, I know the feeling." He paused, then said, "Actually, no, I don't. I always manage to sleep, even when I'm working a big job like this. You've never had a problem with it before either. What gives this time around?"

I gave Tango a half smile. "Oh, probably just the issue of certain doom – pardon the pun – if we fail, not to mention decades of pain for Symkaria and–"

"But that's not your fault."

"What?" I didn't understand what he was saying.

"What's going on in Symkaria… that's not your fault." Tango glanced at me, his eyes dark with concern. "It's a bad spot, for sure, but it's not like you ever invited any of this trouble in. You didn't force all those dictators to take over, you didn't – you didn't *abandon* anyone, Sable. You can't 'abandon' an entire country and have it fail just because of that. The people who live there have to take some responsibility, too, y'know?"

"I beg to differ. I'm a well-known public figure; I have been for a long time." I'd been the leader of the Wild Pack since before I finished school. And before me, it was my father. "People look up to me, but for years I was too busy running around making money to really focus on the needs of Symkaria."

"That's just what I'm talking about. *You* are not Symkaria," he insisted. "Symkaria is a place filled with millions of people. What happens to it isn't solely your call, and it's not solely *your* fault if things go bad, either. You're allowed to have a life beyond an ideal."

Now I knew he was talking crazy. "I don't expect you to understand." I sighed. "But as Spider-Man says, with great power comes great responsibility. If I don't use my power for the greater good of my people, who will?"

"Maybe no one. Or maybe the focus will come down more to individual responsibility, but either way, you don't have to accept responsibility for things that are just… beyond you. You're not like Doom," he clarified, having probably noticed the stirrings of resentment on my face. "He's practically the embodiment of Latveria. That's because he *wants* to be. But you, you can have a life beyond duty. You don't have to hold yourself up to some impossible standard for the sake of a nation that needs to learn to stand on its own feet."

"I won't forever." Because some day I would die, obviously. Or retire, but that seemed unlikely. "But in the meantime, Symkaria was dealt a raw hand, so I'm going to do what I can. Excuse me." I got up and left for the cabin again, deliberately ignoring the silent plea on Tango's face as he watched me go. I didn't want to see it, didn't want to acknowledge it. It promised complications I wasn't ready for, might never be ready for again. Complications like that would make me vulnerable, would require me to let down my guard. It was unthinkable, no matter how much joy it promised.

To think that once, I hadn't shied away from affection. I'd had friends, I'd had lovers. Once, I'd even been married to a man who made me feel like the most precious woman in the world.

And it had all ended so… pathetically. No great final explosion, no terrible tragedy, no desperate attempt to reconcile, just… an end. A leaving. I was grateful Basil had saved me after the debacle with Rhino, happy to have my life, but a part of me still wondered if the horrible pain, the months of rehab, and the slow rebuilding of the Wild Pack had all been worth it.

If I wanted to make sure it stayed worth it, then I needed to make sure we got this job done right.

Come find me, Black Cat. Let's make a deal.

The shenanigans began almost the moment the plane touched down. We got a call from whoever was making the gate assignments that there was an unexpected issue with a fuel truck at ours, and they had been instructed to direct us to a new one.

"Acknowledged," Tango said, then muted his mic and glanced at me. "You ready for this, Sable?"

I smiled. After everything we'd been through in the past two weeks, evading the Black Cat's grasping claws while simultaneously tempting her in close enough to talk to was going to be downright revitalizing. "I'm ready. Lock things down here and get on the road as soon as possible, all right? I'm pretty sure we can trust Doom's intelligence, but–"

"Better safe than sorry," Tango agreed. "I'm on it." And I knew he was. I was confident in my people, confident in being able to get this right, so I didn't fret about Tango. He would take care of his end of things.

Now it was up to me to take care of mine.

I made sure to look the part. I was the tough-as-nails mercenary Silver Sable, from the top of my head to the bottoms of my feet. I wore my body armor, my katana, my derringer, *and* plenty of chais lining my belt. I had the crown jewels in a locked briefcase connected to my wrist by a thin but very tough chain. I had a car waiting for me, an armored SUV complete with chauffeur. I was on this... and if Black Cat hadn't already made half a dozen plans to separate me from my cargo, then I didn't know her as well as I thought I did.

The first attempt came, unsurprisingly, when we pulled in at our new gate. I stepped down out of our jet and headed for the stairs that would take me up into the terminal, when–

"Excuse me! Miss!"

I turned around and saw a short, dark-skinned man driving a baggage cart with one hand and holding a clipboard with the other heading my way. He had his cap pulled down low, and in the early morning darkness I could barely see his face, but I saw enough to know who I was dealing with. *Ah. Dr Korpse.* Right on time. He pulled to a stop in front of me and leapt out of the cart.

"Yes?" I said, schooling my face into a haughty expression. "What is it?"

"You can't bring that into the airport!"

I glanced down at my getup. "Can't bring *what* into the airport?"

"All of it!" he snapped. "You'll have to leave all your personal weapons on the plane, or package them up and send them to wherever you're staying here."

Ah, a good attempt to try and separate me from my gear. Not one that would work, though. "I believe my diplomatic immunity applies here," I said, pulling a badge out from around my neck and holding it out toward him. It clearly stated I was a representative of the Latverian embassy and, as such, wasn't subject to the same rules and regulations as Americans were. "If you'd like to complain about my armaments to my employer, then I'm happy to call up Doctor Doom for you, but it's unlikely he's going to be in the mood to talk."

"Um." His hands tightened a little bit on the clipboard. I wondered what the odds were that it was actually an explosive device. "I... don't think that will be necessary, but we *will* have to inspect the contents of your case, just to be sure you're not bringing anything nuclear in with you. *Which* we have the authority to do," he added before I could do more than scoff. "Diplomatic immunity only goes so far when it comes to protecting the public good."

Luckily for me, I was familiar with the law he was citing. "In that case, I invoke my right to external evaluation." No way was I opening this case in front of a sticky-fingered thief like him.

"Of course you do," he muttered so softly I barely heard it. "I don't have an X-ray machine available here."

"I'll accompany you to the security office, then."

He made a face, but didn't balk the way I was expecting him to. "Very well, let's get going. I'll drive you to the nearest–"

"I prefer to walk." I pointed toward the stairs leading into the gate in the distance. "Can't we just go in there?"

"If that's how you like it," he said, and to my surprise he led the way up the stairs and into the airport, talking on his walkie the whole time. "Yeah, we're coming in from the west side of– yeah, that's the one. Uh-huh. The portable is fine, I don't want to bother with the security lines."

Like there was going to be an issue with lines at five in the morning. I kept my mouth shut, though, interested to see how this played out. Sure enough, by the time we reached the main terminal there was a woman waiting for us with what looked like an old-school overhead projector on a cart. She didn't say anything, didn't even meet my eyes, just grunted and pointed toward the tray. A closer look revealed she was sweating at her temples, and her hands were trembling oh-so-slightly.

An employee who'd given in to bribery, most likely. Not someone I needed to worry about, just someone I needed to get past. I set my case down.

"Take the bracelet off," she said flatly.

"No."

"We can't get a clear image if you don't–"

"Do you want to meet Doctor Doom in person?"

Now she *did* meet my eyes, and hers were full of fear. "No," she whimpered.

"Then take your picture with the bracelet on, or…" I let my sentence drift off, sure that her own mind would fill in the blanks. There really *wasn't* an or. I wasn't about to bring something so minor to the attention of Doom, but I didn't mind banking on his reputation.

"Go ahead and set the case down," she said after a moment. "Leave as much room between your hand and the machine as possible."

I obeyed, and a moment later there was a hum, and a picture appeared on the small screen above the imaging platform. There were the jewels, in all their X-rayed glory, crown on one side and scepter on the other.

"Not a nuke," I pointed out helpfully. "Nor a weapon of any kind. I'll be leaving now." Neither of them tried to stop me, although out of the corner of my eye, I could see Boris talking rapidly into his walkie as I resumed my walk down the terminal hall. What would their next step be?

I checked my phone to keep an eye on Tango's progress, then spoke into my comm as I headed for the main door. "I'm on my way out. Be waiting in the drop-off lane." Innocuous enough, in case someone was listening in. Just as I reentered the cool night air, a heavy-looking armored SUV pulled up from where it had been idling a few meters down. A tall man in a smart uniform got out and nodded to me.

"Ready when you are, ma'am."

And here he was, the next step – Bruno Grainger. "You're not the embassy's usual driver," I pointed out with perfectly justifiable suspicion.

"No, ma'am. Gregor ate some bad borscht. I'm filling in for him. My name is Oleg Imyarek."

"Oleg." I looked him up and down doubtfully. "I'm not in the habit of trusting people I've never worked with before. Are you fully versed on all the embassy's emergency protocols?"

"Yes, ma'am." He tipped his hat. "Believe me, you're in good hands. No harm will come to you with me."

We'd see. Black Cat and her crew had a reputation for being careful when it came to lives – at least innocent ones – but I didn't think I qualified as an innocent bystander in her book. "Very well, then. Let's get going."

As I got into the back of the car, I wondered what tack Bruno would take. Would he simply drive me in the wrong direction, take me somewhere he and Black Cat could try to corner me? Would he fail at driving so miserably that we got stuck in traffic so I became a stationary target?

"We're on the move," I said into my comm. I got two taps

back – confirmation that my people were in place and ready to intervene as needed. Given the likelihood that I was being listened in on right now, that was good enough.

We pulled out from JFK and headed for I-678. So far, so good – that got us onto Grand Central Parkway pretty quickly. Once we were there, it was smooth sailing for a good fifteen minutes – just long enough for a passenger to really let her guard down – and then–

An enormous truck in the right lane pulled over in front of us. "Oleg" cursed and made an effort to go around it, but now the right lane was blocked by a sports car with tinted windows, and the few attempts we made to speed up and get into the left lanes were easily blocked by the truck.

The back of the truck opened up, and a ramp crashed down onto the asphalt, sending up a shower of sparks. The SUV was already slowing down in preparation for driving inside without giving both of us head injuries when–

Smash! A random-seeming car jumped the green space between the lanes up ahead and veered right into the path of the truck. It slammed on the brakes, fishtailing wildly thanks to the lowered ramp, and Oleg had to jerk the wheel to the left to ensure we didn't end up pancaked in our own car. "Faster!" I shouted at him from the backseat. "Get us out of this!" He sped up obediently, and soon we'd left the near-disaster behind us.

I caught a glimpse of the driver of the car as we passed – Tango had an expression of almost comical shock on his face, but he winked when he saw he'd caught my eye.

"That was your idea of driving?" I exclaimed – I had a reputation for being a hardass, and it wouldn't do to tarnish it by being nice at a time like this. "We were almost pinched back there! Get it together, Imyarek."

"Yes, ma'am." He sounded quite serious, and I supposed he was. After all, Black Cat's first real trap had failed. He had to try to make sure her next one succeeded.

What happened next was a masterclass in driving mechanics. Truly, Bruno was one of the best I'd ever seen – he had the ability to make himself seem like he knew what he was doing, while simultaneously feeding into the byways and blockages his boss had laid down in advance to try and get me and the jewels alone, and then react to being stymied by my team each and every time. Construction ahead? Oh look, a new lane *just* opened up! Detour required? Whoops, no, the signs say go the other way! We'd probably have caused half a dozen accidents in the first five miles if this had been a decent hour of the morning, but I'd planned for that, too.

By the time we were within ten minutes of the embassy, it was clear that Bruno was getting tense. His hands were a bit jerkier on the wheel, and he kept looking out the side windows – looking *up*, that is. He was expecting something to happen, someone to rain down from above, which was what I'd been waiting for.

I'd probably already seen Black Cat a few times already since landing in New York – she'd almost certainly been driving the ridiculously expensive sports car that had cut us off – but now she was going to *show* herself.

Perfect. Or purrfect, in this case. It was time to take this heist acapella.

A second after we drove underneath a stoplight, something thudded heavily onto the top of the SUV. A second later, five claws punched through the metal of the roof, twisting sharply to make a fist-sized hole. From there they began peeling the roof back like it was an orange, and that meant it was time to go.

I hefted a chai in my hand, took careful aim, and threw it into the car's dashboard, right below where "Oleg" had his hands on the wheel. He cursed loudly as sparks flew around him, trying to regain control of the vehicle. I couldn't have that. I flung the briefcase forward, hitting him on the right shoulder and knocking him into the door. The car swerved, the person on the roof let out a startled, "Whoa, Boris, what–" and then a second later–

We crashed.

It was a bit more of a dramatic crash than I'd been anticipating. We were supposed to veer off the road, maybe smash into a bus stop or something. But we happened to have just turned onto the bridge over the Harlem River, and instead of taking a few impacts that would be easily mitigated by the SUV's advanced safety features, we went through the guard rail. My stomach leapt into my throat as, for a moment, it felt like we were flying, not falling.

Gravity reasserted itself, and we plunged into the river.

CHAPTER ELEVEN

We hit the water with a noisy *splash*, and seconds later the entire car had gone utterly dark. Water rushed in through the hole in the ceiling, but I was more concerned with getting into the front seat and checking on Boris.

He wasn't moving. A closer look verified he was still breathing, at least, but that wouldn't last for long either if we didn't get out of here fast.

"Sable! Sable, report in, what's going on?" Juliet demanded. "*Silver!* We've lost your clear signal, what happened?"

"We crashed into the river," I said, spluttering as I splashed around in the filthy water trying to locate the button to undo Boris's seat belt.

"Shoot. X-Ray is the closest and she's still three minutes out – she screwed up her car getting you guys out of that last roadblock. Black Cat's been sighted, she's probably–"

"She's here." Or at least, she was somewhere up on dry land, I assumed. "I need to– the driver, he's unconscious, I have to get him out." His face was about to go underwater.

"Let Black Cat get him! He's her guy!"

"And he's here because I put him here," I snapped. "I'm not leaving his fate to chance. Get the others here as fast as you can, I have the feeling I'll need the help." I zoned out after that, not listening to Juliet's increasingly shrill warnings. It was almost a relief when the comm unit fizzled out.

I ended up simply cutting through Bruno's seatbelt and hefting him up out of the narrow seat, which – even with the water's help, this man was big and heavy – was almost too much for me to handle. And I still had to make a hole big enough to get us through, then swim up to the surface...

Don't psych yourself out. First things first – hole. Because we were about to run out of air, and then the timer would really start. I could hold my breath for five minutes under optimal conditions, but while exerting myself in a filthy New York City river that was completely dark? Not likely. A quarter of that, tops.

All right, then. Time to make a hole. I grabbed one of my chais and hammered at the passenger-side window, but the glass didn't even crack. *Fine.* I pulled my gun instead, aiming to fire a hole through the glass.

It still didn't shatter, the bullet simply lodging in the glass itself. It took me five more bullets to remember that this was a vehicle designed with security in mind – every window was likely to be laminate glass. I wasn't going to be able to shoot a hole big enough to get us out that way, definitely not before the water completely filled the car. My hand tightened around the grip of my pistol before my logical mind caught up to me.

Just let the water fill the car. Then I could just open the door once the pressure equalized. I knew that, *knew* it, it was something that should have occurred to me instantly and instead it had taken me almost a minute of processing to come up with it. The effects of adrenaline... and fatigue. If I was going to get through this job alive, I needed to do something about the five hours of sleep out of each forty-eight that I'd been averaging.

The water was almost to our heads. I took a deep breath, then forced away the burning sensation of guilt I felt as the water covered up Bruno. If I got him to the surface fast enough, he wouldn't aspirate enough to be fatal. Right?

Right.

The last of the air vanished, and I reached for the door handle. It opened easily, and I got out and swam into a standing position, bracing my feet on either side of the door, then hoisted Bruno out. A few tiny bubbles escaped from his mouth – I couldn't see them, but I could feel them against my face. I turned my head upward, and now I could see light, faint and wavery, probably about twelve feet up. OK. OK, that was where we had to be. Now it was time to get there. This was going to be a tough swim. I detached my gun and sword and let them sink back down into the car.

At least there were no sharks in the water trying to bite me in two this time. Although, this being a New York City waterway, there really were no guarantees.

I grabbed Bruno with both my arms and kicked off with my legs. That gained us a few feet, but the last ten still loomed over me like the swimming leg of a triathlon.

Kick. Kick. Kick. I was barely moving with each immense effort, struggling to keep my hold on Bruno and manage the floating jewel case and stop myself from doing something really stupid, like gasping, all at once. If I could have spared a hand to let that dumb case drop to the bottom of the river I would have, but I didn't have a spare anything right now. I had to keep going.

Kick. Kick. Kick.

Had to keep working. If there was one thing I was good at, it was working. *Be better. Do more. Harder. HARDER.*

Kick. Kick.

I was getting closer. The lights were getting brighter, almost swimming in front of me, like stars.

Kick…

Kick…

Ki…

A hand reached down and grabbed my upper arm in an iron grip. Water whooshed past me, and a few seconds later I was face-down on the muddy embankment that supported one of the piles of the Robert F. Kennedy Bridge. I sucked in air and coughed it back out just as furiously, my body not quite able to accept that this was really the rescue it looked like. *It's true, we're not dead, now calm down.*

I could hear sirens coming – police? Police I could handle, but Bruno probably needed to be checked out by a doctor, and we couldn't afford delays. I forced my head up to see what was going on–

And saw a remarkably familiar woman in a skintight, soaking-wet black uniform hammering Bruno on the back as he coughed into his fist and waved her away. He was already sitting upright, too. Thank goodness.

"–going with them," she said as I pushed up to my knees, then my feet. The lights were coming closer – not police, but an ambulance. "You inhaled that nasty water, and you probably have a concussion, and *look* how you're holding your arm. You need to go to a hospital."

"It's not that bad!" he snapped at her before coughing again.

"Oh no? Then why are you wincing like you've got a headache? Why did I have to smack you hard enough to bruise to get you to start breathing again?"

"Boss, c'mon."

"Don't you 'boss' me." The woman stood up and crossed her arms. "I pay a ridiculous amount of money for your health insurance. It is literally one of the best policies in the entire nation, and you boys almost never use it. Now that I've got a good reason to get you to go, you'd better believe I'm taking it. Maybe they can do a physical while they're at it."

"I'm in perfect shape!" Bruno protested.

"Save it for the doc, mister."

I walked over to join them, doing my best not to stagger. "You're all right, then?" I said to Bruno, ignoring the woman for the moment.

"Yeah." He looked a little sheepish. "I guess you pulled me out of the car, huh?"

"I did." Not very well, but I did. I turned to look at where it had gone in, then back at him. "We're lucky the river isn't very deep here."

"You're lucky *I* was on hand to save both of you from a watery grave," the woman interjected, and I really couldn't ignore her anymore. I straightened up to my full height – which was still six inches shorter than this woman in her heels, darn her – and raised an eyebrow.

"Black Cat. Fancy meeting you here."

"Oh, you know how it is," she said with a grin. "Can't let a wrong go unrighted and all that. You're lucky I was innocently bystanding nearby and happened to catch sight of this little accident."

"Am I now?" I turned my stare on Bruno, who at least had the decency to look down and shrug. "So, you and 'Oleg' don't have any prior acquaintance?"

"Nope, sure don't, but you know how it is in this town, right?" She tossed her hair over her shoulder and shrugged. "Sometimes you meet somebody, and it's like you've known them all your life."

I was done with the charade at this point. My team had to be close – it was time to get down to business. Except this was the moment the ambulance chose to arrive, and two EMTs jumped out of the back and ran over. They had red shirts and long black pants, and despite the early hour they were both wearing caps.

"We got a call about a vehicle going into the water," the woman in front said briskly as she knelt down next to Bruno. "I take it you were inside?"

"I was, but I'm–"

"He's *not fine*, he needs to be seen to by a professional," Black Cat said.

Bless the emergency medical technician, she didn't even bat an eye at being addressed by a super… something. Hero? Villain? It was hard to say with Felicia Hardy. "I understand," she said as she got out her stethoscope and a blood pressure cuff.

The male half of the duo headed my way, but I waved him off. Five minutes later, a complaining Boris was ushered into the waiting ambulance, which wailed off in a fury of lights and sirens. As it vanished into the distance, the sun finally rose over the horizon, turning the sky pink and making the water look deceptively calm. The distant roar of traffic was more distinct now – the city was waking up.

I was out of time. Things hadn't gone the way I'd expected them to, but I needed to make my play now and hope for the best. "Miss Hardy, I–"

My entreaty was cut off rather abruptly – not to mention rudely – when Black Cat suddenly darted forward, sweeping one arm toward my face as the other slashed down at my left hand. Oh, *come on*, was she still going for the jewels? After this? I jerked the case back as I slipped beneath her claws, then went for my katana, which was…

Not there. Because I'd left it down in the car, *Silvija, you–*

Fine. I'd make do with what I had. I blocked her next strike with the briefcase, counting on her to retract her claws so she didn't risk damaging the jewels. She did, and the strike's stuttering moment of hesitation was enough for me to get off a kick to her midsection. It barely grazed her, as she leapt backward – into a *flip*. Who did she think she was, Spider-Girl? Was I some rube, to be impressed with a few showy acrobatics?

I picked up a rock from the shoreline and hucked it at her just before she landed, which turned her graceful touchdown into more of an arms-akimbo "whoa!" position. She glared at me. I fought the urge to glare back.

"I just want to talk to you," I said, fighting the urge to shiver. It might be summertime, but it was still only dawn, and I was drenched to the skin.

"No, thanks!" Black Cat replied lightly, picking up the same rock I'd just leveled at her and throwing it at me twice as hard. I blocked with the briefcase, but the impact still drove me backward. "I've got better things to do than spend my time in early-morning chats with self-righteous hypocrites, so how about you make this easy on both of us and hand over the goods before someone gets hurt?" She crouched slightly, claws flared, ready to pounce.

Oh, for heaven's sake. Did she really think this kind of intimidation and *banter* would work on me? I scowled at her and tightened my grip on the case. "I'm trying to speak to you in good faith, but even if you turn me away, there is absolutely no chance of me handing the crown jewels of Symkaria over to you without a fight." That we'd barely been tussling now was obvious to me. Also obvious was the fact that I would probably lose an actual fight without better weapons, but if she came at me hard, I would make her earn every carat of this crown. "Do you understand?"

Black Cat paused, then straightened up. "I do," she said. "And believe it or not, I actually respect your tenacity on that front. I'd probably leave with a bald patch. So let's just skip the fight scene."

Wha– A second later there was a strange sound, like a *kachunk-whoosh,* and all of a sudden, I'd been knocked to the ground by a net made of soft black mesh. The more I struggled to free myself, the tighter it held me. *Some sort of smart fabric? How did it get so tight so fast?*

Stop struggling, Silvija, calm down and think your way through this. How do you get out of this? What's the next logical step?

Apparently, the next step was for Black Cat to saunter over, rummage through the folds of the net until she found the briefcase, then reach down and – *snikt* – slice right through the titanium cable holding it to my wrist.

Whoa. Titanium was no adamantium, but still. I would have to update my information about her suit, because those claws were *sharp*.

"And there we go," Black Cat said, a smile wide across her face as she straightened back up. She turned and looked at someone I couldn't see. "Thanks for the assist, Boris!"

"My pleasure," a familiar voice replied. Boris – also known as the airport worker who'd flagged me down almost an hour ago – appeared above me. "I've been wanting to try out the netgun. I think it needs more oomph."

"Any more oomph and you'd have sent her into the river," Black Cat replied. "And then I'd have to fish her out again, and I'm not *that* fond of fishing." She turned her attention back to me. "Well, thanks for everything! I'm sure someone will find you in the next hour or two… or three."

"You're not going to get away with this," I warned her. "All I want is to talk to you."

"Mmm, I think I *am* getting away with this," she replied, tossing her hair – again. Mine was twice as long, and did I feel the need to toss it around like I was making a big blonde salad? No, I did not. "I also know what you really want, and let me assure you, there's no *way* I'm going to work for Doctor Doom." She sighed and patted my head. "He knew just how to get his claws into you, huh? Better luck next time, Silver Sable. If you survive until next time, that is."

"We'd better go," Boris said. "I was able to get ahead of her people, but it's better that we don't get caught by the Wild Pack."

She made a finger-guns sign at him. "Let's roll." They turned around and walked toward the embankment, where Boris's car was waiting for them.

I didn't call after them. Didn't ask for Felicia to reconsider, didn't beg for them to come back. I didn't lie here on the cold, wet ground and stew in my resentments, curse myself for being taken advantage of, decry the unfairness of it all. Nope.

Instead I took a deep, slow inhale and exhale, then stopped moving. Stopped moving *everything* – my limbs, my face, even my eyes. Air trickled in and out of my lungs, so slight my breath probably wouldn't even have fogged a mirror. Ten seconds. Twenty.

At a minute, the net was loose enough that I could wriggle one of my feet free of it. From there, I was able to work the rest of my body free. By the time Tango was running down to the waterfront, I'd folded the net into a tight bundle and tucked it under my arm.

"Silver, are you OK?" he demanded, his hands stretched out like he wanted to check to make sure I wasn't hiding an injury. Or… maybe give me a hug or something. Mm, no. I didn't do hugs. Not even when I was freezing and filthy and could really use a kind touch to help erase the violent ones I'd just endured.

"I'm fine," I assured him, passing him the net so he'd have something else to hold on to. "Mostly annoyed. It's not the best-case scenario, but we should be able to make it work."

He looked at my wrist with a sigh. "They got the goods, huh?"

"They also got the tracking device in the goods, so we've got that going for us." I'd been assured that the bug could evade almost all detection measures, and when it got through the security at JFK with nary a blip, I knew it was worth the exorbitant price I paid for it. "Not to mention, we've got Bruno."

He glanced around. "Should we really be talking about Bruno out in the open like this?"

Probably not. "We can go as soon as I go and get my weapons. Flashlight." I held out a hand, and he shoved his waterproof, crenelated tactical flashlight down in my palm a second later. They were standard issue for my team, and moments like this were why. "Thanks." I turned toward where I estimated we'd gone in and resolutely didn't let myself shiver.

"Wait, Silver, you're not–"

I dove in before he could finish. I was already cold, wet, and tired, and soon I was going to be more of all three. Time to get this done and move on to Persuading Black Cat to Work With Us: Part Two.

CHAPTER TWELVE

An hour later I was curled up on a couch in the Symkarian embassy holding a mug of strong, hot black tea and watching my teamwork. I wasn't generally one for the "sit back and relax while other people are busy bees" approach to management, but in this case, I figured I'd done my day's work before six AM. I was clean, I was dry, and no one had been seriously injured. Not even Bruno, who was sitting next to me with a cup of his own and a rueful expression on his face.

The EMTs – X-Ray and Romeo – had, in fact, taken him to a hospital to be checked for a concussion and treated for a dislocated shoulder. They'd had orders to truss him up like a turkey and haul him back here after that, but Bruno made trussing unnecessary when he promptly fell asleep after taking his pain medicine. He'd just woken up a few minutes ago, feeling better but clearly wondering what the heck was going on.

"You realize it's never a good idea to start things with my

boss, right?" he said to me. "This ain't a threat, by the way. It's just, she tends to be a little..."

"Vengeful?" I offered. "I know. I expect she's furious that we managed to spirit you away. But I hope she keeps in mind that *we* didn't start this game of cat and mouse."

"Didn't you?" Bruno asked, looking far too insightful for someone who probably wanted to curl right back up and go to sleep. "You want her help with something, and she knows it."

"And yet she came after the gems anyway," I mused. "And got them. Speaking of... Foxtrot, have they come to a stop?"

"I've got a signal broadcasting from the south end of Queens," he said, and beside me, Bruno tensed. Not much, not in a way most people would notice, but I was trained to pay attention to these things. This was good intel – probably the location of one of their safehouses, maybe even their home base. "They haven't moved for the last twenty-two minutes."

"That's fine. We know where she is, and she certainly knows how to find us." She'd proven that. "Now we wait." My stomach growled. "Now we eat breakfast while we wait," I amended, putting my mug aside and getting up. "I'll grab some granola bars from the–"

"Sable," Juliet said tensely. "Someone's walking up to the embassy."

"Someone?" I wasn't interested in some random sightseer ambling along, I was interested in potential counterattacks. "Black Cat?"

"Yes, but... dressed in her Felicia Hardy persona. She's holding a big bag in her arms, and–"

Far from the living quarters, a distant doorbell rang. "And

she's here," Juliet finished. I walked over and looked at her monitor. Yes... astonishingly enough, there was Felicia Hardy in all her New York-chic glory. She *did* have what looked like a large takeout bag with her, and as I watched she shifted it from arm to arm, like it was heavy. Heck, with her out of her special catsuit, maybe it actually was.

She rang the bell again and said something. Our security monitors didn't pick up vocals, but I was pretty decent at reading lips, and that looked like... "Hurry up before I eat all the breakfast burritos," I recited.

"Burritos?" Every person on my team suddenly perked up, like hunting dogs catching a scent.

Fine, fine. "X-Ray, Romeo, you go let her in. Make sure she's not carrying anything explosive. Check the burritos before you bring them back here."

"Got it, Sable!" They were gone almost before I finished speaking.

I looked around at everyone else. "Juliet, continue monitoring until they arrive. Foxtrot, make sure nothing funny happens to those jewels. Tango..." He looked at me hopefully, and I smiled at him even though I knew I was about to disappoint him. "Please set the table for eight."

He deflated a little at the impersonal directive, but nodded. "Got it."

Now that everyone had a task, I could take a little more time to finish my tea in peace and quiet. Although... I turned to Bruno. "Does she do this often?"

"Do what?" he asked.

"Come to potential hostiles bearing food and expect everything to go well?"

He chuckled. "You'd be amazed how often it works out. Plenty of people out there are willing to put a hold on their anger when you offer 'em a decent meal or a nice drink. Make 'em feel a little special, you know? Like you care about their comfort."

That was very good negotiation psychology in action. I'd have to keep it in mind for future meetings, not that I planned to charm most of my marks with pretty words and tasty food. The majority of them could consider themselves lucky not to get the sharp side of my katana by the time we'd caught up to them.

Although, actually, when it came to being prepared with bribes... I headed for my room, and the things I'd tucked away for Black Cat's perusal. The hard part was over – she was here. Now I just had to convince the cat that I'd caught a canary for her.

I heard her before I saw her, her tone bright and bubbly. You'd never know she'd been up for probably most of the night and gotten into a fight with me an hour ago. Not that it had been a very *long* fight – cheater – but I had to admit, Black Cat was a heck of an actor.

"...hope you all like chorizo," she was saying as a bag crinkled. Probably distributing food. "There's this great Mexican place just five blocks from here that does the most amazing breakfast burritos, but their chorizo is pretty hot, and their salsa is even hotter. The only person who likes these more than me is Bruno... and where is he, by the way?"

Oooh, there was the stinger behind the honeyed words, waiting to stab someone. Luckily, Bruno was a few steps ahead of me, one arm in a sling but the rest of him looking hale and hearty. "I'm fine, boss. Nothin' to worry about, 'cept my pride."

"I'm glad to hear it," she said, and *now* I could hear the difference in how she spoke to someone she *really* liked. The too-sweet tang had dropped away, leaving genuine affection and a little bit of relief. "I think this proves that it pays to splurge on a private doctor from here on out. There are guys out there who make house calls, and I'm going to get one of them on retainer as soon as we pull in our next big score."

"That could be sooner than you think," I said as I stepped into the dining room. All eyes turned my way. I smiled. "That is, if you're interested in listening to what I have to say now."

I was prepared for her to tell me no, but instead she said, "You've earned a little bit of grace, I suppose. But let's eat first. It's no good negotiating on an empty stomach."

She had a point. My stomach was roiling on nothing but caffeine and painkillers at this point. "Thank you for bringing breakfast."

It was… strange, to eat with someone who wasn't on the team. Eating together was a level of intimacy that I wasn't ready to extend to Black Cat, but grabbing a burrito and scarfing it down back in my room would have been weird. So, I ate and endured my team's little jokes as I used a knife and fork to scoop up each bite instead of eating the burrito out of the wrapper with my hands, and I let Felicia see me vulnerable. It felt like I was missing a layer of skin.

"All right," she said at last after wiping the last remnants of salsa and avocado crema off her lips. "Let's hear it. What do you have that could be so amazing you expect me to work for a maniac like Doctor Doom?" She pointed a finger at me.

Even her regular nails looked suspiciously sharp. "And don't tell me it's those jewels. They're nice, of course, but I'm on to the fact that they're just the way you got me into the room. By the way, should we have any *issues* arise here, I've given Boris permission to blow your briefcase up."

"There won't be any need to blow anything up," I assured her.

"He'll be very sad to hear that," she joked. At least, I think she was joking.

"Here's the situation." *Pride goeth before a fall.* "Yes, we took a job for Doom. We're tracking down a man named–"

"Jamie Tolentino," she interrupted. "Yeah, I know. He's got a future-vision thingy, he sees you coming, you end up causing all sorts of havoc trying to run him down, you've got to deliver, and the clock is ticking away…"

I narrowed my eyes. "How do you know all of that?"

"It's not like you've been paying *that* much attention to operational security," she drawled, kicking her feet up on the antique walnut table. Was that gum on the heel of her right shoe? Ugh, I didn't want to know. "And Johnny Storm is one of my buds. We get sushi together on the third Tuesday of every month, which incidentally was just last week, and he told me about this *crazy* experience he had on a visit out to see his friend Wyatt. Turns out the Wild Pack smashed up a casino trying to get their hands on one of the high rollers, and–"

"Storm did way more property damage than any of us!" X-Ray snapped. "That guy can't keep his power in his freaking pants!"

Black Cat smirked. "Oh, *you've* noticed his pants, too? The way they fit should be illegal–"

"OK, OK." We were veering way off the subject. Time to get back on course. "Yes, we've had some difficulties getting our hands on Tolentino. Yes, we're on a time limit. Yes, I would like you to help us run him down because of your ability to manipulate the odds."

"Black cats *are* traditionally signs of bad luck," she said. God, was she ever *not* smirking? "But I'm still not hearing any good reason for me to join your two-ring circus. I can get all the money and excitement I need by never even leaving this city, and I have no interest in either antagonizing Doom *or* helping him get his hands on something that lets him see the future. That sounds like a good way to get my sushi dates canceled for the rest of my life, and I *like* that place. Johnny always treats."

I reached into the manila envelope I'd carried in with me and removed the contents, then slid them across the table to Black Cat. "Are you sure about that?" I asked, watching her face as she picked up the photocopied piece of paper I'd just handed over. Some parts of it were blacked out, but there should be enough there to pique her interest.

At first she was a study in boredom – far beyond whatever trifles I could offer her. Then she seemed to realize what she was actually holding. Her eyes widened, and her jaw dropped. Her grip on the paper tightened in an uncontrollable squeeze before she smoothed the creases out again, almost apologetically. She looked it over carefully, from multiple angles, even holding it up to the light at one point. By the time she looked at me again, I knew I had her.

"This map is in code," she said at last.

"Yes," I replied.

"Then it's useless to you."

"But not to you." I crossed my arms and sat back. "I assume you know the code he used on the map. After all, the Black Fox was *your* mentor. Practically a second father to you, from what I heard."

I was, perhaps, poking the bear a bit to dig like this into her relationship with the Black Fox. Things between them had ended in a rather permanent way not so long ago, if the perturbations around Manhattan and the subsequent complete and utter absence of the Black Fox was anything to go by. But what the heck. She deserved it after giving me so much trouble in so short a time period.

Black Cat feigned distaste, letting the paper flutter to the tabletop. "Not even close," she said. "Whatever this is a map to, there's no reason for me to go on a treasure hunt for something that might not even exist."

"Not even if it's the greatest haul of his career?" I asked. She stilled, and I continued, "While my father and I were hunting Nazi war criminals across Europe, the Black Fox was doing the same – but for a very different reason. To subsidize their new, undercover lifestyles, many of those Nazis went on the run with loot they'd stolen from the people they'd murdered during the war. The Black Fox was locating them one by one and, ah... *absconding* with their ill-gotten gains." I smiled in remembrance. "He didn't limit himself to stealing from Nazis, of course, but he actually helped us locate several people we'd lost hope of identifying. For all that his focus was on thievery, he was actually a very excellent investigator."

"Yes," Black Cat murmured, "he was."

I'd caught her attention. Now I just needed to lure her

into the story a little deeper, and her sense of curiosity – and greed – would do the rest. "He made Symkaria his base of operations for some time, probably because it had fairly lax border security compared to other European nations. When I eventually caught up with him, he was fencing a handful of very rare gems right here in New York. He got away – not with the gems, thankfully, those we were able to return to the descendants of their rightful owners – but he couldn't return to Symkaria after that, not while we were on the lookout for him. I found that map in his last known location, a small apartment in the capital, Aniara. None of the treasure he'd taken was with it."

"So." Black Cat tapped the document with one long nail. "You think this will lead to where he stowed his stuff?"

"I assume so. I can't know for sure, of course, since I can't read it." I shrugged. "I have to be honest with you – for all I know, that's how he wrote his grocery lists. It's not a cipher I'm familiar with, and while the drawing is suggestive of a map, I was unable to positively correlate it to anywhere *except* Aniara. Without more information, it's useless to me." A shame, too – Symkaria deserved to have its treasures back, but if the map served as a lure for Black Cat, it would still serve my country well. "The jobs that it might lead to represent the pinnacle of the Black Fox's career, though." I leaned forward again. "Do you think you can break the cipher?"

"Possibly," she allowed after a moment. "I'm not positive, but… if anyone could, it's me." She finally made eye contact with me again. "What exactly are you offering here, Sable?"

"A trade," I said. "I'll give you the original of that map in exchange for your assistance in capturing James Tolentino."

Perhaps it was time for a bit of flattery. "I think you might be one of the only people out there capable of getting around the Clairvoyant long enough for us to get our hands on him."

"Hmm." She stared down at the map, then back at me. Down and back. Down and back. I wasn't sure if it was a stalling tactic or just a way to disconcert me, but it wasn't going to work. I was confident that she wanted this. I knew *I* would want one of the last links to my own father if one was suddenly offered up to me.

"Fine, I'm in."

A collective sigh of relief went around the room as her words registered. Even I had to hold back a beaming smile. This was just what we needed – we would be able to make real progress with Black Cat on our side, I knew it. As long as we didn't trust her any farther than I could throw her, we should be fine.

"On two conditions," she went on.

Of course. "Name them," I said.

"One, you keep my name out of this with Doom. I know he's going to see that I'm helping out, but I don't want to sign anything, I don't want to shake his hand, I don't want to even see him across a crowded room. Where dealing with him is concerned, I'm not even a fly on the wall. Clear?"

I nodded. "Done." That was simple enough. "And the second?"

"We bring in my crew to help." She smiled brightly at Bruno. "After all, they're the best in the biz, and we're gonna need the best after all the crap you've pulled so far trying to get this done."

There were some grumbles among the Wild Pack, but

I tuned them out. We knew our own worth. This job was a stumble, nothing more. Soon we'd be done with it, and back to top form. Black Cat would see then who was the best in the business.

"Agreed." I stood up and reached a hand over to her. "Welcome to the team, Black Cat."

"Please," she replied with a wink. "Call me Felicia."

CHAPTER THIRTEEN

A part of me hated to admit it, but Black Ca – no, *Felicia*, really did run a tight crew. By noon they'd consolidated their resources for this job and relocated to the embassy, because, "There's no way I'm having all of you in my place," she'd said. "Talk about an operational security nightmare. Plus, it only has two bathrooms, and that's just asking for trouble after a burrito breakfast."

Boris had even brought the jewels along with him. "Here," he said ungraciously, handing them over to me with a scowl as soon as he arrived. "I expect an explanation, demonstration, and donation of the bug you used in this. I modified the scanner at the airport *myself*; it shouldn't have missed something you could use to track us."

Worth. Every. Penny. "Once the job is done," I agreed, and his scowl got deeper.

"I–"

"Quit arguin' and get in here," Bruno called from farther back. Boris rolled his eyes and went to join him – not, I noticed, bothering to stop arguing. It seemed to be his default state.

"If you'd managed not to drive into the *river*, we wouldn't be in this mess! What happened to Mister 'I Can Drive Anything Under The Sun,' hmm?"

"Sun hadn't risen yet," Bruno said with a shrug.

"Semantics! Don't even think about–"

I closed the embassy door and rearmed the alarm as I mused on how Felicia got anything done with this constant back and forth. Not that my people weren't chatty, but this was a whole new level of "witty repartee."

When I rejoined her at the table, it was like she read my mind. "Music," she said with a smile.

"What?"

"Sometimes I play really loud music to drown them out. Or if I'm not in the mood for that, I've got these noise-canceling headphones that work super well, especially if it's late at night and I really just want to sleep."

"I… see." They shared a house? Wasn't that…

She tilted her head. "Not a problem with your people?"

"No." Because they were my employees, not my roommates. "We – of course I respect and appreciate all of them, they're excellent at their jobs, but when we're not working, we don't…"

"Ah. Yeah, me and the boys are kind of always in each other's pockets, but–" she shrugged "–I wouldn't have it any other way. They've been with me through a lot – gotten me out of some tough scrapes. I know I can rely on them."

I opened my mouth to express some sort of platitude, then slowly shut it again as I actually considered what she was saying. These two bickering, childish, occasionally very professional and competent people were more than her friends. They were her family. That bond was the reason I'd been able to lure her here – the jewels were never a big enough prize for her to consider working with me. But Bruno? She was prepared to do whatever it took to make sure he was all right.

I didn't even really remember what it felt like to have someone who cared about me like that anymore.

I cleared my throat and got my head back where it needed to be. "What do you think?" I asked.

She rolled her eyes. "I think this guy is out of his mind, that's what I think. All of this bouncing around, all the work he's putting into going hither and yon and evading and escaping and… I mean, it's a lot. You guys didn't catch him, no, but you did put a lot of pressure on him. He's had to work harder than ever to stay a few steps ahead of you, and that includes messing with magic, which–" She shuddered dramatically. "Always a risky proposition, if you ask me. One I like to avoid whenever I can."

A memory tickled my brain. "Didn't you get drawn into that golden apple search here in New York? I seem to remember seeing a picture of you at–"

"The MET, yeah." She preened slightly. "'Danny Rand and Felicia Hardy Keep Their Cool in a Hot Spot.' One of my better appearances in the society pages."

I didn't remember the details of it, but I *did* recall that she'd been wearing an absolutely stunning dress, not that you could see all of it when she and her companion were surrounded by a horde of desperate apple-grabbers. I didn't envy her having to put up with that mess.

"What I mean," she continued, "is that one way or the

other, things have got to be wearing on him by now. Tolentino isn't enhanced in any way, is he?"

"Not that I know of."

"Did you ask Spider-Man?"

"Do you think I want him drawn into this?" I snapped. "No, I haven't talked to Spider-Man. I don't want to risk him butting in and making a mess of things." I was irritated by the sudden reminder of the fact that we were both involved – no, not *involved* – connected to Spider-Man. Not in the same way, of course – Felicia couldn't be more obvious about how besotted she was, a constant tease even though Spidey was in a relationship, whereas my relationship with him was purely professional.

OK, so I'd kissed him once. *Once.* But that was just a... friendly kind of... it was a...

Get it together, Silver.

"Approaching him isn't necessary yet," I said. "I've done plenty of research on James Tolentino, and everything I've found identifies him as a very intelligent but unenhanced individual."

"Mmmkay," Felicia replied, one eyebrow raised. She let it go, though. "And you reckon those glasses he wears everywhere are the Clairvoyant, right?"

"They have to be."

"Then from what I can tell, he's got to be *suffering* right now. Look at this video of him escaping you in Montreal." She enlarged it on the tablet. "He's not staggering because people are getting in his way – he is literally exhausted, I can see the veins standing out beneath his skin. I've looked over some of his wins, too, and he's giving up opportunities for bigger

scores. He's made less than a million dollars in the past week –
he could have had ten if he'd played a few hands differently.
He's getting sloppy."

"Or is that what he wants us to think?" I countered. "You
should know I'm not given to false modesty, so believe me
when I say that some of the escapes he's pulled off against us
have been truly... unimaginable. Or at least beyond what *we*
could imagine, which amounts to the same thing."

"Does it though?" She said it with a friendly grin, but I knew
she was being serious. "I mean, yay you guys and your skills,
I say that seriously, but you're a classically trained mercenary
and a bounty hunter for hire. You aren't exactly known for
branching out into more eclectic and creative lines of work."

"And you are?"

She shrugged. "I'm a thief. Creativity comes with the job if
you want to keep working."

Fair enough. "That's why I wanted to get you in on this,"
I said, then gave her a friendly grin of my own. "You're my
effort at creativity, Felicia. And if the best you've got to offer
so far is that Tolentino looks a little tired, then I've got to say,
I'm hoping for more."

Her smile didn't fade, but the character of it changed – oh,
she was sharpening her claws now. "Oh, I'll deliver. You *and*
Tolentino can bet on that. But there's no sense in charging
in, right? You've got a whole–" She dramatically checked her
phone. "Six days, nine hours, and twenty-two minutes before
your little deadline! Well, let's not let that time go to waste,
huh?" *Like it has been*, her eyebrows added as she turned back
to the tablet.

The last person I'd met who could so clearly articulate their thoughts with their eyebrows was… ugh, my ex. No wonder he and Felicia had had a fling together – they were two sides of the same coin. It was a lying, cheating, honorless coin, but one that could be useful if you flipped it just right.

"First things first," Felicia went on, "we're going to have to figure out where he is. You said you had a way of tracking him?"

"One that no longer works, unfortunately." I didn't give her any more information than that. "Unless you've got a trick up your sleeve, we're going to have to do this the old-fashioned way."

"Huh." She stared into the distance for a moment, actually seeming to consider it. "I do have something of a relationship with a guy who knows a lot about magic – just friends, man's best friend, in fact – but he might get kind of confused seeing us side-by-side. Plus, I'd have to break into the Sanctum Sanctorum again, and even then there's no guarantee." She paused then shrugged again. "Nah, better not to risk it. What about you? No magic users on your side who could pick up the slack where technology fails us?"

"If you're talking about Doctor Doom, then no." I wasn't going to go to him or Captain Verlak hat-in-hand and ask for yet another handout, especially after last time. "And I try not to have dealings with many magic users."

"Huh. Welp, we'll see what our people can do, then," she said. "Otherwise start saving your pennies, Silver, because we might be looking at bringing a better hacker on-board, and they don't come cheap."

Didn't I know it. I considered the funds I had in my account, all my potential lines of credit, and what I could get selling off all non-essential Wild Pack gear. Even then, it would be close if

I had to hire out. We'd spent a *lot* of money chasing Tolentino. "Let's hope we can do it without more help." I sighed.

It took a lot of bandwidth – as in linking up all our devices and stealing Wifi from all the neighbors – but we were finally able to get what we needed for two people to go searching for Tolentino. Foxtrot took over the search in the western hemisphere, and Boris started hunting in the eastern half of the world.

Boris hit paydirt first. "Look what we have here," he said with a sly smile as he pulled up video from social media based out of Macau. "One of the big casinos in the city is evacuating. There's been an explosion – minor, it seems – but police have been called." The video, taken on someone's cellphone, showed a fairly orderly scene of people exiting a tall, elegant building by the water. Smoke was billowing out from the top floor, but the rest of the place looked untouched.

"And there he is," I said as I finally caught sight of Tolentino. He was trying to blend in with the crowd but moving twice as fast as most of them – and still wearing the Clairvoyant. Behind him two different teams appeared to be converging, one wearing all black and carrying cheap Eastern European assault rifles, the other in the blue uniforms of the Macau police and holding handguns.

"Mm, yep, that's a triad casino," Felicia said, leaning in to take a closer look. "Not good. Anytime you mix cops and crooks, you're going to get some nasty fallout." Sure enough, as soon as the police and the criminals caught sight of each other there was an outcry. Someone took a shot, there was general screaming, and then the last vestiges of crowd control were gone as pandemonium set in. Whoever was filming had stopped trying to be informative and was booking it instead, the landscape bumping by in a blur as they fled.

"So messy." Felicia clicked her tongue. "Why not just do it all online? He could make a huge amount of money in stocks or playing the currency market. Heck, even with sports betting he'd do better than taking these kinds of risks."

I'd thought about that. "There are still risks, just a different kind," I said. "Most betting sites monitor for suspicious activity, just in case of something like this – someone enhanced trying to play the system. If they get even the slightest inkling that you're consistently beating the odds, they'll lock out your account and blacklist you to everyone else. Same with most trading markets. Nobody wants to be cheated, or known as a venue where they *allow* cheaters."

"Hmm. So he goes in person." She stared at the screen a little longer, then shook her head. "And makes an enemy of the triad while he's at it. That's bad business. The way he's going, he'll run out of places to gamble before he hits whatever goal he's set for himself. We need to figure out what that goal is, because trust me, he's not going to be able to keep this up much longer."

I'd believe it when I saw it. In the meantime, though… "When was this video taken?"

"Just a few minutes ago."

Then he was probably on his way to the airport right now. "Try to find out where his next stop is," I said. "There's no sense in flying to Macau when he'll have flown out before we get there."

"And try to figure out who else is after this guy," Felicia added. "I don't know about the rest of you, but *I* need to maintain good professional relationships, and if Tolentino attracts attention from one of my allies…"

"Then you'll stick with me, because otherwise I'm keeping the map," I said briskly. "If you want to back out, do it, but don't wait to betray me until we've already made a plan. Because if you do, neither Tolentino nor your allies will be a problem for you anymore."

"Aw, I don't know, Silver." She looked me up and down. "I think I could take you."

"You might be able to," I agreed. "But could you take Spider-Man looking at you in disappointment and telling you he feels like he doesn't even know you anymore?"

"You – what–" Her jaw dropped slightly, her cheeks taking on the faintest pink tinge under her foundation. "As if he dictates what I can and can't – I mean! What are you – even talking about, seriously, I don't – you know he's *taken*, right?"

Oh, she was genuinely flustered. Wow, good for me!

"I do know that," I said. "And I–"

"Boss, Tolentino's got triad trouble!"

Oh, crap. I ran over to Boris's computer, followed closely by Felicia, and watched the hijacked video feed from Macau International Airport. For a moment everything looked normal, Tolentino already walking to his departure gate – Sydney, it read. *Interesting* – before I saw the people moving toward him. Three of them, two men and one woman, all of them easy to overlook if you didn't see the way their eyes followed him around the room as they walked. None of them appeared to be armed, but appearances were worse than nothing when all you had was a video feed to go off of.

Tolentino slumped down in a chair by the gate, looking for

all the world like he was on his last legs. "What did I tell you?" Felicia murmured with satisfaction as she watched him rub a trembling hand over his mouth. "He's exhausted. All work and no play makes Jamie a dull boy."

"If the triad gets their hands on him, we're in an even worse place than we were before," I snapped. It was nothing but the truth – Tolentino on his own was a challenge, but he was just one man. If his device fell into the hands of one of the most powerful criminal organizations in the world, the chances of us getting it back for Doctor Doom went from "small" to "infinitesimal."

There had to be someone we could call, someone who could step in if we needed to and–

Wham! Wham! Wham!

Everybody staring at the computer blinked in unison.

"What," Felicia said with forced calm, "exactly *was* that?" She pointed a long, pink nail at the screen. "And who is *that* guy?"

The man she was pointing at looked… well, he looked like just about the most average person I could imagine. He stood about five foot ten, had close-cut dark hair and a vaguely friendly, roundish face. In his plain gray suit and holding a briefcase, he looked like just another face in the crowd at Macau International. Only he'd just knocked out all three of the triad squad, his movements so fast he'd blurred on-screen. They all still seemed to be alive – groaning, but alive – and airport security was moving in already, shouting, guns drawn. The perfectly average looking, completely exceptional man set the briefcase down and raised both hands in the air.

"Who *is* that?" Felicia repeated. "Somebody Tolentino

hired as a bodyguard? You haven't seen any sign of him before this, right?"

"Right," I said, thinking back on all the other attempts we'd made so far. I couldn't recall this exact face, but there was something about the way he moved...

Oh. Oooohhh, what if... "Look for Tolentino," I said to Boris. "Is he still sitting there?"

"Ah... that would be a negative," Boris replied, moving the camera to where Tolentino had been near-collapsed a few moments ago. He was gone.

"So he *is* a bodyguard," Felicia mused. "We can work with that. Bodyguards are bribable, we just have to figure out who he is and make the right kind of approach. I can—"

A sudden memory popped into my head, a picture I'd seen in a wallet. "I don't think he's a bodyguard," I said slowly, interrupting Felicia's monologue about bought loyalty.

Even my own team looked a little dubious at my pronouncement. "Sable," Tango began, "the way they worked together sure makes it seem like he's a bodyguard."

"He's not working with Tolentino." At least I hoped he wasn't. If Tolentino had teamed up with the man I had in mind, things were about to get even more messy.

Felicia snapped her fingers at me. I resisted the urge to snap them off. "Make some sense or go back to bed until you're less delusional," she said.

I wasn't completely sure of what I was about to say, but I thought the odds were in my favor. "How many sticky situations has Tolentino gotten out of so far?" I asked.

"Plenty," Tango said, being my ally without pushing the issue – good man. "But we've put him in all of those."

"Have we? Every single one?" I shook my head. "Some of them, sure. I doubt he chartered a helicopter for anyone but us, but some of his other escapes… I'm thinking someone else is after him as well. He's playing us all against each other whenever he can – which is all the time. He did it in Macau, and *we* weren't even involved in this mess."

"But a bodyguard," Bruno began, but was silenced by a hum from Felicia.

"I might see where you're going with this, but there's no way to prove it until you can figure out where the guy who provided the smackdown this time came from and who he's working for," she said.

"Follow the new guy on the footage," I told Boris. "Watch where he's taken, then watch when he leaves." If my hunch was correct, then I knew exactly how this person had taken down those triad members, not to mention who he was and who he worked for.

After all, I'd moved like that myself once – superspeed, superstrength. It had been liberating… especially while my actual body was broken and bed-bound.

Yeah. Yeah, I was pretty sure I knew who was behind this, but I needed to be positive. Because there was no way I was talking to my ex-husband without being a hundred percent certain that I had to.

CHAPTER FOURTEEN

An uneasy quiet pervaded the room as we followed our two people of interest on camera. Tolentino, who still looked tired but was at least doing a decent job of walking again, had moved on to a flight bound for Brazil. Well, at least it was in our hemisphere. Meanwhile, the man in the suit had been taken to an interrogation room where there were no cameras.

A quick scan of the airport's blueprint – found by Juliet, and if my people kept being this good, I was hopeful we wouldn't need to hire out the job of hacker – noted that it only had one way in.

Five minutes after he was taken in cuffed, the man in the same gray suit emerged again. Only now... now he looked different. He'd gone from looking like a laidback Macau businessman to a man with blond hair, blue eyes, and a jaw square enough to frame a picture with. If the suit hadn't been identical, right down to the square silver belt buckle, I would never have guessed it could be the same person.

Well, *I* would have guessed, but clearly no one else I was

with would have, given how their jaws had dropped. It was nice to be proven right.

"No," Boris said, his eyes narrowed as his hands flew over the keyboard. He zoomed in closer, giving us all a full screen view of the man's face. "It must be a mask."

"It is," I said. "In a way."

"Is it now?" Felicia purred, but there were claws behind her query. "Why don't you confirm it for the rest of us, then? Friends don't leave their friends hanging, Silver."

"That man isn't a real man," I said, as we all watched the figure stride off in the direction of the flight leaving for Rio de Janeiro. "It's controlled by a man, but it's actually a Life Model Decoy."

"An LMD?" Felicia's eyes widened with interest. "Are you sure?"

"As sure as I can be with a remote inspection," I said. "They come with a number of camouflage capabilities built in, including facial remodeling. They've come a long way since the originals, which could only look like the person they'd been designed for. The newest generation is able to switch numerous facets of its appearance as long as the design is coded in." Life Model Decoys were robots that had been used by S.H.I.E.L.D. for decades, near-perfect duplicates of whatever person they'd been modeled after. The tech had gotten out to the larger world after a while, and could be found by almost anyone – for the right price.

"And you know all of this how?" Felicia pressed.

"I know it because…" Ugh, I hated revealing parts of my past – to anyone, really, but most especially to people I didn't trust, and I didn't trust Felicia Hardy. My team knew – no one else had really needed to before now. However, I had no choice but to give her what she wanted. I needed her to know she could rely on me, and she would see right through a lie. "Because I've used one myself recently. After I was attacked by the Rhino here in New York."

"Yeah, we all thought you died," Felicia said. "Spidey was so sad for a while, mourning his old *friend*."

She said it like being Spider-Man's friend was a bad thing. *Easier than being a love interest he'll never want back.* "I was incapacitated," I continued smoothly. "My life was saved, but recuperation was slow. To keep my hand in, I remotely controlled a Life Model Decoy for some time. It had the same capabilities as the one shown here." Stronger, faster, more durable than a human… some of the jobs I did as an LMD were far easier than any I'd taken as a plain old human being. Sometimes I missed it.

"That's interestin' and all," Bruno said, "but I think we're pretty sure you're not controllin' this one." He pointed at the screen, where the LMD had arrived at Tolentino's departure gate – just in time to watch the plane fly off into the sky. "So, who is?"

"Someone I once knew very well," I said, doing my best to keep my voice emotion-free. "I recognize that face from a photo he kept in his wallet of his parents."

Felicia got it first. "Oh *no*," she said, putting one hand briefly over her eyes. "No, come on. Seriously?"

"I'm afraid so."

"Who?" Juliet asked.

"I don't know why I'm surprised," Felicia went on, "and yet here I am, surprised all the same."

I sighed. "Yes, I know. But he has a talent for worming his way into things."

"Who does?" Boris demanded.

"Come to think of it, wasn't he part of that thing at the casino where–"

"That was him," I agreed.

"WHO?" The question was bellowed from half a dozen different mouths at the same time, everyone on our teams annoyed to be left out of the loop. Rather than explain, I let Felicia take point on this part. She might do it with a little more objectivity.

"The man behind the LMD is none other than our dear Basil, aka Rafael Sabitini, aka the Foreigner, aka the guy I was involved with for a while when he was trying to get a super villain crew set up – he didn't manage it, by the way, and I didn't stick around for the fallout – aka Mr Silver Sable."

Welp, not much objectivity there. "Ex-Mr Silver Sable," I said into the uncomfortable silence. "We've been divorced for years."

"This is the guy who set you up after you got hurt," Juliet said quietly, glancing at the other members of the Wild Pack. "He sourced the LMD for you."

I nodded. "He sourced the Infinity Formula for me, too. I wouldn't be able to walk again, much less fight, if he hadn't."

"That's a big favor," Tango said, his hands in his pockets as he looked at me with a troubled expression. "He must care about you an awful lot."

"He did once." But those times were over. As much as he'd done for me after my fight with Rhino, and as grateful as I was to be healthy again, there was too much in our pasts for us to ever hope of reconciling no matter how we felt about each other. I didn't love him anymore, I knew that, but I didn't want to confront him over this either.

I needed to, though. "What he feels right now isn't the point. We need to focus on the fact that the Foreigner is trying to capture James Tolentino. And getting closer than us, in this case," I added.

"He's got to be after the Clairvoyant, right?" Felicia said. "It wouldn't be the first time he's coveted it."

"True." But why now? Why hadn't he gone after it before Tolentino started jumping around the world? What was driving Basil to act… and how badly was he going to get in my way?

"We should call him up," Felicia suggested. "Ask him some questions. He and I didn't part under the best circumstances, but the guy must still have some feelings for you if he went to all that trouble to keep you alive."

"He'd never talk to us over the phone." Basil was a consummate thief and a phenomenal schemer, and you didn't get to be either of those by taking chances on who could be listening in. It had been hard enough to get him to talk to me when I was married to him, never mind how impossible it would be now. He didn't care about what others did or how his actions might impact them – all he cared about was getting things done for himself, as quickly and efficiently as possible.

Even if people got hurt.

Even if they died.

I wanted to go back in time and smack my younger self for ever marrying the guy. He took up way too much real estate in my brain even now. But despite my reservations – and I had a lot of them – I needed answers from him.

Dang it, we were going to have to do the one thing I really, *really* didn't want to do. We were going to have to go visit him in person.

"Felicia, pick one of your guys to come with us. X-Ray, Tango, you're coming, too. We're going to go talk to the Foreigner."

"Road trip!" Felicia crowed, pumping one fist in the air. "Awesome, anything would be better than staying in this dusty old heap for much longer. Besides, I hear he's got quite the collection of art and antiquities stowed away. I'd love to get a look at some of it."

"We're not going to rob him," I reminded her.

"No, no, of course not." She opened her eyes really wide, then blinked them like an owl. She was probably going for "innocent" but came off more as sleep-deprived to me. "I would never treat anything about this job as a chance to snoop. No, ma'am, it's nothing but business with me. Bruno?" She patted her teammate on his good shoulder. "You stay here, rest up, keep an eye out for Tolentino. Boris?" Her smile morphed into a grin. "You're coming with me."

"Excellent," he said with a truly evil smile, steepling his long fingers. "How many explosives would you like me to bring?"

"Oh, as many as you feel comfortable with, you know I trust your judgment when it comes to booms and bangs."

"We're not going to rob him!" I reiterated, louder this time. "Explosives are off the table!"

"They're for self-defense!" Felicia objected. "Like pepper spray!"

"Pepper spray that's weaponized to be capable of burning straight through your sinus walls and leaving you blind for a month," Boris said, rubbing his hands together. "I'm on it, boss."

I glared at them. It didn't have much of an effect.

"Like you'd leave your chais behind when going to talk to somebody like the Foreigner," Felicia said, wrapping one arm around my waist and patting my hip. "You can't even leave them off while walking through your own safehouse."

"Yes, I ca–" Oh wait, no, she was right. I'd tucked two chais into the top of my pants without even thinking about it after my shower. "Fine," I snapped. "But nothing stronger than pepper spray."

"Got it," she said, waltzing off after her henchman.

Her easy agreement made me nervous, but there was no point in overreacting. We'd be out and back from Basil's place in less than three hours, if everything worked out.

"Where are we going?" Tango asked, more subdued than I was used to from him. He was looking at me like he was concerned. There was no need to worry, though. I could handle Basil.

If I had to.

"It's just a short drive from here," I said. "We're going to Jersey."

CHAPTER FIFTEEN

New Jersey might be New York's neighbor, but the character of the state was completely different. In New York, especially in the city, there was drama to be had on every corner. Heroes of all stripes flocked there looking to make names for themselves; reputations were built and ruined in the boroughs of New York, and the battle for territory and recognition was constant.

New Jersey, on the other hand, boasted a more subtle sort of flair. It couldn't compete with New York City when it came to flash, and it didn't want to either. Let the big names duke it out on the streets and in the skies over there – Jersey was for getting things done. Sometimes good things, sometimes bad things, always things that happened behind closed doors, or in whispers, or in the occasional underground bunker.

It was an underground bunker that we were heading to now – or rather, a bunker below a modest bungalow in the scenic town of Montclair. We landed at a regional airport just a few miles outside the city limits, and brought our own ride; one of Felicia's cars was loaded in the back of the plane. I wasn't about to ask a third party for a ride with what I knew these people were packing.

Tango drove, with X-Ray in the passenger seat, both of them watchful and quieter than I was used to. There was none of the playful bickering I usually got from them. I supposed they were following my lead when it came to mood, and I was feeling rather somber.

I needed to snap out of it. The second Basil sensed weakness, he'd attack, vicious as any foxhound. I couldn't show up at his front door, hat in hand, looking like someone asking him for a favor. I was here to tell him to *back off*, and he was going to understand that, or he and I were going to have problems.

And he did not want problems with me.

"This is it?" Felicia asked, one eyebrow raised as we parked in front of the tiny ranch-style home, a monument to 70s style. "Really?"

"It's a lot bigger on the inside," I said as I unbuckled my seatbelt, thinking reluctantly of Doctor Doom's Manhattan mansion. Not *that* big.

"It would have to be, just to squeeze his ego in."

I stifled a smile as I led the way to the front door. "I don't think any building is big enough for that. Tango, please stay with the car." Not that anyone was likely to try anything with it in this neighborhood, but you never knew when the Foreigner was involved. Tango didn't like it, but he nodded reluctantly as he cut the engine.

"And he doesn't even really merit the rep," Felicia agreed as we headed down the front walk to the door. "I mean, yeah, he's pulled off some decent heists from time to time, but he's terrible at managing people, and as far as his performance in other arenas, you'd probably know better than me but–"

Thank god someone opened the door before she could finish. The man standing there was tall, around six foot two, and had the same short, glossy black hair and handsome face that I remembered. His broad shoulders filled out his tailored suit perfectly, and his eyes briefly glittered as they landed on me.

"Well, look who's come to call. If it isn't my darling Silver." Basil glanced at Felicia. "And Black Cat!" He glanced out at the sky. "It doesn't *seem* like the end of the world is here, but it must be if the two of you are working together."

"You're hilarious," I told him flatly. "Let us in, please. We have something to discuss."

"What, all of you?" He looked behind me at X-Ray, and Boris. "And as heavily armed as you all are? I don't think I'm comfortable with that."

"Aw, honey," Felicia said with a smile, "are you really that worried about little old us? Here, in your very own home base? You think we don't know we're stepping into the lion's den? We'll behave. Trust me."

"When pigs fly, Cat." Still, he stepped aside and let us in. The living room we stepped into was typical suburban chic, except for the fact that every doorway leading into it was made from metal, closed, and locked if the blinking red lights were any indicator.

"Now." He sat down on a beige leather loveseat in the middle of the room, crossing one leg over the other. No seats were offered for the rest of us. "What seems to be the problem?

I don't recall crossing either of you recently. In fact," he added with another gleam in his eye, "the last we met, Silver darling, I believe I saved your life."

"I saved my own life first," I said, eyeing his posture, the way he tilted his head, how he folded his hands. Something was wrong. Something was very wrong... but I needed to get him alone to figure out what. Basil would never reveal a weakness if he could help it. "But as for the problem, I think you probably already know what it is. Why did you send an LMD after James Tolentino?"

"What makes you think I did?" he said smoothly, completely unruffled. The corner of his mouth didn't even twitch, a tell I knew from years ago. Had he trained himself out of it? I doubted it. Concern warred with suspicion in my mind. "LMDs aren't exactly privileged material these days. Anybody can get one for the right price."

"Or more than one," I said, just to see what he would do.

"Or more than one," he agreed. The door to our right opened, and a moment later another man strode inside the living room – a blond man, identical to the one we'd seen in the airport in Macau. "I personally find them to be excellent company."

"Why, thank you," the LMD said urbanely.

"You're welcome," Basil replied, then looked at Felicia. "My dear Cat, Silver has been here before, but I don't believe you've ever had the pleasure. Would you care for a tour of the lower level? I promise that Hudson here will be the very soul of gentility."

"How can I possibly refuse an offer like that?" Felicia purred, reaching out and taking the LMD's arm with aplomb.

"What, you're gonna go off with him? Just like that?" X-Ray asked, skepticism clear on her face. "I thought you didn't trust him!"

"Aw, you sweet thing." She gave my team member a smile. "Basil knows perfectly well what I'll do to him if he messes with me. So I trust that he won't!"

"Wouldn't dream of it," Basil lied beautifully. No wonder he and Felicia hadn't worked out – it must have been like dating yourself. Another LMD entered from the other door. "And Hudson Two here would be delighted to show Mr Korpse and Ms Vasilieva the gardens out back."

X-Ray looked at me, aghast, but Boris didn't seem bothered. He didn't seem enthusiastic either, but that seemed to be par for the course when it came to anything that couldn't be converted to a weapon. "Yes, ugh, gardens. If I must. Talk fast, Sable, before my allergies get the better of me." He followed Hudson Two, and after a nod of encouragement from me, X-Ray went with them.

That left Basil and I alone in the living room, just as he'd wanted. "Silver," he said affectionately, indicating the seat next to him. "Please, join me."

I sat down, keeping all the roiling emotions I was feeling trapped deep inside. Something was wrong here, very, very wrong, but I would wait to call it out until I had more information. "Thank you," I said.

"Would you care for some tea? It's been a while since I fired up the samovar, but I'd be happy to dig it out of storage if you'd like a proper cup."

"That's not necessary," I demurred. "I'd prefer if you told me why you're after Tolentino."

"*Why?*" He laughed, as smooth and suave as always. "Darling, I would think that would be obvious. He's gallivanting around the world making a fortune off a device I nearly had in my grasp not so long ago. Apparently, he's worked out the bugs from last time, and I'm eager to see for myself what the future might hold. Not to mention, something like that is worth a lot of money to the right collectors. It's a simple case of self-enrichment, Silver."

"Really?"

"Of course." He smiled charmingly and reached for my hand. I let him take it. His grip was warm and just firm enough. *Perfect.*

Too perfect.

"Once upon a time, you thought more of me than I deserved," Basil said to me, wry yet earnest. "I thought you'd abandoned all those adorable illusions a long time ago, but it's clear you're still harboring one or two. Let me help you get rid of them. I'm an opportunist, and I have both the resources and the time to go after the things I want when they pop up on my radar. That's why I'm after Mr Tolentino. Nothing more subtle *or* more sinister, I'm afraid.

"And why are you after him, darling? Is it as bad as I've heard?" He leaned in close. "Are you really at the beck and call of Doctor Doom? Silver, honestly, I thought *I'd* made some poor choices of allegiance in my past, but this really beats them all. If you were that desperate for help, all you had to do was come to me. I'd never turn you away."

Oh, Basil. "You're such a wonderful liar," I said with genuine admiration. "Sometimes I wish I'd never learned to read you so well. We might still be together if I hadn't."

He tilted his head, like a curious bird. "Whatever do you mean, darling?"

"Basil. Please. I know this isn't you." I gestured to the figure in front of me. "It's been several years since we last met, yet this body is the carbon copy of what I remember, right down to the depth of the wrinkles at the edges of your eyes. You're not above indulging in a beauty treatment or two, but new work wouldn't leave you looking this close to what I remember. People's bodies change." Even if their personalities didn't. "So I ask of you, please, be honest with me. Bring me to your true self, stop trying to fool me with another Life Model Decoy. It isn't working."

The LMD's smile had dropped away completely. Now Basil – the false Basil – looked cold and distant, like a snow-capped mountain that defied any attempts to climb it. "I sometimes forget how clever you are," he murmured. "Not a mistake I'll make in the future. Let me assure you, darling, you're better off talking to this version of me. It's far less distracting than the other."

"And yet I won't be satisfied with anything less than the truth," I replied. "So you either bring me to you, the real you, or I report to my employer that the reason we've been stymied lately is none other than my own ex-husband, the Foreigner, and we see how well he takes that news."

"You wouldn't turn me in to Doom," Basil said, confident as ever. "You're a lot of things, but you're not a betrayer."

"I am, first and foremost, a patriot." I looked his LMD straight in the eyes and saw that glitter again. He was watching me through them, scouring me for my own tells. He wasn't going to find any. "And the deal I've made with Doom is good enough to help every single person in Symkaria live a better life. I won't betray *them*, Basil. Now let me talk to the real you, or we're done here."

The LMD pressed to its feet, urbane expression back in place. "I suppose I'll have to–" It suddenly threw a round kick straight at my head at high speed, the machine's foot little more than a blur.

Good thing I'd been expecting it. I rolled sideways off the couch, came up with a chai in each hand and threw them at the LMD's weak points. The first one went straight into the center of its chest, the second for its head, just above the ridge of the brow.

Both of them hit, but neither penetrated more than a quarter of an inch. The LMD looked at me patronizingly as it tugged the one in its chest free. "Please, darling. That was pathetic, even for y–"

I pulled my gun out and shot him through the base of the throat, the third front-facing weak point that these LMDs were known for. I'd told Felicia she and Boris couldn't bring guns; I'd never said anything about myself. I *knew* Basil, and I wasn't about to give him an advantage, especially because I knew he'd want to get me by myself. He was always best in one-on-one interactions.

The LMD began to list to the side, its eyes glittering overtime as it tried to communicate through its severed neural net. I waited for it to fall over, then used one of my chais to slice the right hand off. It bled disconcertingly for a moment – all part of the sales spiel, "so realistic!" – before I got through the artificial bone and revealed the circuitry running through it. I carried the hand over to the palm reader by the one door that no one had gone through yet, then pressed it to the surface. It beeped, and a second later the door opened into a dark, close-smelling room lit by a single overhead light. That light illuminated a bed, on which a man was lying.

A very familiar man, at that.

CHAPTER SIXTEEN

I dropped the severed hand and walked over to the bed on quiet footsteps, waiting for the man in the bed to come back to himself. It was never nice to be hooked up to an LMD when it experienced catastrophic failure, and he had been controlling at least four at once. The top of his bare head was covered with electrodes, and he was hooked up to several different IVs. The monitor on one of the machines he was hooked up to began to beep more quickly, and after another minute, the Foreigner opened his eyes.

"You," he said hoarsely, "are still as ruthless as you ever were, darling."

"Thank you." I gestured at the equipment surrounding him, trying not to let on how unsettling I found it all to be. "I'm sure under other circumstances you would have put up more of a fight."

"I might have," he said, giving me a faint smile. His lips were dry and cracked. "You always were my greatest weakness, though. I might have let you win."

"You've never let me win at anything."

"But I *have*, darling. I have." He coughed briefly, one trembling hand coming up to cover his mouth. I waited it out, resisting the urge to offer my assistance. He'd helped me at my worst – it would be right for me to help him in return. But until I knew the extent of his involvement in the chase for Tolentino, I couldn't.

"You... you wanted a divorce," he went on once he'd caught his breath. "I gave it to you, no questions asked, no fight put up. I let you have what you desired, even though all I desired was you."

"You killed one of my last family members," I reminded him. "You've tried to kill *me* half a dozen times since then."

"Darling, he tried to kill you first," he pointed out, and, well... that was fair. My uncle Fritz had lost all of his love and loyalty for his family by the end. That didn't mean I liked it, though. "And between people like us, an assassination attempt here and there is the equivalent of a little boy pulling pigtails."

"Little boys shouldn't do that," I said as gently as I could manage. "And neither should you. What's wrong with you, Basil?"

"Now that I've seen you? Nothing. I'm as blissful as a baby."

"You've clearly never spent much time around babies." I came around the side of the bed and carefully took in the setup, catching the label on the side of the IV as I did. Intravenous chemotherapy... "You've got cancer?"

"Of the most malignant sort," Basil said with a sigh. "It hit me like a bolt from the blue. A month ago, I had a simple pain in my arm – now I've got a form of leukemia so deadly that no doctor I've seen can cure it, only slow its progress down."

Oh. Oh, that was awful. "I'm sorry," I said, and reached out to take his hand. Unlike the LMD, his actual flesh was cool and clammy, and his fingers spasmed slightly before they managed to return my grasp. "I wish there was something I could do."

"There is," he replied, his smile a bit more dashing this time around, despite the hint of blood on his teeth. "You can stay out of my way and let me retrieve the Clairvoyant. It's the key to finding a cure for myself."

That wasn't going to happen. "I'm afraid I can't do that."

"Why, because you're afraid of Doctor Doom?" Basil chuckled. "You think I would abandon you to one of the world's greatest sharks, Silver? After all the trouble I've gone to recently to keep you alive? No, darling. After I use the Clairvoyant, I'll ensure it gets handed straight over to you."

My... what did Juliet call it, a bullcrap meter? Whatever it was, it was signaling a warning loud and clear. "That's not an option."

Basil sighed. Lying there on his back, exhausted and sick, with no one around that I could see to take care of him except LMDs, he looked smaller and more human than I'd ever seen him. Not even at our wedding, when he had held my hands and, with tears in his eyes, promised me the world, had he been so vulnerable. So weak.

How you must hate that I'm seeing you this way.

"But," I said, displeased by my own weakness but unable to tamp it down completely, "I promise that once I have the Clairvoyant, I'll use it on your behalf. If there's any way to help you with it, I'll find out for you." Surely I could do that much, couldn't I? Would Doom even know if I did? Not likely... and under the circumstances, it was a risk I was willing to take. Basil might not be my husband anymore, but I didn't want him to die.

"I want to trust that you mean this," Basil said after a moment. "But I'm not sure that I can." His doubt in me hurt more than I expected it to, but I schooled my face to stillness. "Besides, I think the odds of me getting closer to Tolentino with LMDs are better than yours. He doesn't seem to be as attuned to mechanical brains."

"He was attuned enough to escape you in Macau," I pointed out, and gently lowered his hand to the bed. "I'm not going to give up the chase, Basil. I... suppose we have nothing else to talk about then."

"What if we do this as a team?" he asked, a hint of desperation entering his voice. "Bring your people here, work out of my home in concert with me. Together we might stand a better chance than either of us would on our own. I can–"

"Oooh, hey, nope. That's not going to work for me."

I startled so badly I jumped a little, whirling to face Felicia, who was leaning casually against the doorframe with her arms crossed. A little way behind her I could see the body of another Hudson LMD, clicking and twitching in the throes of some sort of major malfunction.

"See, I'm not all that good at sharing," Felicia continued, stepping into the room. "And right now, *I'm* the one who's already made a deal to work with Silver, so mine takes precedence."

Basil regained his voice faster than I did. "Put your claws

away, little kitty. I'm no threat to you. I was merely inquiring about the *possibility* of working with the love of my life again, nothing more. After all, I'm in no position to be making demands." He indicated himself with one hand. "A sickbed doesn't make for the best backdrop for negotiations. Speaking of which… why did you have to go and hurt poor Hudson like that?"

"He kept coming on to me with the *worst* pickup lines," she replied, perfectly deadpan. "And he followed me into the ladies' room. Are these things really modeled after your father? Because if they are, I've got to say, the apple didn't fall far from the tree."

"He's programmed to be charming," Basil snapped. "It's not my fault you're immune to social niceties. And he's *also* programmed to keep people from stealing from me, so the fact that he followed you anywhere probably means he was concerned that you were going to try to rob me."

"You can't prove a thing," she replied blithely, then looked at me. "Are we good here? Because I'm starving."

"Um… yes." I glanced between her and Basil, felt the tension in the air, and decided that discretion was the better part of valor this time around. "You get Boris and X-Ray, I'll meet you out front in a moment."

She winked. "You got it, Silver."

Once Felicia was gone, I turned back to Basil. "I meant what I said earlier. If I can look through the Clairvoyant and find an answer to your problem, I will."

"I know you think you mean that," Basil said tiredly, "but that's not how devices like that work. You can go into it with the best of intentions, wanting to bring about world peace or end hunger, but eventually your interest spirals down into what's waiting for you, what *you* can get out of it. That's how it always goes."

"Not with me," I insisted. "I promise."

"Well." He gave me another smile, small and soft. It was his version of a shark smile, perfectly predatory, designed to incapacitate me with kind thoughts. "Maybe you will, then. And I promise to stop sending my LMDs after Tolentino. I don't think I've gotten very close to catching him anyway."

"Thank you," I said, then leaned down and kissed Basil, very gently, on the forehead. He smelled like sickness and sweat, but there was a hint of his old cologne there as well, leather and smoke and ambergris. It was a scent distinctly his own, and there was something comforting about it despite the circumstances. "Take care of yourself."

"I will if you will," he replied. I gave his hand one last squeeze, and then I left him there, alone in his bed. I stepped over the broken LMDs and out the front door, where everyone was waiting for me out by the car.

"Finally!" Felicia called out. "I thought I was gonna get old waiting for you to say goodbye to that shyster. Let's get out of here."

We were a fairly quiet party on the way back to the airport. X-Ray was silent, her gaze distracted as she looked out the window. She didn't have much to say about her experience there other than, "The gardens were lovely."

"They were intriguing," Boris put in. "The Foreigner might be a shady son of a gun, but he's got an eye for rare plants. I counted three different types of spring weed that have been proven to absorb toxins from the earth, and–"

"Whoa, like the stuff growing out of the old nitramine bomb sites?" Tango asked, carefully encouraging the conversation in a different direction. I ended up talking with Felicia in the middle seat – and not because I wanted to.

"Honestly, how did you ever tolerate being married to a guy like that?" she asked me sotto voce. "He's got to be one of the most self-centered, overrated, verbally abusive pieces of work that I've ever met, and I've met a *lot* of truly terrible people in my time."

I sighed. "*You* dated him, too, you know! What appealed to *you* about him, huh?"

"Hey!" She pointed a finger at me. "Fun and athletic extracurricular activities aren't marriage. And you've never been the type to do anything casually, much less something as serious as tie the knot. So, what gives? What about him made you think, 'Oh, this is definitely the partner I want for life'?"

This wasn't the place I wanted to talk about Basil: baring my heart to another of his exes with two of my people listening in and Boris droning on about the way plants could be used to absorb radiation. Then again, there wasn't *ever* a good time to talk about Basil, and she did have the right to some background given how difficult he might make things for us.

"When he and I got together," I said slowly, trying to push emotions aside and gather my thoughts in a logical way, "I thought… he understood me. I thought he understood what I do, what I stand for. He took the time to listen to me, he gave me every indication that he agreed with my goals and my hopes, and he…" I shrugged. "He paid attention to me in a way that few men ever have."

"You know that's just because you've got such a hard-nosed reputation, right?" Felicia said with a curl of her lips. "It's not because you're not good looking, it's because they think you might bite their heads off if they approach you the wrong way."

"I know," I agreed. "I did it to myself. It doesn't bother me." *Most of the time.* "It was good for a while," I added, because my life wasn't a complete tragedy no matter how it seemed sometimes. Yes, I'd seen my mother murdered, and my father had raised me to be a killer, and all my family was dead now, thanks in part to my ex-husband, and my country was occupied, and I was on the verge of a total meltdown, but… there had been good times, too. Lots of them, some with Basil.

"He was a very attentive partner for the first year. It was only after three jobs in a row went bad that I realized he was playing both sides, trying to make it look like he was helping me while selling information on the side, either to the person I was hunting or to others who were after them. Things started to go downhill after that, and we divorced just before our second anniversary." I shrugged. "But he did save my life, so I owe him for that."

Felicia shook her head. "Mmm, y'know, if saving someone else's life was the metric we used to measure gratitude in this world, then I'd owe all *sorts* of people I have no interest in dealing with, and even more of them would owe me. Heck, Spider-Man has saved both our butts more than once, and you don't see him deploying emotional blackmail missiles at us the second we're on the same continent."

I chuckled. "Basil and Spider-Man are about as different as two people can get."

"It's true, so true. Actually, if we're interested in speaking to someone who might *actually* know something useful." She glanced at me sidelong as Tango pulled up at the airport. "What do you think about going and having a chat with Peter Parker?"

I thought that was a terrible idea, honestly. "What does Peter Parker have to do with any of this? Why do you want to bring him into it?"

"Not, like, *in*-in," Felicia clarified. "But he's another person who's seen James Tolentino in action. They went to school together at Empire State. Peter was there when he was coming up with the original Clairvoyant. He might have some good insight for us."

I pursed my lips. "Are you just using this as an excuse to get some facetime with one of Spider-Man's friends?"

"Hey!" She theatrically whapped my arm with the back of her hand. "I can see Spider-Man any day I want! We're buddies, that's something that buddies can do. And I really do think Peter could be useful." There was a gleam in her eyes that I didn't know how to interpret, but actually, this could be a good idea.

"Well..." I looked at the time. The day was half over already – it wasn't like we were going to be jetting off to South America to go after Tolentino the second we touched down in New York City. "All right. I suppose it wouldn't hurt."

"That's the spirit," Felicia congratulated me.

She might have a point. Not to mention, Peter had connections, thanks to his growing business, that might aid us in keeping track of him.

Fine. We would meet with Peter Parker, but if Felicia got... what did Juliet call it... *schmoopy*, I was out of there.

CHAPTER SEVENTEEN

Peter Parker was the CEO of a globally recognized aerospace and defense company. Or rather, he *used* to be – I knew his business had been through a lot and was technically shuttered, but he'd kept a building in New York for his own personal use. After all, Peter was a scientist first, a businessman second, and scientists needed space to experiment in. He'd kept the top floors for himself and was renting the rest out.

His secretary had been very insistent that his schedule was full today, but Felicia made a quick call to – I don't even know, perhaps she had an in with his secretary or was on a first-name basis with his Aunt May – and all of a sudden he had a free fifteen minutes that very afternoon, just enough time for him to chat with a few of us.

I left everyone else at the embassy – X-Ray seemed tired anyhow, and Boris was pursuing a renewed horticultural obsession. If I never had to hear about radioactive grass strains again, it would be too soon.

So it was just Felicia and me walking into his former New

York headquarters in our civilian clothes. Felicia had changed into a professional suit that made her look like she belonged in the corporate shark tank, while I was wearing my nicest jeans, a silk blouse, and a jacket – no shoulder pads this time – that hid my special ceramic-bladed chais nicely. We still attracted a lot of attention from people milling about in the lobby and in line for the elevators, but I think that was probably because of the strange similarity in our looks.

"It's not," Felicia said as the elevator opened. The two of us got on and pressed the button for the top floor. There were other people waiting, but they opted not to join us for some reason.

"What's not?" I asked. "Not what? What are you talking about?"

"The reason people are looking at us? It's not because of our hair."

How did she even… "I wasn't thinking that."

"Oh no? My bad," she said with perfect insincerity. "But if you *were* thinking that, and you were *interested* in being better informed, then the truth is that they're staring at us because you're walking like you're about to kill someone."

I rolled my eyes. "Oh please."

"They are! You've got a murder walk – don't you realize that?" She tipped her totally unnecessary glasses down and peered at me over the top of them for extra emphasis. "I realize it's just your 'I'm working' walk, but couple the speed with your expression, and I can't fault most people for thinking, 'Oh dang, that woman's gonna cut somebody.'"

Ridiculous. "I walk briskly, that's all."

"You keep telling yourself that," she said as the elevator rose quickly. One wall of it was glass, giving us a beautiful view of the city as we went up. The other walls were mirrored, and I glanced in one of them. Was I really... oh, huh. Hmm. All right, perhaps she had a point about the expression, but to be fair this was how I normally looked. Resting... what did Juliet call it... witch face? Something like that.

"I think they're watching us because your shoes make you look over six feet tall," I countered.

"Six foot two, in fact." She lifted one of her feet up, balancing perfectly on the other one as she inspected her stiletto heel with a smile. "Aren't they lovely? You should try some."

Great, here it comes. "Because I'm short?"

"No, because it's a great way to get an extra set of weapons into any building!"

She had a point. Those heels were deadly. I'd worn my share of stilettos over the years, though, and when it came to stabbing people, I preferred my chais.

The elevator finally came to a stop, and the doors opened to reveal a space that was the exact opposite of how I expected an office to be. There were no internal walls, for starters – no tastefully hung bland corporate artwork or enormous desks with leather chairs. There was a drafting table, and a few tables covered in electronics and computer equipment, but beyond that the place was mostly filled with various projects in situ.

The one spot that did look comfortable enough to sit in, a couch and table with a minifridge next to it, was well off to the side. I could picture Peter's girlfriend or his aunt sitting there, chatting with him as he worked on his latest designs. Was this how he managed all the demands on his time that came from balancing work, family, and "extracurricular" activities? By blurring them all together?

"Peter!" Felicia called out enthusiastically as she sped up for the last few steps to where he was standing in suit pants and a dress shirt, but no tie or jacket. "It feels like it's been forever!" She pulled him into a hug that made *me* blush, never mind the guy she was actually enveloping. Peter handled it well enough, but I could see him breathe a little sigh of relief once she let him go.

"Yes, it's been… like, five days," he said with a laugh.

"So long," Felicia purred. "Thanks for taking the time to talk to us."

"I've always got time for you," he replied, then looked at me and smiled. "Both of you. Silver, it's nice to see you outside of a civil war."

"You as well," I said. "I see you've taken some inspiration from the Tony Stark method of decorating your workplace."

"Oh, well, not exactly? I mean, this isn't really an *office*, it's just a lab," Peter said. "I don't bring businesspeople up here, just friends."

"You're going to make me blush," Felicia said.

"She can do it on command," I added, and she glared at me. I ignored her. We weren't here to flirt. "Peter, we need to ask you some questions about an old acquaintance of yours."

His smile faded away. "Sounds serious. Go ahead."

"His name is James Tolentino. He's the inventor of a device called–"

"The Clairvoyant," Peter interjected, running a hand through his thick brown hair. He looked resigned, as though this wasn't a surprise. Had he *expected* Tolentino to make another version of the device? "Right, yeah. Shoot. Is he using again?"

"Using?" I glanced at Felicia. "He doesn't seem to have a drug problem…"

"Not a drug problem, exactly, but he does have an issue with addiction," Peter said. "It's… let's talk over here." He led us over to the couch, grabbed us some bottled water, then flopped down next to us with a troubled expression on his face.

"Jamie and I were never best friends or anything, but I knew him pretty well in school. He was brilliant, but he was also easily distractable. I'm not surprised he managed to invent something like the Clairvoyant – it's the ultimate entertainment. He used to spend hours watching it in the lab. I practically had to pry him out of it to get him to remember to eat and sleep."

That reminded me. "Couldn't he simply take it with him?"

"No. It used too much power – he had to leave it plugged in all the time at first," Peter said. "And even then, he couldn't see more than one or two alternate realities until he started using something really hefty to run it."

"Until he started powering it with the Catalyst, right?" Felicia asked.

"Right." He looked at me. "How is he powering it now, out of curiosity?"

"I… don't know, actually." That was a very good question. "I can't see any sort of battery, and I know that anybody else who uses it is going to need one." I didn't know how Doom was planning on powering the thing, but I wasn't about to ask him either.

"Huh. Weird."

"Why?" Felicia pressed. "This isn't the original device. He must have made it more energy efficient."

"Maybe, but it's still going to take a lot of juice to run no matter how efficient it is," Peter replied. "You don't power a device that will shuffle realities like a deck of cards with double-As. Unless he's running it with magic, but that doesn't sound like Jamie. He never liked magic – it did weird things to the odds, and he never liked it when somebody messed with his odds. That's his real addiction – gambling. He's gotten into trouble with it before."

Peter looked down at the floor. "I should have checked in on him more. I said I'd help him out, and I did for a while, but then life got… busy." He winced. "And I know that's not an excuse for being a bad friend, but honestly, I thought he'd come to me if he was having problems."

What nonsense. I shook my head. "Right, because that's what people with a lot of pride and a gambling addiction do when their back is to the wall – blatantly disappoint the people who've already given them a second chance."

Peter sighed glumly. "Rub it in, why don't you?"

"So he hasn't been in touch," Felicia interjected, putting us back on track. I had to admit, she was good at managing a conversation. "That's really all we needed to know. If he *does* reach out, please contact us. He's being hunted by some very dangerous people right now, and we want to make sure he gets the help he needs before they catch him."

Peter raised an eyebrow. "Are those very dangerous people *you* guys? Because I'm not going to help you run Jamie down, if that's the case."

"We have no plans to hurt him," I said. "We do intend to stop him from using the Clairvoyant to help him fleece casinos, though."

"And there are other people running him down who have none of our hang-ups with morality," Felicia added.

Peter chuckled as he pulled out his phone. "Only you would refer to having morals as a 'hang-up.' Look, how about we exchange numbers? If he pops up on my radar I'll call you, and if you need help with him, you can do the same for me."

"Since when have you started using a new number?" Felicia asked with more than a hint of suspicion in her voice as I turned my phone so Peter could read the number. "Are you trying to ghost me?"

"Not everything is about *you*, Felicia," Peter replied with a sigh as he texted me. *Bzzz.* "I'm trying to ghost someone *else*. I've got your number memorized. Besides, you've got MJ's number, too."

"Good point."

"Thank you for your offer of help," I said, tucking my phone back in my jacket as I stood up. "I appreciate it."

"I'm happy to do what I can. Silver..." Peter's expression was troubled. "Be careful, OK? There's more at stake here than Jamie's fate, and if you need my help, you can–"

"I'll be fine," I said firmly. Lord, why did *everyone* think I was in over my head just because word had somehow gotten out that I'd made a deal with Doom?

"She will," Felicia said, immediately earning points for sticking up for me. "Because I'll be here to hold her hand every step of the way."

Points removed. You now have negative points, Hardy.

We said our goodbyes, and I hustled Felicia out of there before she could coopt the conversation anymore.

"Well, that could have gone better," I said as we rode the elevator down.

"On the contrary, it went great," Felicia said. "I got to check out Peter's newest toys – did you see the grappling setup he's making? Who do you think it's for? Not to mention, we now know how Tolentino is powering his device."

I thought about it for a moment. Either he had the world's smallest nuclear power source strapped to his body somewhere – not a good idea – or... "He's using himself as a battery."

"And probably running a fever to do it," Felicia said. "Good information to have if we need to identify him via thermal imaging or something like that."

If James Tolentino had been running the Clairvoyant off his own body's energy since before the Wild Pack had been after him, *and* he was doing the bare minimum necessary when it came to sleep in order to stay one step ahead of the game, then he had to be getting close to the limit of what he was capable of. He'd been at this for over a month, first chased by Doom's forces, now by us. We really *might* be able to wait him out and let him exhaust himself, then sweep in to gather up the pieces.

Except for the fact that he had people like the Foreigner and maybe even the triad after him now. They were waiting for their chance, too, and they'd be a lot less concerned with Tolentino's wellbeing than I was.

"We'd better find him fast if we're going to save his life," I said as we hit the ground floor.

Felicia looked surprised. "I didn't know life-saving was in your mission brief. Aren't you supposed to be after the Clairvoyant at all costs?"

I shook my head. "That's the primary goal, but I'm adding a secondary one: get James Tolentino the help he needs. If he's doing this because he's battling an addiction, then he's probably not going to be able to break the cycle on his own." I nodded toward her phone. "Make sure you keep Peter's number handy. If everything goes well, we'll need it."

"Aww, Silver." Felicia put her arm around me and pulled me into a side-hug. I resisted the urge to punch her in the kidney. "Look at you with your soft heart."

"That's me," I said blandly. "So soft." I shrugged her arm off, then walked over to a tall man with a baseball cap perusing his phone a few meters away from where we'd parked the car, pulled out a chai, and stabbed him just below the sternum with it. The Hudson model stumbled slightly, then turned sad eyes on me.

"Darling, really, was that necessary? It's not even a show-stopping blow."

"Just a reminder that I'm going to be looking for you," I snapped, angrier now than I'd been at his house earlier. I hated being stalked. "And the next one of you I see won't get a little love tap from me. I'll let Boris blow you up instead. *Back. Off.* Is that clear?"

The Hudson smiled urbanely. "Perfectly clear, darling."

CHAPTER EIGHTEEN

Another five hours of searching with Foxtrot's custom facial recognition algorithm finally got us a hit in Las Vegas, Nevada. Of course. It was the jewel of the American gambling industry, the best place for making a big score, the most golden of all fleeces. It was also highly monitored, heavily secured, and a nightmare when it came to infiltration. Every casino had its own tricks, and none of them liked to share – not security information, not personnel, and definitely not the whereabouts of their potential clients. Tolentino would have a tough time pulling something big off here, but if he managed it, the rewards might be enormous.

We were at least able to figure out which hotel-casino he was staying in. The Diadem was an old casino that had just gotten a major facelift, and we were all going to be present for the grand re-opening of it, which was tomorrow. The tickets had cost a mint, but it promised a party for the ages: free drinks, fine cuisine, live shows, and huge giveaways, all things that drew people like honey drew flies.

We got a set of two suites, connected, and I pointedly gave

Felicia and her guys one set of rooms for themselves while gathering my people in the other. We'd hardly been working with them for more than a day, and I was already exhausted by Black Cat and her crew. It was nice to settle in and take care of my own people, for now... and from the look of things, they needed taking care of.

Foxtrot was setting up our computer equipment, but he was moving slowly, blinking every couple of seconds like he could barely stay awake. Juliet was a little better, but she'd gotten to the point where she barely spoke to anyone, just huddled deeper into her hoodie and texted her girlfriend almost as often as she checked the cameras. Tango was unaccountably quiet, and apparently X-Ray's melancholia was catching, because after she slumped down on the couch, Romeo settled in next to her, close enough that their shoulders were touching. He didn't even say anything, just sat there leaning into her, like they needed each other's support.

"Hey," I said quietly to my team, who stopped what they were doing to listen in. "If you want to do some recon in the hotel, feel free." It was as close as I could get to offering them a night off while we were working a job. "Check the exits, visit some of the stores and restaurants... Tolentino just got here, he's going to be on high alert. We won't grab him tonight. I'll work with Felicia and her crew on getting surveillance set up, all right? And I'll get some food brought up if you'd rather stay in," I added.

There was a moment of silence, and then – "Sold," Foxtrot said with a faint groan. "I've got a migraine the size of Manhattan right now. Too much screen time. I'm going to sleep."

"Take the bedroom," I told him.

"I'm going to call my bestie. Actually *call* her," Juliet said, "and talk to her like a normal person instead of over text. I barely remember what her voice sounds like." She headed for the balcony, and I turned to X-Ray and Romeo, who were–

Already up off the couch and headed for the door. Gosh. Fast movers. "We're gonna go check out the shops," Romeo called back to me. "Don't wait up, we'll have our comms with us, goodni–" The door closed before he finished his sentence.

Tango sighed. "I guess I'll go do some gambling. I can get recon in on the floor that way."

I smiled. "Try to have some fun while you're doing it, huh?"

"Yeah, sure. I might… actually." He paused and turned to look at me hopefully. "Would you like to get dinner with me once I'm done? I know you've got work to do, but it wouldn't take all that long. There's a restaurant on the first floor that specializes in Eastern European food, we could–"

"No, thank you." It was a kind offer, but I wasn't about to get in the way of his enjoyment. Tango was almost as kind to me as Juliet when it came to making me feel included, but I knew the truth. I was the boss first and foremost. "I'm sure you'll have more fun without me."

Tango opened his mouth, then closed it, shook his head, and left the room. *Curious.*

"You are one of the most obtuse people I've ever met," Felicia drawled from our connecting door. "And I know *Bats*, for crying out loud."

"What bats?" I asked as I joined her.

"Bats, he's a ghost dog who belongs to Doctor Strange, very sweet but gullible. Definitely don't listen to him if he tells you he's ever met you before," she said briskly, then led the way back into her suite. Boris had already put a decent command center together, complete with multiple monitors and some good views of the casino's main floor.

"It's smart giving your people a night off," she continued as she poured herself a drink from the minibar. "They're good, but they've been going at top speed for a long time now. You're going to burn them out if you're not careful."

"Worry about your own people," I said coldly, refusing the drink she offered me.

"I do," she replied. "That's why Boris is over here playing piece-together-the-jigsaw puzzle with hotel security while Bruno chills with the sports network." She nodded toward the couch, where her hitter was sitting with his feet up and a beer in one hand as he watched someone talk about draft prospects.

"Number one draft pick, my *butt*," he muttered as he tapped a message into his phone with his free hand. "The Browns are going to lose harder than ever."

Felicia laughed, then called out, "How's Casey?"

"Wrong about football, like usual."

"Mmm, give her my love, OK?"

"You got it, boss."

Casey? I'd never heard of Black Cat working with someone named Casey before. "Do you have another team member?" I asked.

"No, not exactly." She made a face. "Well, more like kind of? An *honorary* member, let's put it that way. My *point* is, I know when to push my people and when to let them have a break. Right now, it's push time for Boris, while Bruno gets some more time to baby his shoulder. Your people? They look like they could have used a break days ago."

"It wasn't an option days ago," I said stiffly. "If you're done criticizing how I handle my team, let's move on. Boris, have you hacked into the hotel's computer?"

"Not exaaaaactly," he said. "But I've hacked into the phone of someone who has access to the hotel's computer, which is almost as good."

"How did you manage that?" Felicia asked.

"Diadem's head hotelier is putting his family up in one of the other suites for tomorrow's grand re-opening," he said, pulling up a quick picture of them. "Apparently his five year-old likes to play with daddy's phone. I traded her an Avengers coloring book in the atrium downstairs in exchange for two minutes with the device."

That was lucky, but… "Why did you have an Avengers coloring book with you?"

"Have you ever flown commercial?" he asked with a sour expression. "And been surrounded by hordes of hellspawn eager to interrupt your serenity with their kicking and screaming and crying? Do you know what distracts little nuisances like that? I pack coloring books *and* crayons every time I leave New York – the good crayons, not those little rinky-dink primary trios. I have *standards* for bribery."

"We didn't fly commercial," Felicia pointed out.

"Depending on how well you and Sable get along from here on out, we might very well be flying commercial to get back home," he muttered, stabbing the keyboard vociferously. "I like to be prepared. There are seven potential James

Tolentinos in the hotel, all single men who fit the bill as far as time of arrival go."

"Great." That was good work. "Once you've narrowed it down a little more, Felicia and I can bug their rooms. Once we have Tolentino targeted, we can start making a plan of action." In a hotel this size, the more specific we could be, the better.

"Sounds like fun!" Felicia said brightly, pouring me yet another drink. I accepted it this time, and took a tiny sip. *Mmm,* warm and spicy. It would go well with a hot, fresh *burek,* one of the crispy, filling meat pies I used to get back home. *Burek* was the last thing my mother had ever made for me.

Maybe they had it in the restaurant downstairs. Maybe it wasn't too late for me to join Tango for a meal, to sit and share a drink with him and just be a *person* for a while, a person who deserved to have a moment of easy pleasure rather than...

No. I was working, I couldn't. I walked over to my bag and grabbed a protein bar instead. I bit into it viciously and refused to feel sorry for myself, no matter how much sympathy was in Felicia's eyes. Let the others have their fun. Someone had to stay on point here.

In the end, Felicia and I ended up bugging three rooms with some very nice, nearly invisible directional bugs that I'd bought off a wholesaler in France the last time we'd had business in Paris. Two of them were on the same floor, close to the ground level. Felicia claimed those ones with a declaration of, "I want to go down and look at the Cartier boutique anyhow." That left the room at the very end of the hall on the seventeenth story for me.

The bugs were good once in place, but they weren't drones –

you couldn't place and activate them remotely. I could walk down that corridor, but the security cameras would see me, and I didn't trust that Tolentino wasn't monitoring his own room for signs of interference. So how best to do it?

"Boris," I asked after my stomach growled – so spoiled, a protein bar should be keeping it quiet – "can you check and see if any orders have been made in the kitchens for room 1721?"

"I thought you had a challenge for me," he muttered, shifting away from a screen that had something to do with mushrooms and opening up the ordering system. "It looks like... actually, yes." He sounded surprised. "How did you know?"

"Tolentino usually orders room service when he's working from a hotel. What's his order?"

"A bacon double cheeseburger, fries, a chocolate malt, an ice cream sundae... ugh, he eats like a child."

Or like a man who didn't care if his arteries clogged up. "Give me the order number, please," I said, standing up and heading for the door.

"2248... but you better hurry, it looks like it's already on the move from the kitchens," he warned me.

Shoot. I headed for the stairs instead of the elevator, rushing down to the seventeenth story. I opened the stairwell door on the opposite end of the hall from Tolentino's room just as the elevator went *ding,* then sprinted over, almost running into the person pushing the cart.

"Oh!" I exclaimed, steadying myself on the edge of the cart. I surreptitiously checked the ticket stuck to the outside of the silver delivery tray – 2248. This was it. "I'm so sorry, I... I was expecting someone else." I palmed the bug and maintained eye contact with the server as I carefully pressed it to the outside of the tray. The optics in it would make it appear as reflective as its surroundings.

"Oh, gosh. Who were you looking for?" the server asked, flipping their long black bangs out of their face.

"Just a guy. He invited me up to his room, but…" I scuffed my toe against the carpet, kind of hating myself for the ruse I was going with. "He, ah, hasn't shown up yet, and I'm getting kind of antsy."

"Um." The server looked me up and down, then leaned in a little closer and said quietly, "I totally get wanting to hang out in your spare time, but shouldn't you be in rehearsal? You all have three full shows to do tomorrow, right? I swear I just heard the director shouting at one of the rubies – he's not going to like it if he has to track you down, too."

Uh… what? Rubies? Director? Who exactly did this person think I was? I glanced down at myself surreptitiously: my usual lightweight silver top, skintight silver pants, silver boots, all rated to deflect knives and small caliber bullets… the usual. The person was staring at me like they'd just done me a favor, though. "Ah. Thank you. I'll handle it."

"No worries, just wanted to give you a heads-up. By the way," they added, "love how you matched your hair to your costume!" They gave me a smile, then headed down the hall toward Tolentino's room.

Still curious but happy the job was done, I got into the elevator and headed back up to my own room. Felicia wasn't back yet, but her bugs were live, and Boris had all three of them up on screen and was running a language detection program listening in for key words and phrases to keep from losing his mind bouncing back and forth.

"I think we've got something with the one you placed," he told me. "I'm going to record it separately. Here." He pointed to the chair next to him. "Take notes."

I settled in and, a second later, a familiar voice came out of the speaker. "…sure that she gets it three times a week, right? That's what the doctor said, isn't it?"

"Who's been doing this alone ever since you left?" an exasperated young woman's voice replied. It was a little tinny, but pretty clear – Tolentino was probably talking to her on speakerphone. "I know how to take care of Mom. My question is, who's taking care of you?"

"I am," Tolentino replied.

"Not to be harsh, Jamie, but you're kind of rubbish at that. I bet you haven't showered in days."

"Now who's being harsh?"

"Dude, I shared a room with you until the fourth grade, I know how you live."

Oh. I leaned in closer. This wasn't just a caregiver looking after his mother, this was probably his sister Rosamie. She'd fallen off the grid almost as effectively as Tolentino had, and I hadn't bothered tracking her or their mother down because it didn't seem to have much relevance, and I wasn't going to threaten someone through their family. If that technique worked, no doubt Doom would have already tried it.

"Talk to me," his sister went on. "You've been at this for a while now. You said once you got us enough money for that designer treatment that you'd come back, but I enrolled Mom in it three days ago. It ate up most of the funds you sent us, but that's fine! We don't need any more money, Jamie. We need *you*."

"No, you don't." He sounded resolute... almost unsettlingly so.

"Jamie..." His sister's voice was soft. "Of course we do. You know Mom wants to see you, and when she gets better, she's going to–"

"Mom's not going to get better, Rosie."

There was a long moment of silence, then his sister said, "What are you talking about? That's what all this has been for, making enough money to get her into the special treatment. It's going to save her, isn't it? You said it would, you looked through the Clairvoyant and–"

"I lied." Tolentino's voice was full of self-loathing. "I lied to you both. I said I saw a future that would fix things, but the truth is that no matter how much money I send on, there's no future where Mom lives for much longer. I couldn't... I didn't want to stick around and watch her die, so I told you I could fix it and left you there with her, alone. Because I'm the most worthless son and brother in all of Brooklyn, and I'm a coward, too."

"That's not true!" his sister shot back immediately. "That's not true at all! You've had your problems, but that's not – nobody is perfect, Jamie. Not even the people you feel like you've got to compare yourself to, and *don't* say you don't compare yourself to Peter Parker, because I know you do. But you don't have to be like him. All you have to be is *you*. Mom wants to see you so bad, so why don't you just come home already? If she's..." Rosamie's voice wavered for a moment. "If she really is dying, then it's even more important that you come home and get the chance to say goodbye to her, and let her say goodbye to you. She didn't get to say that to Dad, Jamie, so don't do that to her now."

There was a muffled sob, and my heart panged in concert as I heard it. God, he sounded *broken*. Felicia entered the room, but I waved her to silence before she could speak. I didn't want to miss a word.

"No, I can't. I just can't. You don't know what I've done, who I've crossed. If I go back home, they'll come after you and Mom."

"Who will?" his sister begged. "Who's coming after you?"

"People who won't stop for anything. They've followed me around the entire world. I've gone into other *dimensions* to try to knock them off the trail, but it's not working. It's not working, and I'm so tired, Rosie. I have to plug the Clairvoyant straight into my nervous system to power it, and I'm running low on juice. I'm seeing fewer and fewer futures, and almost none of them are any good."

Other dimensions? Felicia mouthed at me. *What the he–*

I waved her away and refocused on Tolentino – no, Jamie. It was hard to think about him dispassionately when he was on the verge of tears.

"I won't bring them down on you," Jamie promised his sister. "Just… take care of Mom, OK? Tell her I love her. Tell her you're gonna be set for life before I'm through here."

Set for life? What did that mean?

"Jamie, stop it, please," his sister begged. "Come home, or we – maybe we can meet you somewhere else, I can hire a travel nurse to come with us and we can all get together again. It's not hopeless. It can't be!"

"Love you, Rosie," Jamie murmured.

"Jamie, *no!* Don't–"

He ended the call. Boris left the bug recording but silenced the speaker so we could talk amongst ourselves. He started things off with, "Well, that explains why he never takes those sunglasses off."

It was the perfect remark to jolt me out of my depressing contemplation of Jamie Tolentino's life. "What do you mean?"

Boris sighed heavily. "If he's powering the Clairvoyant with his own body, there must be some sort of neural interface between them. He probably *can't* take the glasses off without losing power, and I doubt he has the skills to reattach them if he pulls them out. It takes a very competent cybernetic surgeon to install this sort of thing... or you can get it done cheaply, which means it's going to be unreliable and most likely painful."

I remembered the trails of light I thought I'd seen under Tolentino's skin a few times and winced. Using himself as a battery was undoubtedly a constant source of aggravation, both physical and mental.

"Ouch," Felicia said with a grimace. "That's not fun."

"He sounds like he's given up," I said. I felt vaguely guilty about that. "I didn't mean to push him so hard that he *hurt* himself over it."

Felicia shook her head. "*You* didn't. Tolentino made his own choices, and those choices included defrauding a bunch of casinos. Sure, you're after him so that you can steal the Clairvoyant for Doctor Doom, but it's not like you're the *only* person after him – the Foreigner is evidence of that, not to mention the triad. He put himself into this position, and the real kicker is he *knew* he was doing it, way back when this all started."

It seemed like she was building up to something. "What exactly are you saying?" I asked, resisting the urge to cross my arms defensively. I had no need to be defensive, but I felt it anyway.

"I'm saying that he's an addict," Felicia replied. "And at his core, he's using the Clairvoyant to fulfill that addiction. He could have done a lot of stuff to help his mother, up to and including asking Peter for a loan, which you *know* he would have given him, but Tolentino chose this path instead. He did it for the high, for the thrill. Not because it was the smart call or because he was backed into a corner. I don't know which future he saw that he thought he'd shoot the moon for, but whether or not it turned out that way isn't on you, Silver."

It was bizarre that Felicia Hardy was trying to make *me* feel better, of all people. Even stranger was the fact that it was working. I nodded, then took a deep breath to try to clear my head.

Jamie Tolentino was at the end of his rope. His mother was dying, his sister wanted him to come home, and he *still* wasn't budging from Vegas. He told Rosamie that she was going to be set for life by the time he was through here.

"He's planning a major heist of some kind," I said. "His final objective may have changed, but his means of fulfillment hasn't."

"Mmyep," Felicia agreed.

"I think we should approach him directly."

"Mmnope."

"It makes sense!" I insisted. "He's primed for intervention

right now. He's vulnerable, he's alone – we should make it clear to him that we're not his enemies, that we can help him."

"He doesn't want help," Felicia pointed out. "If he was interested in help, he'd have accepted it from his family or friends."

"He doesn't want to involve them."

"Are you kidding me?" She threw her hands up in the air. "I can think of a bajillion ways to get in touch with people without subjecting them to surveillance! I could probably think up *two* bajillion if I had something like the Clairvoyant going for me!"

I pondered that for a second before saying, "I don't think bajillion is a real number."

"It's *not*, it's a metaphor – shut up," she snapped at Boris, who was snickering in his chair.

"I think you mean it's hyperbole, boss," Bruno added from the couch.

"You can shut up, too! I'm making a *point* here, which is …" Felicia frowned. "Wait, where was I going with this?"

"Something about Jamie not wanting help, perhaps?" I offered.

"Yes, that's it. He doesn't really want help." She was pacing now, treading the same ten feet over and over again as she gesticulated broadly with her hands, one of them still holding her half-full drink. "He's caught in a trap of his own making, and he thinks that the only way out is through – whether that means finding that sliver of a remaining future that lets him survive this, or going down in a burst of glory. My money's on burst of glory, it's the sort of thing that occurs to people when they get riled up like this."

I couldn't exactly rebut her assertions, given that I would give my life for Symkaria in a heartbeat. I understood feeling like there was no way out, but I also knew the value of having staunch allies around me to help keep me on the path, to keep my head clear and my soul uncluttered. That was what the Wild Pack did for me. They were my people, however distant and awkward we were at times, and I would die for any one of them. I would certainly do my utmost to *live* for them.

Jamie wasn't even willing to live for the sake of his mother and sister. His circumstances were grave.

"You think he would resist our intervention," I said.

"I think he's determined to pull this last big job off," she replied. "So why not let him? Let him have a win, get his endorphins flowing, make him less desperate once his addiction has been satisfied. Let's make him *happy* first." She grinned. "After all, happy people are the easiest people to manipulate."

Her plan had merit, but… ignoring the heist ignored the very real danger that Tolentino was going to put people at risk while he pulled off his "set for life" scheme. I couldn't just stand by and let it happen, not when there was a good chance that we could bring Tolentino in *and* stymie whatever plan he had before people got hurt. "I want to go after him now."

"Are you even listening to me?" Felicia snapped. "Do you actually want my opinions, or does it feed your ego to get my advice and then do the exact opposite?"

"I *do* want your opinions, but that doesn't mean I'm always going to follow your advice." I reached for my comm unit and turned it on.

"At *least* give your people the rest of the night off! You

pull the rug out from under them now, and I guarantee nobody's going to be happy when it comes to going after Mr Gamblepants at… what is it, ten at night? Come on."

My fingers trembled on the comm as I considered my options. I wanted to call them all in, make a plan, get going as soon as possible – after all, the more time we gave Tolentino, the more time he'd have to plot against us right back. But he sounded even more tired than we were, and I was close to staggering at this point.

"Fine," I said at last, setting the comm back down. Felicia shot me a big, fake smile.

"Greeeeat," she said. "Now that that's settled, I'm going to go try my own luck downstairs. You game?"

"No." Much as I hated to admit to any weakness, my eyes were blurry with exhaustion. "I'm going to sleep for a bit."

"Good, you have fun with that." She drained her drink, then picked mine up and drank it down, too.

"Hey!" I'd barely touched it, but still!

"Gotta make the most of the minibar while we have it." She left without another word.

Bruno was watching the TV again, Boris was monitoring the computers, Juliet was on the balcony… I had time to catch a good five hours or so before I needed to get up and start making plans.

When's the last time you slept in when an injury didn't force you to? Do you even remember?

I didn't.

CHAPTER NINETEEN

The Diadem's grand re-opening was happening in stages. The doors wouldn't open to the public until ten o'clock in the morning, so that the guests who'd made reservations here could enjoy the promotions, food, drinks, and deals at the tables by themselves until then. After ten, the doors would open to all, and the madding crowd would stream into the place, and that's when the craziness would really begin.

Part of the casino's marketing revolved around promoting its name – Diadem. It had a real, genuine gemstone diadem – rumored to have been a gift to the owner by a member of the Atlantean royal family – on display in the center of the casino to help with that promotion. The diadem was valued at one million dollars, mostly for the notoriety of its previous owners.

Everyone who entered the casino would get a diadem-themed ticket with a scratch-off number on the back. At noon, the doors would close, the tickets would stop flowing, and after some sort of entertainment to catch everyone's attention, the diadem would be removed from its case so that the number hidden beneath it was revealed. Whoever's ticket matched that hidden number would win the crown.

It was such a gimmick of a giveaway. What was your average person going to do with a crown, after all? I mean, yes, they could be useful when it came to luring Black Cats into your clutches, but the *real* value of the diadem was in the Atlantean artifact collectors vying to purchase it from whoever won it.

"Private bidding is at two-point-five million and counting," Juliet informed me that morning at eight AM as we all sat around the suite's table. "Naturally the casino is keeping tabs on it all, since they're going to want to get their cut in promotion pictures and probably even a handling fee."

"Probably." Because they were jackals, and that was what jackals did. "Two and a half million would be a very good nest egg, don't you think?" There were a few other games running in the casino that would give a bigger payout, but none of our surveillance had turned up any sign that Tolentino was interested in them, whereas he'd gone to inspect the case holding the diadem twice last night. Besides, it would be more thrilling to walk away with a crown, wouldn't it?

More of a last score, no matter how ridiculous it was.

"What's the plan, Sable?" Tango asked me, his eyes a little pinched in the corners. Everyone was tense this morning except for Felicia. She was sipping a mimosa with her bare feet propped up on a spare chair, and Bruno and Boris weren't even awake yet.

Fine. She wanted to let them slack, that was her call, but if we didn't walk out of here with Tolentino, she would never get Black Fox's map. I'd take that secret to my grave if I had to… which I very well might, if we didn't pull this off.

"We have eyes in Tolentino's room." He hadn't put the tray out to be picked up yet. The bug I'd attached to it was facing the wall, but at least we knew he was in there. We'd heard the shuffling of feet, a few jaw-cracking yawns, and the sound of the shower going so far this morning. Overnight there had been a few thuds, and a sound like someone in another room had left a TV going, but nothing apart from that. "Let's get everyone into position. As soon as Tolentino leaves his room, we move in."

"It's a waste of tiiiiime," Felicia sang around her straw. "He's not going to let you corner him."

"I don't want to corner him, I want to *speak* to him." Felicia might be right, but I at least needed to *try* to reach out without resorting to violence first. I knew how it felt to be desperate, to be ready to abandon all your sense for the chance at one final act of revenge… or atonement, as the case may be. "I think he's ready to talk. He must see that we're the better option, and if he doesn't? We won't give him the choice to walk away." I gestured at her bedtime attire. "Are you planning on helping with any of this, by the way?"

"I'll keep eyes on the sparklies, how about that?" Felicia said. "Make sure nobody carries them off prematurely. Not even me." We'd already talked about how stealing them ourselves in advance was a waste of time. Tolentino probably wouldn't bother to come after the diadem if it wasn't fairly easy pickings.

"Perfect. Thank you." I looked back at my people. "All right, you've got your assignments. Let's get this done. It's got to happen today." *Because we aren't going to have time to plot another attempt.*

The Wild Pack dispersed without another word, not even from Tango or Juliet. Romeo headed for the tables close to the diadem, X-Ray was going to be hanging out near the stationary security booth at the back of the main floor "checking" her phone, Foxtrot was keeping eyes on the stairwells and elevators, and Juliet was going to coordinate between us all.

Me? I was going to go talk to Jamie Tolentino. I was going to make him see reason. I was going to offer him a lifeline and hope against hope that he reached out to take it. I stood up and double-checked my gear – chais at my hips, my gun in the small of my back, sword hidden beneath the swirl of my long jacket. I didn't think I'd need the hardware, but I wanted to be prepared.

"Good luck," Felicia said to me as I got to the door. I glanced back at her. She was still stretched out and casual, polishing off the dregs of her mimosa, but her eyes were perfectly serious.

"Thanks," I said, and headed out.

I took the stairs down – I didn't trust elevators – and jogged until I reached the seventh floor. Just like last night, I entered the hall and walked toward the far end, past the elevator and to Tolentino's room at the very end. Taking a deep breath, I knocked on the door.

No one answered. Not surprising. Of course he knew what I was here to do. He was probably weighing his options even now. "Mr Tolentino?" I called out. Still nothing. "Jamie?"

I tried. No response. Finally, I tried the door, which was unlocked.

Uh-oh.

"We have a situation here," I murmured as I stepped inside. The noises were still going – I could hear the toilet flush – but I wasn't getting that prickle of awareness that came from sharing space with another person.

"What kind of situation?" Juliet asked.

I glanced into the bathroom. Empty. "Tolentino's not here."

"That's strange," Foxtrot said. "I've been monitoring the stairwells *and* the elevators. He hasn't moved, as far as I can tell."

I walked further into the room. The bed was a mess, like someone had been tossing and turning in it all night. Looking a little closer, I could see spots of blood on the pillows. Had Tolentino gotten a nosebleed, or was this evidence of his hack-job version of turning himself into a battery? There was a phone on the nightstand, turned on.

"It's a recording," I said grimly as I stared at the phone. "He's been playing a recording in here. He could have gone downstairs hours ago."

"No, I still would have caught it," Foxtrot insisted. "We've been monitoring for plenty of time, he–"

"Went out the window." It was closed, but there was a black scuffmark from a shoe's heel on the edge of the white frame. I could see some of the sole's pattern in it. Why had I forgotten to aim a camera there? I could have kicked myself. "He went out the window. He's got to be downstairs somewhere." I whirled and headed for the door. "Everybody, heads up, keep your eyes open for Tolentino; he's mixing with the crowd."

If he intended to get his hands on the diadem, then he'd be down there right now – the winning ticket and the presentation that went with it would happen in ten minutes. That would be the ideal time for him to make off with it. The people who collected things like that, they didn't care about maintaining legal provenance – what they wanted was a piece of Atlantis.

"Tango, keep your eyes open, too," I went on as I exited Tolentino's room. "Look for vehicles that are lingering out front, anything he might choose to use as his getaway vehic–"

The elevator dinged, and the doors opened. A woman a head taller than me, with hair up in a bun stuck through with at least half a dozen pens, rampaged out into the hall. Rather than avoiding me, she came right over and confronted me. "There you are! Dang it, Chantal, when I say it's call time I mean *right now!* Where's your badge? Is your earpiece not working? I've been calling you for the past fifteen minutes!"

"I–" I had to admit, I was nonplussed. "I'm not–"

"Oh my god," she wailed despairingly, scrunching the ends of my hair in her hands as she stared at my outfit. "This is what the costume designer went with? Seriously? You look like you're about to punch someone!"

I *was.* "Listen, I need to–"

"Come downstairs right now and get in line before it's too late to salvage this cluster bomb of a performance? *Yes,* you do." She grabbed my hand and tugged. "Honestly, if that guy hadn't mentioned seeing you on this floor we'd *all* be out of luck, and you would be the first to get fired, and then *I'd* get fired, and then the director would get fired, and for the love of Pete, would you *get onto the elevator already*?"

Well. Clearly Tolentino had pointed her in my direction, but why? What did he get out of this, apart from the joy of messing with me? Was this an effort to get me out of the way? What had he heard between me and the waiter I'd chatted with in the hall last night?

The mistakes were piling up – I was losing my edge.

On the other hand, did it really matter? She thought I was some sort of performer – where were the performers going to be? Close to the diadem. It wasn't a bad charade to go along with and might keep me from having to deal with this woman's rage, panic, and subsequent meltdown. I was no good with tears. "All right," I said, and let her pull me onto the elevator. "Sorry for the trouble."

"You should be! We have *three minutes* to get you in line, and I swear, if you don't can-can your heart out like the rest of the girls I'm going to scream, do you hear me? I will scream, and then I'll get arrested, and then I'll make sure *you* get arrested, and–"

Mkay. The best thing at this point was for me to go with the flow. We made it to the ground floor, and as soon as the doors opened she hustled me through the crowd toward the stage, where the diadem and the owner of the casino – along with plenty of security staff – were standing. And to the side of the stage was a row of women in jewel-toned outfits, every one of them unique except in how much skimpier they were than what I was wearing.

"Silver!" the woman shouted, and I actually thought she was speaking to the real me for a moment before she shoved me into line beside a gorgeous black woman in a gold bikini top and sequined skirt. "Great, now where's Diamond? *Diamond!*"

"You're not Chantal," the woman next to me observed.

"No, I'm not," I agreed. "But go with it, please."

"Eh." She shrugged her shoulders, looking bored. "I get paid either way."

"Silver? Silver! What's going on?" The voices coming through my comm finally registered. I saw X-Ray in my peripheral vision, looking at me worriedly, which meant Romeo probably wasn't far behind.

"It's fine. Little change in plans is all," I murmured. "Does anyone see Tolentino?"

"A few glimpses in the crowd about fifteen minutes ago," Juliet confirmed. "It's hard to track anyone for long with this many people crammed in here, though."

"He'll show himself soon enough."

"Maybe," Felicia put in for the first time. "Did you guys know this casino uses a Pinwheel safe?"

"Is that supposed to mean something?" I asked. The clipboard-bearing banshee was still shrieking, pulling people into and out of the line and looking one step away from a breakdown. The music was starting to swell – we were going to be headed onto the stage soon. I'd break away just before we went up there.

"Not really, but it's an old safe. Like, eighties-era old. I guess when they upgraded the rest of this place, they decided not to bother with that. It's hardly better than a cardboard box if you have the right equipment, though."

"Why does it matter?"

"It might not," she said slowly, "but then again…"

"I see him!" Juliet suddenly called out. "Middle of the crowd, wearing a hat, looks like he's moving in closer to the stage."

"Got it. Romeo, X-Ray, get him boxed." Once they had the escape routes covered, I would move in to apprehend him with Felicia in backup position. "Juliet, do *not* lose him, he–"

"Sable." That was Foxtrot, sounding perturbed.

"What is it?"

"I double-checked the elevator and stairwell feeds, and… Tolentino used a keycard to access a restricted floor underground."

I frowned. "Do you know what's on that floor?"

"It's got to be the–"

"The vault," Felicia cut in. "He was going after the casino's money."

What? "Does he still have it on him?" I demanded.

"He didn't come to this level first after finishing up," Foxtrot went on. "He went to *our* floor, with two big bags."

Oh, no. "We have to get him, now," I urged, beginning to push through the crowd. "Before–"

"Excuse me, sir." That wasn't my comm – that was on someone else's end. "We need you to come with us."

"Romeo is being arrested," Juliet said tensely.

"On what charges?"

"I don't know yet, but – now they've got X-Ray!"

A surround-sound blare of brass instruments and a thudding drumbeat erupted at the base of the stage. People began to cheer, and a second later the line of dancers began to move.

What should I do? Stick to the original plan and get close to the diadem to keep Tolentino from going after it? Or disengage now and go after him before he pulled off whatever he was planning with the money he'd stolen? Ahead of me, I could see the owner of the casino removing the diadem from its display case and holding it up like a trophy.

"Keep an eye on Tolentino – don't let him get away!" I shouted into my comm as I kept in line with the ladies. "Felicia, move in now! I'll cover from the stage!" I would be able to see better from up there.

"*Smile!*" the frazzled woman shouted at me right before I headed up the stairs onto the stage. "For god's sake, look like you're having fun, or I'll *murder you!*"

The noise, the smells, the press of people, and the terrible, loud music that rang in my head even as I worried about my people and scoured the crowd for Tolentino – it was the most disoriented I could remember being in a long time. I reached the stage, did exactly *one* synchronized leg kick, then pulled away and approached the owner. "Sir," I said, reaching out a hand, "Please, I'm here to–"

"Ah, you're the model! Perfect, perfect!" Beaming, he reached out and placed the diadem down on my head, then grabbed me by the shoulders and spun me around to face the crowd.

Eh, it wasn't what I'd expected, but I'd take it. I stared out there looking for Tolentino and – aha! There he was, not ten feet away, crouching down at the edge of the space they'd cleared in front of the stage for... for... what was *that?* It looked like some sort of launcher, or cannon, or...

Oh, *no.*

Tolentino looked right up at me and grinned. Then he took careful aim at me, pressed a button on the back of the cannon, and–

Everything dissolved in a swathe of suffocating glitter.

CHAPTER TWENTY

"Is she all right?" The careful, worried familiar voice was the first thing to cut through the fog surrounding me since the explosion of silver glitter had blocked my view of... of... What had I been doing again? I couldn't quite place it – it was like my mind just didn't want to focus, not on the past, the future, and certainly *not* on the present. My brain was wrapped in clouds, cold and shivery, but that was OK. Better than confronting that I was a complete and utter failure.

"She's not injured," another, louder voice said. It cut a line right through the brain fog, like a beam of sunshine parting a perfectly good rainy day. "She's just overwhelmed, I think. Who wouldn't be, if they took a party cannon to the face? C'mon." Strong hands slid beneath my upper arms, grasping tightly as they levered me to my feet. I wobbled, and was instantly braced by someone on either side. "Let's get her somewhere quiet, huh? We'll work it out."

Work what out? What was there to work out? I didn't want to do any work right now, I just wanted to sit and not think and not feel and not... not...

His kiss is mocking, an ill-wish blown on a sour wind.

Crap, *Tolentino*!

I jerked my head up, dislodging the hands on the left – Juliet, of course, that was *Juliet* – but not the ones on the right. "Where is he?" I gasped. "Where… oh no, what happened to Romeo? Is he all right? Did X-Ray–"

"They're all being questioned right now except for Juliet," Felicia said from my right side as she kept me moving toward the door of the casino. "Hotel security has footage of them in… compromising positions, is the best way to put it. There are good reasons for all of them, of course, but Tolentino took them in such a way that it casts reasonable doubt on things. It doesn't help that he managed to stash a bunch of empty cash bags into the laundry service that was delivered to your room right after Juliet escaped."

"Wait, so… he *did* rob the casino?"

"Yep," Felicia confirmed.

"What about the diadem?"

"He got that, too," Juliet said with a sigh. "The casino owner lost his grip on it when the glitter took you both out, and by the time things settled down again, it was gone. I'm not surprised you don't remember, you were… kind of out of it by then."

"How long was I out of it?" I asked with a sense of growing embarrassment.

"It's just been fifteen minutes, Silver."

A quarter of an hour… it could have been worse, but *any* time with a loss of control over my own mind was too much time.

Stepping outside was like stepping into a furnace. It was

bright and hot and dry, and my body immediately started working on homeostasis by making me sweat like a horse. It also blew the last of the cobwebs out of my mind. The job had gone *so* wrong. So terribly, predictably wrong.

I was screwed. We were *all* screwed.

I stopped in the middle of the sidewalk and stared at Felicia. My eyelashes were limned with silver glitter – a keepsake from that awful cannon. It made her sparkle like the diamonds she loved so much.

I expected her to look smug. She'd *told* me my plan wasn't going to work, after all, and I hadn't believed her. She'd warned me I was being manipulated, toyed with by a master, but there was something about the desperate nature of his plight that spoke to me. It mirrored how I felt about Symkaria – a need to do what I deemed necessary at any cost. I'd tried, for once, to dredge up my faith in humanity and make the effort to reach out to Tolentino, rather than hunt him down, and he'd repaid me by making an absolute fool of me, and getting away with his grand heist to boot.

It must have been the ultimate high, seeing me humbled with the knowledge that he'd pulled off his plan right before my brain seized up. "What else has happened?" I asked, fighting back the numbness that was trying to take over again. I turned to Juliet, who looked exhausted – even her dark purple hair seemed bleached and lessened in the light of the sun. "Are you OK?"

"I'm all right," she said immediately. "I was in the bathroom when hotel security broke in. They got Foxtrot, but he distracted them well enough that I was able to get to the balcony and rappel to the ground."

"Oh." I sometimes forgot that although Juliet preferred to oversee things from headquarters, she was fully field-trained as well. "Good."

"Felicia found me a few minutes after that and told me to stay outside until things settled down," Juliet continued. "Everybody's been picked up, but the evidence against them is all circumstantial."

"Boris and Bruno are getting into their lawyer clothes as we speak," Felicia added. "They'll put the fear of god into these wannabe cops and get your people out soon."

That should make me happy. It *did* make me happy, but I was also confronted with the reality that when my people got out, I was going to have to tell all of *them* that we'd failed. Not only had we not prevented Tolentino from carrying out his heist, we'd let him escape altogether, *with* the Clairvoyant. We had four days left before Doom expected it in his hands, and given our track record, I couldn't see us pulling this off. It wasn't going to happen, not even with the Black Cat's skills on our side.

"I wish I hadn't involved you in this," I said to Felicia, who shook her head.

"No, I'm glad you did. It's been interesting, I'll say that much."

"Interesting isn't going to seem like a lot of recompense when we come up short." Although of course I would keep her out of it as much as I could.

Felicia tossed her hair over her shoulder. "You're talking like it's over already, Silver." Her eyes seemed to sparkle, and I was pretty sure it wasn't the glitter in my own doing it to them. "Let me assure you, it's *not*."

"We should find somewhere to sit down," Juliet said, staring distrustfully at the hordes of tourists walking around us. "Somewhere more private."

"Let's. We'll find a place to wash the worst of that glitter off you, and then..." Felicia grinned at me. "I'll tell you our next step."

The coffee shop was uninspiring, but it was only a block from the Diadem, and it had caffeine. I downed twenty ounces of coffee that was almost as black as my mood and felt much better, while Juliet had tea and Felicia helped herself to a scone.

"Here's the thing," she said as we settled in to snack. It felt almost friendly, like we were just three ladies getting together for coffee to chat about our families, our lovers, our lives. Ridiculous.

Just because you want something soft doesn't make it ridiculous, Basil's unwelcome voice reminded me. I silenced him. This wasn't the time to get distracted.

"My probability generator doesn't work in a perfectly predictable way. If it did, it could be countered. If I could have made your plan work, I would have," she said, and it almost didn't sound like a reprimand. "If Tolentino was the person you thought he was, it probably *would* have worked. But the guy who's running the show right now isn't the son or the brother or the friend – it's the addict, it's the mastermind, it's the narcissist. Because let's face it, this dude is totally a narcissist. If he indulged his whims any harder, he'd be bathing in a chocolate fountain."

"That sounds like *your* whim," Juliet said wryly, and Felicia laughed and nodded.

Since when had they started getting along so well? Dang, I was missing *everything* lately.

"It is, but my point is that I wasn't able to affect the outcome to get you what you wanted this time. *However*," she went on before I could point out how obvious she was being, "that doesn't mean that Tolentino got what he wanted either."

"Are you kidding me?" I demanded. "He's got five million dollars in cash stashed someplace *and* the diadem! He got exactly what he wanted!"

"Mm, no," Felicia said slyly. "He's got the stuff, yeah. But what he *didn't* get is a clean escape."

What? Surely that couldn't be right. "But he's…"

"Did you know that *all* the guest floors of the casino are on lockdown right now? And probably will be for the next few hours, just to make sure no stones are left unturned? Once people realize the Wild Pack doesn't have the goods, there's going to be a room-by-room search."

"But he won't be in his room." He wouldn't. That would be ridiculous.

"Well, he *wouldn't* have been," Felicia allowed. "See, he got into the elevator and tried to go down to the parking garage. But a funny thing happened. The lift went the other way, instead."

I stared at her, then at Juliet. "Your probability generator…"

"Yep! It sent him back up to his floor," Felicia confirmed. "And the lockdown was announced right after that. So now, yeah, he's got the stuff, but he can't move it somewhere safe."

"He'll figure it out, though," Juliet said, always playing devil's advocate. "And it's not like we can reach him there either."

Felicia arched an eyebrow. "A simple casino lockdown is no big deal for someone like me, but sure, let's assume you're right. He's locked up there, we're down here, at least for another hour or so."

"So... how do we get him?" I asked. I felt like she was guiding me toward an answer, but I genuinely couldn't see it right now. "He can see every future, he can certainly see a way to hide his loot and evade us and–"

"Ah-ah-ah." She shook her head. "This is where my original plan comes in. I can make chaos with my device, but that chaos only goes so far. You know what makes a *lot* of chaos, a lot more easily?"

Now I saw where she was going. "Fun," I said slowly. "People having... fun."

"Yes! Gold star for you! Or maybe silver, to match your glitter and glam," she said. "And nothing makes people more fun than getting them liquored up."

"I wish that weren't true," Juliet said. "I mean, I get the whole lowering of inhibitions things, but it's just so... vapid."

Felicia shrugged. "We can't all be satisfied with an evening of *D&D*."

"Actually, we're playing *Zombicide* right now."

"Same difference."

"What *exactly* is your plan?" I said, forestalling an argument that seemed like it might just go on and on.

"Over the next hour, I'm going to buy every adult of legal age in the casino – every single one, staff included – rounds of drinks," Felicia said. "Not just the people playing the games, not just the people holding Diadem tickets – *everyone*. I'm going to fill the halls with people who are tipsy and good-natured and who have completely forgotten all their stress, and Tolentino is going to watch them all as he comes down from his high, and he's going to join in. Anything to put off the sting of reality coming back into his life."

"He hasn't done a lot of drinking in any of the other locations, from what I've seen," I said. "Only enough to sell a cover. I'm not sure this is going to work."

"Well, if it doesn't, we're not out anything but money," Felicia replied.

Money wasn't something I had an unending supply of, particularly not at this point in the hunt, but... what the heck? I'd done my best, and I'd failed. We might as well try it Felicia's way. "All right, fine," I said after a moment, and both the other ladies grinned. "Let's go buy everyone drinks."

"I *may* already have put that into motion," Felicia said as she rose to her feet. "Let's just say the other girls from your ill-fated dance routine are making a mint in tips right now moonlighting for the casino's bars. C'mon." She held her hand out to me. "Let's go see how things are working out, huh?"

I stared at her hand for a moment. I was steady now; it wasn't like I *needed* the help up. But... maybe I did need someone to hold my hand. I took it, and sure enough, after I was upright, she didn't let go, just laced our fingers together and led the way out of the coffee shop. With Juliet on my other side again, not touching but still close, I felt a strange sense of comfort come over me. Everything had gone to hell, and we might not be able to salvage this job, but right now, in this moment, I had friends. I didn't have to do this alone. Felicia and Juliet staved off the fugue that had overtaken me earlier – something I hadn't experienced since I was almost crushed to death – and hopefully the caffeine would keep me on an even keel until I could take some time off for recovery.

"Party" was a light way of putting things when we reentered the casino. I don't know what Felicia was paying the Jewels to hand out drinks and make merry, but those women had *committed* to their roles. People everywhere had glasses in hand, the music over the stereo system had been turned up to facilitate dancing, and with the way the light sparkled off the chandeliers and mirrored walls, it was like a daytime rave.

Not that I had ever been to a rave.

"That's what I'm talking about!" Felicia said, moving her hips to the beat and putting her free hand above her head. Someone held out a glass of champagne, which she took immediately.

"You can't drink and work!" I exclaimed.

"In this instance, drinking *is* working," she said to me, then turned around and looked at Boris and…

Wait, Boris? Where had he come from? He looked a little incongruous in a blue suit with a crisp white shirt, very much like a lawyer and not a mad scientist.

"Where is everyone?" Felicia asked, still bumping and grinding against thin air. Somehow she made it look natural.

"Bruno's in talks with security, assuring them that the Wild Pack are innocent victims of circumstance," Boris said with a smirk. "Meanwhile, Tolentino's room has just been checked for the goods. They didn't find anything, of course – he'd never do anything so prosaic as hide it in the air conditioning vent. I think he stashes it on top of the elevator.

Speaking of air conditioning, though, I've ensured that his air conditioning is malfunctioning. Even if he didn't have anything in the vents, he wouldn't be able to cool himself down in there."

"Excellent," she said. "And the shower?"

"Only gives hot water."

"Even better!"

Ah, I got it now. "You're overheating him."

"He's already overheated," she said. "All that hardware plugged into his body, using up his reserves, making him feverish. Well, now instead of hanging out in a cool seventy-degree room, it's more like ninety degrees. And the balcony won't give him any relief. If he wants cooler air, he has to be in the hall. And you know what you can hear really well from the hall?" She smiled as she let go of my arm and turned in a circle. "The *music*, baby! Broadcast on every floor, management's way of reminding everyone that better times are coming as soon as their rooms are inspected because it's a *party!*"

"His floor has been cleared," Boris announced, glancing at his phone. "People are free to leave if they like."

"He could escape now," I said.

"He won't want to take the chance," Felicia replied. "Tolentino knows that your team is in custody talking about him right now, probably trying to convince them to go after him. He's going to come down and check things out here by himself first, and when he does? He's going to get wasted. Now come on." She took my arm again and pulled me into the crowd. "Stop standing there like a bump on a log and start trying to blend in."

Blend in? How did someone blend into a crowd like this? By, what, gyrating? I've never gyrated! I bounced back and forth a little, if only because it helped keep me light on my feet so I could avoid the partiers next to me. Juliet tugged on my hand.

"I'll keep an eye on the elevators," she said, tapping the comm unit in her ear. "Let you know when he shows up."

"Thank you." She vanished into the crowd, and I quashed the part of me that wished I could go be a wallflower with her.

"You've got to relax!" Felicia insisted. "You think the Clairvoyant doesn't sense your own intensity? Stop focusing on the plan and start focusing on the *fun*, girl!"

"I don't know anything about fun!" I shouted back over the loud music. I didn't – not about *this* sort of fun, this helter-skelter, crazy-wild fun. I knew satisfaction, I knew affection, I knew devotion – or at least I thought I did – but "fun"? No way.

"Well, you're gonna learn! Here, let me show you a move. Focus on what I'm doing, OK?"

She's trying to help you, she's trying to help you, she's trying to help… I gave in and let Felicia teach me a complex dance move that she'd learned on TikTok. Then I learned to do it with champagne in my hand, then before I knew it, we were teaching it to a bunch of people around us. It wasn't exactly *fun*, but it was absorbing enough that I was genuinely startled when I heard Juliet's voice sound in my ear. "He's here, Sable. No bags, he's just looking around."

"Keep your eyes on him," I snarled as I started to head toward the elevators. Felicia caught me by the arm.

"Uh-uh," she said firmly. "Ignore him."

"He's less than a hundred feet away!" I said desperately. "I could corner him in a minute!"

"We don't *want* to corner him. We want him to feel relaxed and high on life and envious of everybody else's happiness. Here, dance with me." She tugged me in close and spun me around in a circle.

"I don't dance," I reiterated. Hadn't my abysmal attempt to blend in earlier proven that?

"Well, you're doing a pretty good job of it right now," Felicia replied. "Come on, just some spins, a few little steps... one and two, one and two, one and two..." It was embarrassing to be led about the two square feet of floorspace we were occupying like a child, but at least the dance was easy enough. "There, nice job. You're even better at this than Odessa."

"Odessa?" I knew of an Odessa... "Are you talking about the head of the Thieves' Guild?"

"That's the one."

My jaw dropped. "You taught her this dance?"

"I tried to," Felicia demurred. "But she didn't really have the patience for it. She was more interested in *other* things, if you know what I mean."

I didn't. "Like what?"

Felicia laughed, hard. "God, you're funny! Nobody would ever believe me if I told them you were so hilarious. Hang on, I'm going to do a twirl, then a dip. Are you ready?"

"A twirl, then a – *whoa!*" I wasn't ready for the twirl, and I *really* wasn't ready for the dip, but years of honing my reflexes allowed me to follow along well enough that when Felicia bent me over backward, I didn't let it faze me.

No. What fazed me was seeing James Tolentino standing right there beside me, an empty glass in one hand and a dazed expression on his face, not even noticing us. I couldn't see his eyes, of course, they were hidden behind the Clairvoyant, but his jaw was dropped, and his fingers were slack – he'd nearly dropped the glass.

"Gotcha," Felicia said smugly.

"Get me up!" I hissed at her. This was our chance to get him, when he was so focused on the present and far from the future.

Felicia obliged, pulling me up and spinning me into another twirl as she let go of my hand. I stopped my spin, one hand going to a chai at my belt as I faced Tolentino, and then–

Before I could take a step, he really *had* dropped his glass, letting it tumble to the rug to be trampled to sand beneath people's feet as both his hands suddenly rose to the Clairvoyant. "No," he muttered, halfway bent at the waist, like if he just went a little bit farther whatever he was seeing would change. "No! *No!*"

Felicia reached him before I did, pressing her fingers against two divots at the very back of the Clairvoyant's frame. The eyepieces detached from Tolentino's head, leaving behind attachments that sparked and sputtered fitfully where they'd been drilled into Tolentino's scalp.

She'd done it. She'd retrieved the Clairvoyant. I was stunned but elated – she'd actually gotten the drop on Tolentino. Her power had *worked*. Now I needed to make sure the plan kept working.

I ran over to him and clapped a hand over his mouth right

before he got himself together enough to scream. The sound still came out, it was just muffled against my palm, but no one else heard it over the chaos of raucous laughter and thumping bass. He stared at me and blinked, once, twice, then again, like he wasn't sure that what he was seeing was real. A second later, he collapsed.

CHAPTER TWENTY-ONE

It was all I could do to catch him before he hit the floor, I was so astonished.

I managed to scoop him up into a fireman's carry over my shoulders. My grip was tight around his wrist – even if he wasn't feigning a faint, I wasn't about to let my guard down. I turned to Felicia, who had the Clairvoyant up to her eyes and was tapping it on the side irritably.

"Come on! Let's get back up to our rooms!"

"Stupid thing," she muttered, lowering the device from her face and glaring at it. "Fine."

"You didn't actually think it was going to work without a battery, did you?" I asked as we headed for the elevator. Juliet was waiting for us there, along with Boris. Boris looked pleased, while Juliet looked half like laughing and half like she wanted to jerk Tolentino out of my arms and dance on his body in her steel-toed boots.

"No," Felicia said with a sigh. "I suppose not. Would've been nice, though." The five of us got into the elevator and headed up to our floor. By the time the door opened, I felt ready to take control of the situation. We had who we'd come here for. Now it was time to start cleaning things up.

"We need to get the Wild Pack out of holding. Juliet, use one of the burner phones to tip hotel security off about where Tolentino hid the loot." Although, the last thing we needed was them coming for him. My job had been to retrieve the Clairvoyant, and now we had it, but I wasn't about to hand Tolentino over to people who had no idea who they were dealing with.

He needs help.

Screw that, he'd had his chance.

You don't mean that.

Maybe I didn't… but either way, I wasn't leaving him here. "Actually, first we should move it. Felicia, could you–"

"Boris can do it," she said, opening the door to the suite and leading the way in. "He's almost as good at sneaking in and out of tight spots as I am, and I want to be here for the shakedown."

"Why?"

She smiled beatifically at me. "Because I love to see a grown man cry."

She probably did. "Fine."

"Give me ten minutes," Boris said, his eyes alight as he took off his suit jacket and switched it out for a familiar EMS uniform coat he'd borrowed from X-Ray's bag. "I'll leave the stuff in the owner's office. He'll be too busy explaining how it got in there to be bothered with hunting down whoever stole it for a while."

"Thank you," I said. He shrugged, picked up a tool bag, and

headed out. Juliet was already going back to her monitors, ready to keep an eye on things. She'd get the Wild Pack out of trouble as soon as possible.

That just left dealing with Mr Tolentino here. I tilted my upper body and poured him out onto the couch none too gently. He landed without a sound, still unconscious, and I took advantage of his stillness to truly look at him.

That he'd run himself ragged, to the very edge of his endurance, was clear. He'd lost weight, and the skin beneath his eyes and along his temples seemed thinned, grainy and dark with fatigue. The connections behind his ears where he'd kept the Clairvoyant plugged in were still sparking fitfully, and the area around them looked painfully swollen. He'd been wearing the Clairvoyant for so long that it had dug bloody divots into the bridge of his nose, and his lips were chapped and bitten.

Worst of all, beneath his skin ran dozens of wires, glowing with electrical impulses as they spread down his neck and into his arms and, presumably, his legs. He'd literally turned himself into a battery pack for the Clairvoyant, and if the way he was bruising around every wire was an indicator, it had to be terribly painful.

This was the price of the high, the price of his quest to make his family rich by gambling on futures he was certain only he could see. *Expect the unexpected* should have been a moot point when it came to him, but he hadn't expected the Black Cat.

"Thank you," I said quietly to Felicia, who was still holding the Clairvoyant, inspecting it from all angles with a collector's eye.

"For what?"

"For doing what I couldn't do." It hurt to admit it, but I wasn't going to lie to myself. The last really correct thing I'd done throughout this whole mess was bring Felicia and her team on.

"Hey, don't sell yourself short," she quipped. "You primed him for me. Part of the reason I was able to short-circuit his little gadget is because he was so ready for anything *you* could throw at him, he didn't look hard enough to see me coming. Although judging from the look of him, he was probably losing the ability to shuffle more than a couple futures with this baby. Too much power." She tossed the Clairvoyant up in the air, catching it by one eyepiece, and I flinched. "Why did he make them look like *these*, that's what I want to know. He could have gone way more designer, but he went with the mid-aughts version of every high-schoolers dream shades in *neon blue*? I mean, come on."

I was about to ask her to hand them over to me when Tolentino groaned. I refocused my attention on him, ignoring my momentary impulse to handcuff his wrists to his ankles. Now that we had taken away his advantage, I was pretty sure I had nothing to fear.

If the way he blinked his eyes open, looked at me, and began to sob was any indication, I was right.

The tears were sad, but they were also rather pathetic. "James," I said sternly after the first thirty seconds had elapsed without even a pause for breath. "*James.* Try to control yourself, please."

"I – I c-c I can't, I c-c-c–"

"James, really–"

"I *lost*!" he wailed, hands clutching the ports on his head as he stared at me. "I wasn't supposed to lose! It wasn't supposed to happen this way!"

Good lord. What had happened to the confident, abrasive, reckless man I'd been chasing for weeks? "Yet here we are," I said briskly. "Now, I need to talk to you about–"

"This wasn't supposed to *happen*! I only saw this outcome three times, and only once from this location! There were hundreds of other futures vying for supremacy; how could *this* be the one that won out?"

"Just once, huh?" Felicia put in before I could try to get us back on track. "Interesting. What happened next in your vision?"

"Uh… what?"

"You heard me, hon. What happens next?"

A glimmer of hope speared in Tolentino's eyes. "If… if you let me go, I'll tell you."

"No deal," I said before Felicia could. "We're taking you back to New York."

"I can't go back to New York! There are people looking for me there!"

"Hon, I think you already know this but I'm going to say it anyway, just to drive the point home – you've got people looking for you everywhere," Felicia said. "There are authorities on practically every continent trying to get their hands on you, and here's the bad news – most of them don't care about the Clairvoyant. They're more concerned with the fact that you've been stealing from their business interests."

"That's not really provable," Tolentino said, but his voice was weak.

"The triad doesn't care about proof," I told him. "They care about the guy who won half a million dollars in a game that was rigged for you to lose. And they're not the only ones who want to get their hands on you." I hadn't seen any of Basil's LMDs here yet, but I knew better than to count him out.

"I know, I know, but..."

"But *what*?" My patience was gone. "But you thought you could just waltz across the world without a care stealing from people and not get caught? You thought you could outsmart everyone who came for you until you went out in some grand finale, while your mother dies, and your sister is left in mourning for both of you? Is that what you thought?" I pointed a finger at him. "Well, let me tell you something, Mr Tolentino. *Nobody* lives like that. Nobody can make a life out of outrunning and outsmarting the entire world forever and expect to have anything but regrets and emptiness at the end of it all!"

"But..." He pointed at Felicia. "She does."

"Hey! I never abandoned *my* mother when she needed me the most," Felicia snapped. "I manipulated everybody from Nick Fury to my favorite booty call to save her life, thank you very much. And if that had been impossible somehow? I *still* wouldn't have left her to suffer through everything alone. I'd have been with her, helping out where I could, because I *love* her." She paused, letting her words sink in for a second, before adding, "The rest of it, I mean, yeah. That's basically my life."

"You are incorrigible," I told her.

"I know." She straightened up and clapped her hands together. "So! I propose we call everybody's favorite wall-crawler and let him deal with Jamie here, because the odds that I'm going to give in to my urge to make him call his mother and tell her what a bad boy he is are going up every second he sits here."

"No, please," he moaned. "I can't talk to my mother about this. I'm not… this isn't… it wasn't supposed to *happen* like this!"

"That's life," I said with all the sympathy he'd earned for himself, which after realizing how he'd been playing me earlier, was exactly none. "If you're lucky, your mother will be well enough to tell you to your face that she's disappointed and expected more of you. Honestly, James. You don't actually think you're going to be able to *keep* the money you've stolen so far, do you? There will be an inquiry from the IRS, the casinos might sue, you– *hey*! Don't even try it, mister!"

CHAPTER TWENTY-TWO

By that evening we'd successfully prevented Tolentino from throwing himself off the balcony, arranged for his haul to be found by Diadem security, and freed the Wild Pack. Now my people were all sitting in the suite's living room around two massive pizzas, casting furtive glances at the Clairvoyant as Felicia and her guys prepped for Peter to pick Tolentino up at a private airfield just out of the city.

Peter would help James, I was sure of it. Now was the time to make sure that *we* got through the rest of this all right. I'd been thinking a lot about what Felicia had said, about letting people wind down, giving them a chance to breathe and relax. We were still ahead of our deadline. As far as I knew, nobody else in this hotel was aware that we were the ones with the Clairvoyant – not even the indomitable Captain Verlak had set my phone to ringing yet. If even Doom didn't know that we'd finished the job, and we still had four days to get the device back to him, then...

"So, what's next, Sable?" Tango asked as he polished off

another piece of extra meat, extra cheese, sauce-doesn't-count-as-a-veggie pizza. "Do we call Doom to come and pick the Clairvoyant up, or should we take it to him in New York?"

"If he's even *in* New York anymore," Romeo said, looking tensely at the device that, for lack of a better spot to put it, I'd perched on top of my head like a regular pair of sunglasses. "We've got to find him before we can deliver anything to him."

"That shouldn't be too hard," Foxtrot said. "Sable's got his number. He *wants* this thing, remember? This is the end goal. He's going to make it easy for her to hand it over."

"That's what worries me," X-Ray put in. "What's to hold him to his word once we hand over the Clairvoyant?"

Success, it seemed, had made my people paranoid. "I signed a binding contract with him," I said. "I trust him to abide by it."

"Yeah? Do you also trust that he won't immediately go and steal the nearest means of powering this thing, then end up implicating us in the theft since *we're* the ones who got him the Clairvoyant?" she asked. "Because I don't! I don't trust Doom farther than I could throw him."

"We need to scout a neutral location to hand it over," Romeo agreed. "Someplace nobody can get the drop on us. Let me get you a safe for it at least, Sable, the ones in this hotel are complete pieces of—"

"Please." I held up a hand. "I appreciate you all being so concerned with our next move, but I think you're overreacting."

"We're not—"

"You can't—"

"You've seen what—"

"I'm not saying you don't have good reason for caution," I interjected over the jumble of worries, "but in this matter, I trust Doom. He has good reason for following through on our deal, and I'm not going to give him cause to think *we're* being the distrustful ones by setting all sorts of conditions on the handover. Besides, this is *Victor von Doom* we're talking about here," I added a bit fatalistically. "If he wanted to take the Clairvoyant from us, he could have done so the moment it came off Tolentino. We don't have a way to power it, and from what Boris could tell of Tolentino's neural interface, it's highly complex." He'd hooked up everything from the twitches of his muscle fibers to the peristalsis of his intestines to keep the Clairvoyant going. That wasn't the sort of thing we could jury-rig.

"I propose, instead of worrying and planning and making our next moves, that we all take the night off instead. For real, not as a scouting expedition."

My team stared at me as if I'd suddenly grown another head, or perhaps been replaced by a Skrull. "Are you feeling all right?" Juliet asked. "A little feverish, maybe?"

"Like a sudden breeze might just knock you over?" Tango suggested, but he was smiling. "Lightheaded, weak in the knees…"

"A night off?" X-Ray said, glancing at Romeo. "I didn't think that was something you did, Sable."

"I don't," I replied. "But I think you all deserve it."

I got the expected chorus of "nos" and "we're in this togethers" and the like. It was nice, but it wasn't what I wanted right now. I wanted to show them that I was more than just a taskmaster, that I could relax enough in the face of triumph to let them have a little time to themselves. After all, we *had* the Clairvoyant. Working or not, we'd done it! The precise terms of the deal with Doom had been met. Whether he made a power source for it himself or stole the Catalyst that Tolentino had once used to power it out of wherever it was stored in New York City, that was up to him and nothing to do with us. I'd nearly met my end of the bargain. I could afford to be gracious with my employees, my teammates.

My... friends? Perhaps one day they would be. Until then, I could at least give them this.

"I insist," I said. "I want you all to go out and have a good time tonight. I'll stay in and babysit the Clairvoyant, and tomorrow we'll arrange our next move with Doom. Is that acceptable?"

"I mean..." X-Ray smiled at Romeo. "Yeah, it is for me. Last night's fun was rushed, and today has been a total washout so far, but–"

"I can get us Cirque du Soleil tickets," he told her.

"Sold," she said instantly.

"Oooh, I want to see that," Juliet piped up. "Can I come along?"

There was a pause, then, "You bet," Romeo said, smiling widely as he stood up. "The more the merrier. Foxtrot, Tango? You guys want to get in on some acrobat action?"

"Nope," Foxtrot said, standing up and stretching his shoulders out. "I'm going to the spa. I need a massage, and maybe a facial. And some time in a sauna."

"Gonna get your nails done, too?" X-Ray snarked.

"Maybe, yeah! Hey, I work on the computer all day long,

that means a lot of time using my hands. They deserve to be pampered."

"Tango, tell us you're in at least," Romeo called out. "Unless you want to get in on some spa time with Mr Handiwork over there."

Tango looked at me for a long moment. "I'd be just as happy staying in with you," he said quietly. "We could order in some dessert. Find some of that mango ice cream you love so much."

Oh my god. I *did* love mango ice cream. I almost never ate it, but I loved it. When had he noticed? How had he... no, how had *I* missed this? Was he... *attracted* to me?

A dozen previous encounters suddenly took on a new shape. Oh no. I couldn't encourage it. We were in the middle of a job. "I'll be fine," I assured him, pushing my fresh realization forcibly aside. "Felicia and her crew will be back any moment. I need to go over the details of getting her the map, and..." And I was making excuses. Was I really not interested in what I was pretty sure that Tango was putting out there – or was it that I was just... scared, after everything that had happened with Basil? "And perhaps," I finished, "when we're done, I'll text you and we can meet up afterward."

Tango smiled. "I hope so." He didn't wait around any longer, just got up and followed the others out the door. I wasn't *glad* to see him go, but I was relieved. Being open with others was hard for me, and I had been hyper-conscious of how I appeared to the people I was leading since I had been old enough for my first command at the age of fourteen.

"You're the person in charge," I remember my father telling me sternly as he handed over a loaded derringer. I had lost that original years ago, but I kept replacing it. Outdated as it was, there was something comforting about carrying a piece of my past with me. "You can ask for advice, you can seek other opinions, but when it comes down to it, the success or failure of every venture you undertake is *your* responsibility. You have to look at all the angles, and if something happens that you didn't expect, you learn from it and hope that no one died from your ignorance."

"I understand," I'd told him seriously. "I won't let you down." For a moment after that he'd clasped my shoulder, his smile warm even if his eyes were as cold as ever – as cold as they'd been since my mother's death.

"Better you don't let yourself down instead," he'd said. "Don't rely on others for validation, Silvija. You can't count on them to have the same values as you, after all."

Hadn't that turned out truer than I'd ever expected? Not long after that I lost my father, lost the original Wild Pack, rebuilt, lost it again, lost my uncle and my husband as a result of it… I had lost far more than I'd gained over the years, I thought. When did I give up and stop fighting? When did I let myself have the freedom to fail, or better yet, permission never to force myself to try in the first place?

When did I give *myself* a chance to rest, a real one?

"Well, don't you look miserable."

I didn't startle. I'd heard her open the door, after all, and I'd listened to her walk around enough at this point that I could identify the sound of her footsteps. I *hadn't* intended for her to catch me in such a pensive mood, but it didn't bother me that she had. Mostly. "How did the meeting with Peter go?" I asked.

"Awkwardly," she said, flopping down on the couch and putting her feet up on the coffee table as she leaned back against the leather seat. "There were tears. Don't get me wrong, I respect anyone who can let themselves cry in front of others, but there's a stylish sob, and then there's the absolute *blubbering* that Jamie started in with as soon as Peter got within ten feet of him."

"Do you think he's going to be able to play Peter?" Not that it really mattered, but I didn't want our mutual friend to end up regretting helping us.

"Nah. Peter's a lot of things, but willfully naïve isn't one of them," Felicia said. "He's come a long way from his early years."

"I suppose he has," I agreed quietly. I didn't know him as well as Felicia did, but he seemed like a reasonable person, and with Spider-Man's influence on him he could be a valuable ally. "He'll do right by Tolentino. It's the best the guy could hope for."

"It is," Felicia agreed. "Let's hope he's properly grateful, huh? Sooooo…" She glanced over at me and arched an eyebrow. "You let everybody off for the night, then?"

"It seemed like the right thing to do," I said, not mentioning the fact that she'd recommended the course of action to me. We didn't acknowledge things like that between us, after all. "They can get some rest and relaxation, and I can reach out to Doom about the Clairvoyant and get some more work–"

"No."

I frowned. "What do you mean, no?"

"I mean you're ridiculously strict with yourself, and it's time you let your hair down for a night."

"I *did*," I said. "Didn't I just tell you about what the rest of the Wild Pack is doing tonight?"

"That's *them*," Felicia said with a groan of frustration. "Not *you*. My god, you might be the most self-effacing person I know, and I know a lot of people! I know *Daredevil*. You think he doesn't know how to flog himself over his wants and needs with the best of them?"

"There's no need to be rude about it."

"It's not rudeness, it's honesty." She shook her head. "Your team clearly loves you. They want to see you succeed. They want you to *unwind*, to get as much of a chance to relax as any of them, instead of running yourself into the ground!"

I shook my head. "I'm the leader. The success of our missions relies on my attention to detail, so I'm not going to compromise that by letting myself get distracted when–"

A golden throw pillow suddenly smacked me in the face. "No!" Felicia snapped. "You're not listening to me!"

I glared at her as I reached up and, very carefully, took the Clairvoyant off the top of my head and set it to the side. Then I picked up the pillow she'd just chucked at me and threw it back twice as fast. She tried to dodge, but I'd anticipated that – *ha*, yeah, even us regular people could do that sometimes – and got her in the shoulder. "Say something worth listening to, and maybe I'd pay better attention," I snarked.

"Oh," she growled. "Oh, I will."

Two throw pillows were lobbed in quick succession, gold and purple. I evaded one and kicked the other in midair, sending it whirling back at her. Felicia caught it and boomeranged it, hitting me in the stomach and sending me tipping over the arm of the couch. I rolled up into a crouch, ready to defend myself.

I caught three more pillows – how many decorative pillows did one room *need*, anyway, what kind of maniac had designed this place? – before Felicia resorted to heavier firepower, actually picking up one of the couch cushions and throwing it at me. It got me right at the ankles, and I had to do a front flip to keep from landing flat on my face. I landed flat on my *back* instead, but the cushion actually did its job there.

I picked the nearest squishy footstool up with my feet and fended off Felicia's next attacks, then transferred it to my hands and used it like a battering ram to drive her back into the wall.

"What is wrong with you?" I snarled, pressing hard against her with the yellow leather pouf – *yellow leather*, what a disgraceful combination.

"What's wrong with *you*?" she replied, digging her hand into the soft top of the pouf and ripping it out of my grasp. I backed up just as she heaved it over her head and brought it smashing down where I'd been standing, like a hammer. Unfortunately, I backed right into the computers. Two of the laptops crashed to the ground – it was all I could do not to step on them.

"You are allergic to fun!" Felicia went on, completely ignoring the mess I'd just made. "You are anathema to relaxation! You're going to give yourself a heart attack if you keep up like this, Silver!"

"What do you care?" I demanded, backing up as she menaced me with the fluorescent furnishing. "I practically forced you to help me with this anyway, you should be glad it's almost over. You should be off celebrating with the others!"

"I don't let killjoys tell me how to celebrate!" she replied, and hurled the pouf at me. Before I could stop myself, I pulled my chais and sliced through the leather, deflecting the attack.

Unfortunately, the pouf was stuffed with down. A pile of it *whooshed* up into the air as the footstool hit the floor, covering both of us in fluffy white feathers. For a second we were silent, staring around us at the mess we'd made in here. The couch had completely tipped over, the pillows were all over the room, the control station was a wreck, and now it was raining feathers all over us. They stuck to my sweaty skin like they'd been glued there, almost as bad as the glitter from before.

I was surprised when Felicia started laughing. "God, you look like a – a little lost chick!" she chortled. "Like you – aha – like you've never been in a pillow fight before!" She sobered a bit at the response she read on my face. "It's OK, everybody has to have a first pillow fight," she said, reaching out and brushing a few feathers off my shoulder. "It's just most of them don't get quite so vigorous."

"Oh," I said. "So, more like this?" I toed the pillow closest to me up to my hand and walloped Felicia right across the face with it. She stared at me, mouth gaping. "I don't know, I like this better." I ripped the pillow open in the middle, then smacked her in the midsection. This one was filled with some sort of artificial foam, though, and only a few chunks of it fell out as I hit her. Very disappointing. I dropped it and prepared for a counterattack.

It didn't come. "Girl, I knew you could have fun," Felicia

congratulated me, slinging her arm around my shoulder and giving me a squeeze. "You know what comes next, of course."

Oh god. "What?" I asked apprehensively.

"Drinks!"

I made a face. "I didn't like the one you gave me before."

"Makes sense, not everybody is a gin person. That's fine." She brushed a few feathers off my head, then pointed to the bedroom door. "I know a bartender here who makes themed shots. We can get him to do one for both of us. Let's see what goes into a Silver Sable, huh?"

No way. "I can't go barhopping when I've got the Clairvoyant to look after," I reminded her. "You go, I'll stay here."

Felicia shook her head. "Mmm, no, that's not how this works. I'm introducing you to how Black Cat and her team wind down after a successful job tonight, and that means letting your hair down."

"My hair *is* down."

She pointed a finger at me. "Stop taking me literally when you know I'm speaking figuratively, Silver. Let's do this! You can bring the Clairvoyant with, or we can ask one of our respective people to babysit it for a while. Boris can count cards some other time. But *you*, you seriously need to relax. Let someone else carry the load for a bit. OK? After all." She leaned in toward me and winked. "What happens in Vegas, huh?"

"What about what happens in Vegas?" I asked, genuinely confused. Was something supposed to happen here? Something other than everything that already *had*? I hoped not.

"It... never mind."

"It's not that I don't want to go," I finally said, because there was a part of me that *did* want to go out on the town. I wanted to see somewhere I'd never been before we hunted down Tolentino here, experience a taste of a life I already knew I would never get to have for myself. The idea of letting go of all the weights and worries I carried with me every second of every day was appealing, but...

The door opened. Felicia and I turned as one to face it, stirring up a cloud of feathers at our feet. To my surprise, X-Ray stepped inside. She looked at us, then around the room, then back at us. "So... uh. Should I go, or..."

"We're not doing anything *too* fun right now, don't worry," Felicia assured her with a grin. "Just testing the pillows' durability. What's up, buttercup?"

"I thought you were going to a Cirque du Soleil show," I added.

"Yeah, well..." X-Ray rubbed at the back of her neck. "It turns out watching people bounce around on tethers makes me more dizzy than anything else. I figured I'd leave the others be and hang out here instead."

"Perfect!" Felicia gleefully punched me on the shoulder. I resisted the urge to punch her back. It would undoubtedly lead to us ripping up the rest of the room. "You can watch the Clairvoyant while I take your boss here out on the town. What do you say?"

"Oh, yeah?" X-Ray brightened as she looked at me. "That sounds fun. We can keep an open channel if you want to check in, but I'm fine with that."

"Great. I'll get changed," Felicia said, heading for her

bedroom. "Let me know if you need help plucking your feathers, Silver!"

"You don't have to do this," I said to X-Ray as soon as the door was closed. "I'm fine staying here. I know you need a chance to unwind and relax and–"

"I can do that here," she interjected, her mouth a line of tension. "I mean, yes, I'd like that, but I'm just feeling... a bit insular tonight. You know how it is."

Did I ever. "If you're sure..."

"I am. It's going to be fine." She held out a hand. I reluctantly passed the Clairvoyant over – not because I didn't trust X-Ray, but because it signified handing off responsibility. Was I really going to do this? Was I really going to give in to a night of indolence, just because I could?

I didn't even have anything to wear, other than that damn silver dress.

I took a deep breath, put on a smile, and consciously let go. "Thank you." Then I headed for *my* room.

The silver dress would be fine.

CHAPTER TWENTY-THREE

"Aww, you look like a prom queen," Felicia said when we met again five minutes later. "Don't worry, it's a good look for you. Makes you seem younger."

I rolled my eyes. "I don't want to look so young that I get carded at these bars."

"Oh, honey. Nobody is going to card you. Trust me, they'll *want* you in their bars." Felicia, looking very much like herself in a sparkly blue dress and high heels, linked her arm in mine. I felt like her diminutive shadow. "Let's go!" She led the way to the elevator.

"We should take the stairs, it's safer," I pointed out.

"Not in these shoes it's not," she replied, punching the button for the ground floor. "Trust me, the last thing you want is to pick me up off the ground when I trip over one of these babies."

"You would never do that." I didn't know a lot about Felicia Hardy, but I knew she had gracefulness down to a science.

"Neither would you. Where are *your* heels?" she asked as we watched the numbers go by. 3… 2… 1… *ding*.

"I'm wearing them."

"Anything under four inches doesn't count," she said as we got out. "I guess we know our first stop. We'll get you knee high to a grasshopper ASAP."

"I'm not short."

"If you're afraid to wear real heels, just tell me and I'll stop pushing," she said with infuriating smugness as we headed for the front door. The party was still in full swing down here, but I didn't want to be in the Diadem right now – too much chance of being recognized as that girl from the show who took a glitter bomb to the face.

I caught a glimpse of Romeo headed across the main floor as we left. Apparently, he'd given up on Cirque du Soleil as well. Or maybe…

"I think two of my teammates might be in a relationship," I said to Felicia as we headed for a row of stores.

"Who, X-Ray and Romeo? I'd say so, yeah." We entered the first store in line, and Felicia waved off a sales associate and led me over to the shoes herself. "It's obvious from the way they interact, isn't it?"

"What do you mean, obvious?" I frowned.

"I mean when you've worked as hard as I have at learning to size people up, these things are easy to spot," she said, looking at my feet. "You're what, like an eight? Eight and a half?"

"A thirty-nine," I replied automatically. She handed me the shoe, five-inch stilettos with a strap that wrapped around the ankle.

"Try this on. And don't tell me you're surprised," she added. "Romantic entanglements in the workplace are bound to happen."

"No they're not! They don't even know each other's real names! *I* don't even know their names!" Felicia's eyes widened, and I clarified as I slid into the shoes. "I mean, I don't call them by their names. When we're working, it's code names only. That helps keep things professional at all times."

"And that's … good?" she asked me dubiously. "Here, stand up, let me – hmm. No. Try these instead."

"Yes, it's good," I replied, handing back the original pair and accepting another, four inches high with a chunkier heel. "Becoming overly involved with the people you work with hampers your effectiveness in the field. You can't allow old grudges or personal enmities to get in the way of the job at hand."

"Hmm." Felicia paused in her browsing and looked at me. "From almost anyone else I would think that was lip service to a larger ideal, but from you … I mean, you're working for *Doom*. After everything he's done to you, after what he did to your friends and especially to–"

I cut her off with a sharp gesture. "I don't think about it. I can't. Not if I want to protect Symkaria. That's my first and most important goal."

"Wow. That… sounds awful, and you're gonna tell me all about it," Felicia said. "But not here. You know what? None of those work for you, try mine." We traded shoes. "What do you think?"

I could almost look her directly in the eye now. Walking on six-inch heels was worth it for that. "Perfect."

If I were less honest with myself, I would say that I didn't enjoy the rest of the night. After all, it was so far from my comfort zone that it might as well have blown it to bits –

going from bar to club to restaurant, eating fine food, dancing with people I'd never met before, and finally settling into the Las Vegas version of the super hero-themed bar my team had been to in New York City to drink truly disgusting beverages with plenty of commentary to go with each one.

"Do I even want to know what's in an Iron Man?" I asked as I stared at the list of drinks drawn on the wall.

"No, but it comes with a sprinkling of gold dust," the bartender said stoically. "Probably not your style."

Definitely not.

"What about the Fin Fang Foom?" Felicia asked, licking her lips as she put down her empty glass. She'd just had a Squirrel Girl, which was just a pink squirrel cocktail served in a plastic mug in the shape of a woodchuck. "Eh, it's still a rodent," the bartender had said when Felicia complained.

"Fin Fang Foom is everything green you can dig up plus an Alka-Seltzer."

"That sounds hideous."

"They're all going to be hideous," Felicia said, "that's the point. Get over it and pick one so we can get down to the serious business. I'll have a Black Cat," she added, and even though it wasn't on the menu, the bartender nodded and began mixing up a drink. It came in a martini glass and was topped off with a twist of lime.

"I'll have... a Silver Sable," I said, unable to help my curiosity. The bartender squinted at me, then at Felicia, who was sipping her drink with an innocent expression on her face.

"Y'all must be bored as all get out to be spending your evening here," the guy said at last.

"You'd be surprised," I replied. "Would you ..."

"Yeah, sure. It's your dime." He grabbed a few different bottles and a minute later handed over a martini glass edged in sugar, smelling faintly of lemon, and topped off with a spritz from a cloudy blue spray bottle.

I peered at the bottle. "Is that colloidal silver? *Really?*"

"A little won't kill you," Felicia assured me before grabbing my hand and dragging me over to a booth. The leather was worn, the wooden tabletop was sticky, and something unsavory was crunching beneath my heel. She held up her drink, dark and murky in the dim light, and grinned at me. "Here's to learning to unwind."

Oh, what the heck. "Noroc," I replied before taking a sip. It was ... hmm. Strong. I'd have to be careful.

"Now." My companion set her glass down and gave me a look that was a hundred percent sassy Black Cat. "Spill."

"Spill what?"

"Whatever you want," she replied easily. "As long as it's something you've never told anyone else before. Something interesting. Something special."

I shook my head. "Are you trying to steal my secrets? Pretty obvious attempt."

"If I wanted your secrets, I'd have already stolen them," she said. "I'm asking, as a *friend*, to learn something about you. What makes Silvija Sablinova tick, huh? Was it really as simple as doing something nice for your country that you decided to work with *Doom*, of all people? Didn't he kill a friend of yours?"

My heart hurt too much to let me think about Amy for long. Her loss was one of those things I packed away, deep inside myself, so that I could still function. My family, Basil – until he started interfering in this mission – and Amy were no-go zones for the sake of my sanity. "I'm a mercenary," I said, trying for cold but probably coming off just sad. "I work for whoever pays me."

"You're a mercenary, sure, but you're principled," Felicia replied, stirring her drink with its straw. "Don't your principles prevent you from working with madmen and dictators?"

"If I didn't let myself work with madmen, I'd have no work at all."

"Fair point."

"The truth is, there are no hard lines in this world," I said, taking another long sip of my drink. This Silver Sable... huh, it was growing on me. "There is so much *power* to be had, so many exceptional individuals, so many changes in fortune and destiny... as much as I'd love it to be true, the world isn't black and white. Someone who is a villain today may repent tomorrow, and they shouldn't be forced to remain in their old role just because it's more convenient for me. I myself have been involved in conflicts which I now... regret." I hadn't always been Spider-Man's ally, after all. "All I can do is my best, in the moment. The only person I can really take responsibility for is myself, no matter how hard I try, so... that has to be enough."

Felicia stared at me for a long, quiet moment before reaching out with her glass and touching its rim to mine. They made a little chiming sound that seemed to linger. "I'll drink to that," she said.

She did, and then I did, and before I knew it, we needed to order new drinks because our narcissism cocktails were all gone. We tried a Captain America (red, white, and blue, made with vanilla ice cream and moonshine), a Green Goblin (mostly olive juice, absolutely foul), and a Spider-Man, which was pretty good, but the glass was wound with dental floss and kind of hard to hang onto. Drinks turned into a cutthroat round of darts, which I won, followed by a game of pool, which Felicia won. Then we both won by offending the head of a local biker gang when we turned down his advances, which became a rather delightful brawl.

I had never fought with a pool cue before, but it wasn't so dissimilar from a staff. If anything, the tip on the tapered end made simple work of targeting the eyes, and the blunter end was ideal for walloping overenthusiastic, undertrained men in the family jewels. It wasn't very well made, though – I broke it after the third strike.

"Just use one of your shoes!" Felicia called out as she smashed a beer bottle against one very large, very menacing man's face. He went down like a swatted mosquito.

"I refuse to go barefoot on this floor, it's filthy!" I replied. I spun into a heel kick and sliced six inches of designer shoe across my next would-be attacker's face, breaking his nose and sending him into a spin.

A chain came flying at me from the right – a woman half as big but twice as fierce as any of the men in this gang was trying to whip me with it. *Someone's identifying a little too much with Ghost Rider.* I caught the chain around my arm, jerked her in close, wrapped her up with her own weapon, and put her in a chokehold until she went limp.

"You're so picky," Felicia said as she stomped on a biker's boot. Her stiletto penetrated the leather, eliciting a high-pitched scream as he bent over to save his foot, and met her knee with his forehead on the way up. "Here I am, trying to show you a good time–"

"You brought me to a *biker bar*–"

"And buy you a bunch of fun drinks–"

"I've paid for half of them, don't even try it!"

"And offered up a floor show, and all you can do is complain that it's not Cirque du Soleil!"

A pair of brawny arms grabbed me from behind, trying to crush me against my attacker's sweaty barrel chest. I threw my head backward into his face as I reached over my shoulder and grabbed the back of his collar, and the second he dropped his hold I tugged him into a hip throw and sent him flying into the nearest pool table, which crashed to the floor under his weight.

There was a moment of perfect silence, broken by someone's pitiful moan. Nobody moved except to cradle their own injuries. Even the bartender looked impressed. "Actually," I said, grinning at Felicia, "I like this show much better than Cirque du Soleil."

The bartender treated us to a round of Bloodstones after that, then someone else bought us some Marvel Girls, and by the time we made it back to our suite at the Diadem I was nearly stumbling. Almost anyone else in six-inch heels would have broken an ankle at that point, so I still felt there was reason to be proud of myself. It might have been the first time I ever let myself get this tipsy – beyond the occasional poisoning from a rival merc or a villain. It was… interesting. Freeing, in a way. Probably not something I'd ever do again, but valuable for the originality factor.

"Yeah, yeah, you can just tell me you had fun," Felicia said as she stepped over a snoring Boris, who had fallen asleep on the carpet wearing one of the Diadem's cheap plastic novelty crowns and clutching a pile of one-dollar bills. Various members of our teams were scattered around the furniture, and the doors to the bedrooms were open, with more people sleeping within.

Goodness, had we really stayed out later than everyone else?

"Of course we did! You think I'm not gonna fight until dawn?"

Wait a second… was I saying all of my thoughts out loud?

Felicia laughed and tucked her hand into my elbow. "Yeah, you are. C'mon. I've got a California king in the other room. Let's sleep it off, Silver."

I could have shrugged her off, but I didn't. Instead, I let her guide me back into the bedroom, pour me a huge glass of water, take my shoes off, then cover me up. No one had covered me up like this since Basil. I hadn't *missed* it, but…

It was kind of nice to have someone around to bother.

You could have this with your own team, at least some of them. Be a friend, not just an employer. Juliet, Tango… maybe the others. Wouldn't it be nice?

Wouldn't the risk be worth the reward?

I fell asleep before my mind could answer the question. When I woke up, it felt like two of my chais had taken up residence in my eye sockets, and my mouth was a mystical combination of swamp and desert. Ugh… why *was* I awake?

Ah, because Juliet was shaking me by the shoulder. "Sable," she said urgently. "Sable! It's gone!"

"What's gone?" I mumbled, sitting up. On the other side of the bed, Felicia rolled over, pulling most of the blanket with her and groaning about it being too early.

"The Clairvoyant, Sable! It's gone! X-Ray and Romeo took it!"

A numbing chill swept over me. Lo and behold, Juliet had just invented a new hangover cure – instill a sense of impending doom in the person in question. Only in my case, the impending Doom was quite literal.

If I didn't get the Clairvoyant back, I would indeed be Doomed.

CHAPTER TWENTY-FOUR

I sprang into action mode immediately, getting out of bed and stalking into the shared living room. Sure enough, everyone was there except for X-Ray and Romeo, but every single person looked guilty for some reason.

Ridiculous. They had no reason to look guilty. If anyone here was guilty, it was me, for letting my guard down. "All right, where are they now and where are they headed?" I snapped, going straight for Foxtrot, who was at least trying to look busy.

"They slipped out at two AM, before you even got back," he replied. "They just landed in New Jersey."

"Do we have footage?"

"... yes..."

Why was he so nervous to tell me? "Then show it to me," I said between gritted teeth.

He switched the screen's view. I recognized the small, rural airport we'd visited so recently. No wonder he was able to get a visual so fast. We'd left our own surveillance there. And our cameras were currently picking up X-Ray and Romeo walking toward the parking lot, bags slung over their shoulders, holding each other's hands so tightly their knuckles were blanched as they headed for a car. Someone got out of it and smiled in welcome at them. Someone I recognized.

Not a woman. Not a man, either, although it looked like one.

"It's a Hudson LMD."

Two of my people… two of the people I trusted to be loyal to me, to stick with me on a job to the end, had betrayed me to the Foreigner. My ex-husband.

"Basil must have made some sort of offer to X-Ray when we went to visit him," I said, and my tone was almost level. "Something she decided she couldn't refuse." And Romeo had gone with her, because while *I* hadn't allowed myself to have relationships with the people I worked with, apparently, I was the only one.

"They must have a good reason," Juliet offered weakly. "They would never do this otherwise."

I laughed. It sounded more like breaking glass. "They're mercenaries, like all of us are. All Basil had to do to buy their loyalty was offer more money."

"That's not true," Tango said. "We're all Symkarian. We all know how to put country before self."

"Apparently not."

I wasn't even surprised. This had happened before, after all. The Wild Pack had broken down, become an instrument of individual greed and infighting. When everything fell apart, my only recourse had been to disband them altogether and start anew. I was intimately familiar with the consequences of someone you cared for going too far, and as painful as it had been to cut ties back then, it had taught me this valuable lesson: keep your personal life and your professional life separate.

To think I had been considering otherwise, that I'd been daydreaming about having *friends*. Ridiculous. I had just learned the hard way, yet again, that the only person I could truly trust was myself.

"We're done," I said. My people looked at me apprehensively. "The Wild Pack is over. I'll pay your severance fees and ensure you get a good recommendation, but–"

"No!" Juliet snapped, putting herself squarely in front of me. "No, Silver, I'm not letting you fire me!"

"That isn't your choice!"

"The heck it isn't! You're upset, I understand that, I *do*, but if you want to have any hope of getting the Clairvoyant back from your evil ex and into Doom's hands before the deadline, you need to bring the rest of us in *closer*, not push us away!"

"How do I know I can trust you?" I demanded, stepping into her space. To her credit, Juliet didn't back away. Tango picked up the conversation from there, though.

"We're still here," he said gently, one hand reaching out and landing very softly on my shoulder. "We've been with you through over a dozen missions, haven't we? We've all saved each other over and over again – Silver, we want to be a part of this. We want to help you. Foxtrot and Juliet and I, we *want* to help you."

"You can't–" I shook my head, trying to get back to my state of pure, elevated anger. "No, I don't need help, I don't need a team, this was a mistake–"

"Everybody needs a team," Felicia put in from where she was sitting on the couch. She paused to take the fresh cup of coffee that Bruno offered her. "The only thing you accomplish by being a lone wolf is dying alone," she said bluntly. "Even Spider-Man relies on others when he's off doing his crimefighting thing. So, yeah, you've got a couple of turncoats, and it blindsided you. It happens. *I'm* a really good judge of character and had no preconceptions about your people, and *I* didn't see this coming. So maybe it's worth asking yourself *why* they're turncoats?"

"That's a good question," Foxtrot said, his fingers flying across the keyboard. "Money would never be enough. Romeo has made a fortune in crypto, and X-Ray inherited plenty of money from her older sister when she died a few months back."

"Why didn't I know any of this?" I demanded.

"Probably because you never wanted to," Tango replied with a shrug. "We all got that. No telling you personal stuff, that's like an unwritten rule of being a member of the Wild Pack. That doesn't mean we didn't talk amongst ourselves."

"Oh my god," Juliet whispered, pressing one hand to her mouth. "Foxtrot, check on Ana!"

I was so far out of my depth. "Who is Ana?"

"X-Ray's niece. She was made her guardian after her sister's death, she's got the girl in a boarding school in Switzerland…"

"There was a break-in there," Foxtrot confirmed. "Ana is officially missing. There are no firm suspects other than a… ah. A blond man with an American accent." Foxtrot looked grim as he showed the still from the security footage.

Another Hudson LMD. Basil had stolen X-Ray's niece and used the child as leverage against the Clairvoyant. X-Ray had obeyed him because she wanted to save her family, and Romeo had helped because he loved her.

It was an excuse I could understand, if not one I could forgive. If they had just come to me, explained what Basil had done and asked me for help...

No personal business. Keep your private lives private. Don't ask and don't tell, because I don't want to know. NO PARTNERS.

I sighed, all the fight going out of my body. In a way, I had done this to myself. I hadn't abducted a child or forced others to do my bidding, but I hadn't made it clear to my team that they could bring their problems to me. I thought it was safer not to know, when really it was anything but.

"All right," I said at last. "All right, we're not disbanding." *Not yet.* Perhaps not at all, but that wasn't something I could think about yet. "But I'm not dragging the rest of you back into the fray, either."

"Silver–"

"Sable, come on–"

"We *just* said that–"

"No." I looked each of my people in the eyes. "Basil has proven that he's willing to go to extreme lengths to get the Clairvoyant. I don't know what he has planned for X-Ray and Romeo now that they've given it to him, but I'm sure it's nothing good. I'm going to go after him personally, and I don't want to give him the chance to use you all as hostages against me."

"Can't rely on a tactic that won't work," Tango pointed out with a shrug. "I'm sure he knows that you wouldn't comply no matter how he threatened us."

"I would," I said, and the room went silent again. The Wild Pack looked at me with wide eyes. "I would," I repeated, tired of lying to myself and everyone else about the quality of my heart and the content of my soul. These people were more than comrades-in-arms, and had been for a while. I hadn't wanted to see that, but now I didn't have a choice. "So I would prefer not to give him the option. I want you all to head back to the embassy in New York and prepare to assist me remotely." That way they would still feel included. "I don't know what Basil's next move will be, but–"

"He's going to have to find a way to power it, of course," Felicia said.

Oh, of course. Basil didn't have any of the extensive internal wiring that Tolentino had carved into himself. He was going to need an external power source, which meant...

"The Catalyst." He was almost certainly going after the Catalyst, the original power source Tolentino had used – more like stolen – for the Clairvoyant the first time around. I didn't understand the mechanics of it, but the last I knew it was under lock and key at Empire State University in New York City. Well, we all might be going to the same place anyway. "I'm sure he's thinking of using the Catalyst for it."

"Ah, the Catalyst. I know it well," Felicia said. "Too big to easily steal, until Tolentino started slinging Pym particles around, which–" She wrinkled her nose. "There's risky, and then there's *risky*. I prefer not to risk being shrunk."

"You don't have to risk anything," I told her. "Your part in this is done. You stuck to your side of the bargain." Fair was fair, and the last thing I needed right now was for the Black Cat to give me trouble as I tried to finish this job because she thought I was going to stiff her. "I'll make arrangements for the map to be delivered to you before I go after Basil."

"Mm, no." She shook her head. "I mean, don't get me wrong, I love it when other people take the blame for things, but in this case you're gonna have to share it with me. I'm the one who dragged you out for a night on the town, after all. If you'd been here, your people would never have gotten the Clairvoyant out of the room, much less out of the state. So me and the boys are going to stick with you."

"I…" It didn't feel right to let her take this kind of responsibility, and yet… she wasn't wrong, either. And if I was honest, it *would* be easier to hunt down my ex-husband with the help of someone who knew all his tricks. "We can talk about it on the way back to New York," I said, because there was being in agreement and then there was folding like a bad hand. "We can figure out our next steps there."

"Mm, no," Boris said.

Everyone turned to look at him. "Mm, no what?" Felicia asked.

"Mm, no, we're not going to New York," Boris said, fiddling with his phone. "That's not where the Catalyst is."

Oh, for… "Tell me he didn't steal it already," I said.

"Oh no, not at all. According to last month's issue of *Fission and Scission*, the Catalyst has been loaned out to a foreign university in order to promote scientific cooperation and joint research developments."

"Fission and what?" Bruno asked, scratching behind one ear.

"*Scission*. Both are references to nuclear energy, of course," Boris said, raising one eyebrow. "Every time I begin to think you weren't raised in a barn or under a rock, you surprise me."

That wasn't the part that concerned me. "Which foreign university did they loan it to?" I asked with a sense of growing dread.

"The Latverian Academy of the Sciences, naturally."

Naturally. Of course the device that had the capacity to run the Clairvoyant was already in Doomstadt. Doom had undoubtedly planned that out well in advance. Only now, it was Basil who had his greedy hands on the Clairvoyant, and Basil who was going to have to go to Latveria to make it work.

Actually… this could play in our favor. Even at his best, I doubted that Basil could have pulled off a heist against Doom himself, and he was far from his best right now.

Unfortunately, for this to *really* play in our favor, I was going to have to come clean to Doom. But better to be honest and upfront about it now than have it blow up in our faces after the deadline, which was in… two days.

"I'm calling Captain Verlak," I said, heading for my phone. "Either she can coordinate an operation there to grab Basil when he comes after the Catalyst, or we can do it ourselves."

"You really want to spill the beans?" Felicia asked with a frown. "I'm sure we can get this done without her help."

"Maybe we can, but I don't want to leave anything to chance." I opened her contact information and hit send. The phone rang… and rang… and rang.

No answer, and no way to leave a message.

"Shoot," I muttered. My next call was to the Latverian embassy in New York.

"Szia, miben segíthetek?"

I mentally rerouted from English to Hungarian, one of the major languages used in Latveria. "Yes, hello. I'm…" Oof, I hadn't thought this through. I couldn't just say, "Hi, I'm Silver Sable, mercenary currently working for Doctor Doom who's trying to find him so I can confess just how greatly I screwed up the job he gave me. Can you find the captain of his personal guard so I can let her know all of this?" No.

"I'm a reporter with the *Daily Herald*, hoping to interview Doctor Doom about his recent collaborations with Empire State University. Is it possible to speak with his personal staff about this?"

"I'm sorry," the receptionist said, "but Doctor Doom is unavailable to the media for the foreseeable future."

"Unavailable how?" I pressed.

"Unavailable as in unavailable," the man snarked, then ended the call with a huff.

"Rude," I muttered.

"He's either off planet or in another dimension," Foxtrot said with a grimace from where he was watching his computer. "Nobody is entirely sure, but he *definitely* isn't in Latveria or New York right now."

It wasn't good news, but it wasn't the worst either. If Doom was unavailable, then Captain Verlak was probably in charge of keeping Latveria from catching fire or sinking into the Underworld, or whatever trial Doom had set it up for today. No wonder she wasn't answering her phone.

"That's perfect!" Felicia exclaimed. Well, apparently *someone* thought it was good news. "Now we have the chance to get the Clairvoyant back before anyone is the wiser. Don't beg for forgiveness before you have to," she said to me in an aside. "You never know when you're going to pull off a Hail Mary, and lucky for you, I specialize in Hail Marys."

I didn't like it, but I also didn't mind a bit of a reprieve to try to take care of this ourselves. "As soon as we confirm that Basil is off to Latveria, that's where you and I go," I told Felicia.

"Oh, he's going," she said confidently. "Time is of the essence with issues like his. He's got to be on hand to use the Clairvoyant as quickly as possible, or he's risking his life."

He was risking his life going against *me* like this, something he would soon discover to his detriment. "Wild Pack, do your best to locate Romeo, X-Ray, and Ana."

"Silver," Tango spoke up. "Let me fly you. I'm the best pilot on the team, I'll get you there fast and safe."

"You…" I wanted to say he was needed here, but that would be a lie. Tango wasn't like Foxtrot and Juliet; he didn't work best on a computer. He was an operations guy, a driver, reliable and steadfast.

Maybe it was time I gave him the trust he had so determinedly earned.

"All right," I agreed. "You're in charge of flying."

"Boris and Bruno, you're with us," Felicia said. "Let's go do what we do best!"

Ugh, stealing… theft was never the ideal solution to anything as far as I was concerned, but in this case I had to make an exception. If a little harmless thievery – harmless to the people I cared about, at least – was called for, who was I to say no?

It was time to track down the Catalyst before Basil got to it first.

CHAPTER TWENTY-FIVE

We made it to Latveria in record time, which was good, because we then wasted five hours negotiating air space restrictions and talking through layers of bureaucracy in order to put the plane down at Doomstadt's international airport. I had never wanted to get Captain Verlak on the phone so badly in all my life – in fact, I'd really never wanted that before at all. She could have cut through the red tape for us with a word, but whatever was going on with Doom had obviously affected her as well.

By the time we were on the ground in Doomstadt, it was evening, and every public institution in the country was closing. I hustled our group to the Academy of the Sciences in a rush – I wanted at least to be able to *see* the Catalyst in person before we tried to break it out, and Doomstadt was a frustratingly modern and security-conscious city. Their surveillance was nearly impossible to penetrate, and they were very cagey about showing maps of the interiors of city buildings.

For all that it was modern, the city also reminded me greatly of Aniara in its heyday, or the less-touristy sections of Bavaria in nearby Germany. The buildings were made of stone or heavy wood, plastered in white and roofed with cheerful red tiles that spoke of decades, even centuries of love and care. There were still old-fashioned iron streetlamps along the streets, which were twisty and narrow. The air smelled of woodsmoke and damp, and if I walked briskly enough, I could almost block out how at least a quarter of the homes were undergoing repairs, and how many of the old, worn roof tiles had been replaced with almost garishly bright ones, standing out like tiny blemishes against the face of the city. For all that Symkaria had endured far more war than any nation should, Latveria had more than its fair share of invasions and civil strife.

Or perhaps what it got was *exactly* its fair share, considering who ran this place. I picked up the pace, anxious to get some actionable intelligence.

"The academy doesn't close for another fifteen minutes!" Felicia huffed as she tried to keep pace with me along the cobblestone street. I had long since changed into a more suitable pair of shoes, but she'd gone with another pair of something fashionable and impractical. She was light on her feet, but cobblestones were a whole new challenge for shoes like those. "We can always sweet talk the security guards into letting us stay a little longer."

"Not in Doomstadt we can't."

"Sweet talk works everywhere," she informed me. "Trust me, I'd know."

"Not in Doomstadt," I reiterated. "Doom has eyes

everywhere, and his people know it. He's committed to Latverians, and they are to him, but that commitment is reinforced by the constant threat of retribution if people *don't* do what he tells them to do. Trust me, you're not going to convince a security guard at one of the premier institutes in the country that it's just fine for you to wander around in there after hours."

We turned left off Victory Street, and there, in the distance, was the Academy of the Sciences. It was, like many of the Latverian government buildings, repurposed from its original use. It had once been a monastery, and the grandiose yet solemn architecture reflected that. I could have sworn there were gargoyles peeking around some of the corners of this place. At least the windows were still lit up. I marched up to the front entrance and inside.

"We close in five minutes," the receptionist, an elderly white-haired woman, said from within the bulletproof enclosure built into the far wall. "I'm afraid I can't allow new visitors in."

Felicia stepped forward, apparently as confident in her ability to sweet talk old women as anybody else. "Are you sure we can't just dart down to take a quick look at the Catalyst exhibit?" she asked, wide-eyed and clutching a pen and notebook – where the heck had those appeared from? "My advisor said I've got to see it in person if I want to use it as a primary source for the paper I'm writing, which seems unreasonable, but what can I do? Please?"

It was a pretty decent desperate student schtick, but the receptionist remained unmoved. "You should have budgeted your time more carefully." Felicia opened her mouth to continue the con, no doubt, when the woman said, "It's not here now anyhow. Our king had the Catalyst moved to his castle for personal study."

Of course he had. Of freaking *course* he had.

"You'll have to make a request of the science staff there if you want to get a closer look. Now." She pointedly turned over the sign that read "Closed" in English, German, Hungarian, Romanian, Latverian, and Romani. "Please leave."

"Rude," Felicia muttered as we turned and headed for the exit.

"That's far from our biggest problem," I replied. "The Catalyst is already in Doom's possession. I'm sure the Foreigner knows that, too. That means he's either sending Romeo and X-Ray in after it, or–" I stopped in astonishment, all parts of me, as I took in the man in the wheelchair at the bottom of the academy's stairs. He had a blanket across his lap and was slightly slouched to the side, and I saw an IV needle entering the back of his right hand. He was being pushed by yet another familiar blond man.

"My dears." Basil looked up at us, a ghastly smile on his wasted face. "I'm so glad you've finally arrived. Please, won't you join me for dinner?"

I stepped forward, one hand going to the throwing daggers at my waist. "Tell me where my people are."

"Tut tut, my love," he said, shaking his head slightly. "You wouldn't threaten me in a space as public as this, would you? When there are so many eyes watching us already?"

"I would cut your head off with absolutely no compunction," I said, so furious that my treacherous heart didn't even twinge. "You've abused every faith I ever had in you. Now tell me where my people are, or see just how willing I am to do more than *threaten* you."

"If you kill me, you'll never get your people back," he replied. His smile was faint but confident.

Felicia tossed her hair over her shoulder. "You know what they say, Basil. The proof is in the pudding. Show us proof of life and we can talk."

I didn't want to talk, I wanted to *maim*, but I knew I needed to be patient. This wasn't just about me, and it wasn't just about the Wild Pack. This was about a young girl who Basil had ruthlessly pulled into his schemes in an effort to manipulate me, and it was *working*. I hated that it was working.

I was going to pull him apart one nerve cluster at a time when this was over.

"Come back to my hotel with me, and I'll show you there," he said. "Or cut my head off, get arrested, and lose your window to get this all wrapped up before Doom returns from wherever he's scuttled off to."

I was a hairsbreadth away from killing him anyway, but Felicia stepped in front of me and shook her head. "It can't hurt to hear him out," she murmured. "And I don't want to have to break out of a Latverian prison if I can avoid it."

Reining in my ire was hard, but she had a point. "Fine," I said, glaring at Basil. "Lead the way."

He nodded, and with an unspoken signal to the Hudson LMD, turned and trundled down the street. A few people who were out glanced our way, but the streets were largely deserted, even though it had just touched on eight o'clock.

"I like this place," Basil remarked as we headed down a side street toward an old rathaus that had been converted into a hotel and restaurant. "People leave each other alone here, for the most part. One can really take the time to think, to get introspective. I've been doing a lot of that since I became sick, my dears, but Latveria is bringing my personal insights to new heights."

"Oh?" I asked. "It seems rather that you've discovered new *lows*."

"No, no." We entered the expansive hall, and a quiet host escorted us to a private dining room. Once we were seated and the host had vanished, Basil continued, "There's a lot to be learned from the way things are done here in Latveria, Doomstadt in particular. These people, most of them adore Doom even though he's the cause of almost every single problem that they face. His hubris is legend, he practically invites attack, and his experiments and quests for glory have led to this entire city being nearly razed to the ground numerous times. People suffer, they *die,* and still he rules."

"Yes, that's what authoritarians do," I said. "Are you seeing a style which you wish to emulate? Because let me tell you, you're not half as clever or a tenth as powerful as Doctor Doom."

Basil's smile thinned. "Perhaps not. But I *am* more clever than you."

"Ruthlessness and cleverness aren't the same thing."

"They might as well be." He turned to Felicia. "Black Cat, darling, why are you even still here? The game is over, and I've won. I'm willing to let you walk away from this right now, free and clear. Go play somewhere else, hmm?"

She laughed. "When do cats ever do what they're told? Now, if you can tempt me with a prettier prize, that would be one thing, but all I hear right now is blah-blah-blah."

I resisted the urge to stare at her. She wasn't being serious right now. She *wasn't*. I'd already told her she could go, and she hadn't taken the out. Surely she wasn't going to be tempted by our awful ex, of all people.

"What if I gave you the freedom to pilfer and pillage my New Jersey home for as long as you wished, unassailed?" He winked at her. "I've got some rare French impressionists down there that you didn't get a chance to see last time."

"Oh please, French impressionists? Really? You think you can throw me a Monet or a Seurat and expect me to bite?" She rolled her eyes. "As if I couldn't take half a dozen of them out of any museum in Manhattan."

His lips thinned. "Real estate, then. I have ownership of half a dozen properties in New York, and–"

"Basil. Stop. You're embarrassing yourself." Felicia looked over at me, then back at him. "You might have been able to get me to switch sides back at your place, if you'd buttered me up nicely enough, but I'm afraid I've gotten a bit attached since then. You know what I like about working with Silver?" She leaned in slightly. "She hasn't lied to me once. Not once! It's so novel, I almost don't know what to do with it. And I'm not going to repay that novelty with a betrayal this late in the game. Besides–" she shrugged "– she's got better puzzles than you do."

"I should have known better than to try to be nice to you," Basil said on a sigh. "All right. It's your funeral if this goes wrong, which it better not for your friends' sakes. Speaking of." He held up a hand, and the Hudson LMD handed over a phone. Basil turned it so we could look at it.

Front and center on the screen was a video feed with three

people pictured in it: Romeo with his jacket off, X-Ray who was sitting down with crossed legs next to him, and a little girl with uneven pigtails sat in her lap, covered with the borrowed jacket. There were a few bags of chips lying against the wall next to them and an empty soda can at the edge of the frame, but no other extraneous items were visible. "It's live," he informed me. "And so are they, for now. Get me the Catalyst and they'll stay that way."

"How do I know you won't betray me?" I asked coldly.

"You don't," he replied. "But I think it's a risk you're going to take, because if you don't, you *know* I'll let them die. And believe me, you'll never find them without my help."

"And the Clairvoyant?" I asked.

Basil smirked and passed the phone back to the LMD. "Again, somewhere you'll never find it. Ah," he said as the door behind us opened again, "dinner's here. Excellent."

I stood up. "I'll have to turn down dinner. Eating with you would only turn my stomach."

"As you wish." He stared at the food set down in front of him with the avarice of a man who was about to enjoy his last meal… or the first meal of his new life. "You'll have more time to get me the Catalyst that way. You'll find me here. Be good, Silver, and I might give both devices to you in time to make your meeting with Doom."

I walked around the table until I was beside Basil and leaned over next to him. "That's one of your greatest flaws, you know," I told him with quiet menace. "You never understand when to stop with the carrot and the stick. You offer and retract, offer and retract… it makes you impossible to trust."

"You trusted me once," he replied, interest sparking in his

eyes. "It's not too late to do so again. With me healed and a working Clairvoyant, we could be an incredible team."

I straightened. "I'm already part of an incredible team. Enjoy dining alone." I turned and shoulder-checked the Hudson LMD as I left, making it give a wounded sound and an "Oof, honestly, what did I ever do to you?" on my way out. Felicia followed me.

Outside, the sky was dark and the street nearly deserted. I stopped and inhaled deeply, centering myself after being thrown off-kilter by my regrettable-in-every-way ex. Felicia put a hand on my shoulder. "You OK? I know it's hard to watch your people being threatened, but I'm sure we can..." Her voice trailed off as I pulled the phone Basil had used to taunt us with out of my pocket and handed it over. Yeah, Felicia wasn't the only one here who could pick a pocket.

"I'm pretty sure they're in New York City somewhere," I said, bringing up the video feed again. "Those chips are made by a local company there, right?"

"Right," she said, looking carefully at the picture. "Yeah, you can find them in a lot of bodegas, but–"

"They're being held captive by four people, probably more LMDs." Who *else* would be able to put up with Basil?

"How do you know *that*?" Felicia demanded.

"Look at their hands." Both X-Ray and Romeo only had one hand visible to the camera, with their thumbs tucked against their palms. "If there were more, they'd be showing five fingers, or eight, or however many we needed to deal with. We're looking at a building with air conditioning, too – Romeo has goosebumps. He hates being cold, so he'd be wearing that jacket if Ana didn't need it.

"It can't be that hard to identify the buildings in New York City that Basil owns, and LMDs have a very identifiable energy signature if you've got the right scanner. We need to relay this information to my people back in New York so they can get to work on finding them."

Felicia stared at me like I'd just grown five inches. "How did you figure all this out so fast?"

"I'm a professional mercenary," I scoffed. "I run one of the top outfits in all of Europe, probably in the world. What, you think hunting people down is as simple as firing a gun?"

"I think you'd make a decent thief with the way you pickpocketed that phone, is what I'm thinking."

I smiled. "I've been known to dabble here and there. Now come on. We've got a Catalyst to steal, people to save, and an ex to teach a lesson to."

It would be the kind of lesson Basil might not survive learning. We'd see where my mood was at by then.

CHAPTER TWENTY-SIX

It was amazing what you could get done when motivated by the rocket fuel of spite.

Over the past three hours I had coordinated a rescue mission in New York City *and* identified the best option when it came to breaking into Doom's castle. Finding my people turned out to be as easy as calling in a favor to a person with the right kind of drone and, after Juliet identified Basil's likely New York assets, scanning them until they detected his squad of LMDs. Juliet and Foxtrot might spend most of their time behind computers, but they were both fully trained operatives and more than capable of taking a few overly suave LMDs down.

"We don't want the Foreigner to run with the Clairvoyant once he finds he's been compromised," I warned them. "So don't move on them until I send you word, or until four AM your time." That would be ten in the morning here in Doomstadt, and give us all the time we needed to get our hands on the Catalyst. If we didn't have the job done by then…

It would be because we weren't around anymore.

I'd passed responsibility for figuring out a way into Doom's castle to Felicia. I was good at breaking and entering, but that kind of thing was literally the Black Cat's meow. It helped that the job she'd set Boris and Bruno to the moment we touched down here was making inroads with the local anarchist community. Doom had been involved in a guerrilla war with a group of his deposed nobles for some time, and while they'd been soundly defeated, some of them still lingered on the outskirts of the city, trying to find ways to make trouble.

"It's the perfect job for Boris," Felicia told me as she listened in on her people's meeting with the head of an underground "resistance" group. "He's got a reputation as an explosives expert, enough to get him through a lot of doors. Then you find a rebel who knows a rebel, grease a few palms, promise a little mayhem, and we can walk through the front doors like we own the place."

Well, not really the front doors, and not *exactly* like we owned the place. Castle Doom, for all its Gothic architecture and ancient facades, was as contemporary as the rest of the city was – more, in fact, because it housed Doom's personal laboratories, his private collections, and his most daring experiments. I didn't like Kariana Verlak, but I did admire her dedication to her work. She, undoubtedly with Doom's oversight, had turned his medieval castle into a modern fortress. There were motion sensors, facial recognition, laser arrays armed with percussive *and* chemical deterrents, and a guard seemingly every ten feet. I didn't know how we were going to get in.

Felicia did. And the plan started with Tango.

"This uniform is too tight," he groused, pulling at his collar as he stared at himself in the mirror. "And I'm not so sure the makeup is believable."

"Trust me, I've worked a security system like this before," Felicia assured him. "The makeup isn't there to be believable to *people*, it's there to fool the system into thinking you look like Harald von Schwinn, who is unfortunately going to come down with a stomach bug about a hundred yards from where he's supposed to clock in. This pattern of lights and darks will get you through the door without the facial recognition software knowing any differently."

"And how will I explain how I look to the actual *people* who see me like this?" he asked.

"Tell them you got into a fight, tell them you let your kid do your makeup, tell them you lost a bet." She shrugged. "Tell them whatever you think will work in the moment, just make sure you commit to it. Commitment is key to pulling off a con. If worst comes to worst, you'll have Bruno as backup until you reach the inner wall."

Bruno was clearly annoyed that he was being sidelined by something as trite as recovering from his dislocated shoulder, but he didn't say anything about it, just tossed off a salute before going back to loading magazines single-handed.

"Tell me the rest of the plan," I said to Tango as I detached his hands from his collar, patting it smooth. We'd gotten the uniforms from one of the anarchist groups, and fussing at it wouldn't make it fit any better. "Go through it one last time for me."

He steadied as he stared into my eyes, his breaths slowing

and the high color in his cheeks receding. It was humbling to have such power over another person.

"My name is Harald von Schwinn," he said in perfectly German-accented Latverian. Harald had been born in Latveria, but his parents were immigrants. "I am going on duty tonight at 0200 hours. I will display my credentials at the eastern gate, walk through the curtain wall to the checkpoint at the gatehouse, and check in for my shift. Once I'm within the inner wall, I will proceed to the easternmost point in the fortification, set the smoke bombs, and detonate them remotely. At that point, I will extricate myself by any means necessary."

"Good," I told him.

He put his hands over mine, which were still lingering against his collar. "Now you tell me *your* part of the plan," Tango said softly.

I swallowed, then cleared my throat. "We follow the underground route provided to us by the conspirators," I said. "It should lead us to a section of inner wall that has been hollowed out and will require minimal effort to break through. We utilize your distraction to get inside the castle, proceed to the most likely location for the Catalyst, and grab it. We make a new distraction, return to our exit point, and get out of Castle Doom as fast as we can."

"Then we rendezvous with the Foreigner, get the location of the Clairvoyant out of him, and somehow resist the urge to shoot him in the face," Felicia put in with a saucy smile.

"Don't resist it on my account." I had learned my lesson with Basil. There was no redemption for him, no coming back from this. It was something I'd already known, but time and

distance had softened his rough edges and made it harder for
me to remember all the reasons I'd tried to kill him before.

"All right, then." Felicia topped her stolen guard's uniform
off with a cap on top of her short brown wig and tossed me a
salute. "Let's get this party started, hmm?"

The first part of the plan, and the easiest to enact, was to get
Felicia and I into position. Doomstadt was as modern as could
be – from the street level up. Their sewers, however, were as
antiquated as any medieval town's, and just as unpleasant to
wander through.

"It could be worse," I said when Felicia swore for the fifth
time at a rat eyeballing us from the far side of the tunnel. "We
could be doing this back in New York. That's one of the few
places I won't take a job underground. If you want a fool to go
into the sewers, find a hero to do it."

"I've ventured into them before, but only because I had
absolutely no other choice," she said with a grimace. "The
number of people who put their valuables in the sewers is
higher than you'd think."

I preferred not to think about it at all. I shone my infrared
light on the wall and made sure we were still following the
marked trail, bypassing the occasional iron ladders up to
the surface. The rebels had been very thorough when they
planned their attack. Not thorough enough to conquer Doom,
but their loss was our gain. I hoped the map they'd given us
of the inside of the place was as good as their description of
its sewers.

We passed under the castle's outer wall, noticeable thanks
to marked reinforcements of the stonework. Castles were

heavy beasts. The sewer got smaller, and we had to hunch over to continue. The rats grew bolder as well, scurrying across the stones right in front of us. One of them tried to run right between my feet. I kicked it into the water, and it surfaced moments later with a look of beady-eyed hatred, but didn't swim back over to accost me a second time.

We walked another twenty feet or so before the infrared light turned, heading up again. None of the tunnels beneath the castle would lead *directly* into the castle, but I could see where the stones above us had been carefully removed. Through the hole in the ceiling of the sewer tunnel was another type of stone, the dark gray granite that was reserved for Castle Doom itself. The ones I could see had been chiseled and chipped at until they were practically hollow. This, then, was our entrance in.

I touched my earpiece. "We're in position. Time?"

"ETA two minutes. Good work," Bruno said. He was our command hub this time around – Tango was the infiltrator, and Boris was placing a few "Plan Bs" in strategic places near the castle ground just in case we needed a little extra firepower on our way out. "Tango's closing in on the eastern gate. You want to listen in?"

I wasn't going to be happy unless I *could* listen in. "Yes." I glanced at Felicia and pointed at the hole above us. She pulled her duct-tape-wrapped package of explosives out and nodded. "On it," she said, then pulled herself up to place the bomb.

I settled in to listen to my teammate. My friend.

Arriving at the gate went well enough – Tango was one of several new people checking in for their shift. The darkness of the city played to his advantage. No one asked about his face until after he scanned in his ID card. "Von Schwinn?" a masculine voice suddenly cut into the quiet of beeps and steps. "What on earth happened to your face?"

"Fell off my motorbike," Tango said ruefully as he kept walking. "I got some nasty scrapes from it. Did my best to cover them up with this stuff my girlfriend recommended, but... yeah, it's not that great, is it?"

"You put *makeup* on top of open wounds? What kind of moron are you?"

"The kind that's more afraid of annoying his girlfriend than he is of you."

"Wait a second," another voice said from a little farther away – they sounded a bit hollow, like their noise was bouncing off a stone wall before making it to the microphone. "Since when have you been dating again? You told me you were done for a year after what happened with Martine."

"An entire year?" Tango sounded surprised. "Did I really say that? I was far more ambitious when I was fresh off Martine, wasn't I?" He and the other man chuckled, but the new voice sounded annoyed.

"Yeah, well, you weren't so fresh off Martine when you told me you couldn't go on a date with my sister because you were still so *wounded* just last week!"

Tango sighed. I heard the sound of a hand striking a body – not in a violent way, more in that comrade-like, shoulder-clasping sort of manner. "Look, I'm sorry about that, and I really was determined to stay to the single path for a while, but... this woman, you'd have to see her to believe her. She's beyond anyone I've ever met before. I've only known her for a little while, but I already feel like I would die for her."

"Huh." The second speaker sounded slightly appeased. "Beautiful, I guess?"

"She could be an angel come down from Heaven."

"Hmph. And nice? Because my sister *is* nice, and she wouldn't just throw someone to the side like that–"

"Oh, this lady can be nice. She's also *fierce*." The admiration in his voice was clear. "Like a lioness. Once she sets her sights on a goal, she won't be denied it, no matter how tough it is. She's amazing, really."

"Aww, he's talking about youuuuu," Felicia whispered from up above me, adding a kissy sound at the end of it.

"Shut up," I snapped at her, aware my cheeks were probably bright red. Good thing it was so dark in here. I kept listening. Because I had to for the sake of oversight, obviously, not because I wanted to hear Tango say more nice things about someone who *might* be me.

The first speaker scoffed. "If she's so wonderful, what is she doing with *you*, Harald?"

"That is an excellent question, and one I hope to have an answer to soon," Tango said cheekily. A chime sounded, signifying the formal shift change. "Better get inside." He began to move.

"Better pull your hat down and hide what you can of your face," the second speaker called after him. Tango just laughed.

"I didn't expect him to be so good at the interactive side of operations," Felicia said as she dropped down next to me. She had a remote detonator in her left hand that had a blinking red light placed over an enormous red button, apparently because Boris was keen on irony. "I thought Tango was your wheelman."

"He's got hidden depths," I replied, but honestly, I was a little surprised myself by how well he was doing. I'd missed so much...

We listened to him make his way from the outer wall to the inner one, beep himself in through another door, then begin the walk which would take him from the eastern side of the castle to where we were crouched in the southwestern corner. One minute, at the most, and then–

"You! Hey, you!"

Tango's footsteps stopped. "Yes, sir?" he asked in his pleasant Harald voice.

"Where do you think you're going?"

"I just came on duty, sir, so I'm going to my checkpoint."

"No, no, no!" Whoever he was speaking to sounded incensed. "We went through this yesterday! Tonight is the special event planned by Captain Verlak, and we need to run through the placements for it again."

"But..." Tango's voice tensed even as he maintained his facade.

"Roll with it, roll with it," Felicia muttered. "Give him something, anything..."

"I thought the captain was unavailable," Tango said after another moment's pause.

"And you think that gives us the freedom to disregard her direct orders? The event goes on whether she is here or not. I wouldn't be surprised if she put this together solely to test our readiness, and if you're the reason our shift gets less than a stellar rating, Von Schwinn, you can…" The voice trailed off for a moment. "What's wrong with your face?"

"Oh, I was in a motorbike accident. I covered up the worst of it, but–"

"Noooo." The voice drew out the word. "No, that's not it. You look… you…"

A second later there was the impact of fist against body, nothing friendly like the backslap we'd heard before. I heard a grunt, then the very start of a yell which was immediately choked off.

Come on, come on, give me something more… tell me that he isn't…

"Hostiles incoming," Tango murmured, his voice barely discernible. "I'm not going to be able to get to your location."

"Set off your smoke bombs now and get out of there," I ordered him, not letting any of my concern for him bleed through my voice. He needed to focus on his escape. "We'll create our own distraction." That was the entire point of Plan B, after all. I had been hoping to hold off on deploying it, but needs must when the devil – and Doom – drive. "Get yourself out of there, Tango, now."

"I – shouldn't I I–" There was shouting coming toward him, and the sudden ringing of an alarm. Over my own head, very faintly, I could hear that same alarm going off.

"*Go now!*" I barked. "That's an order!"

"Yes, ma'am." A second later I heard a sound like an airbag deploying, followed by bouts of coughing. Then, a moment later, the line cut off.

"He did the right thing and ditched the comm," Felicia assured me.

"I know." Of course he did – Tango would never let one of our communication devices fall into enemy hands. We'd be ditching our own once we were in the castle, just in case. But that didn't mean I had to like the fact that it meant I couldn't hear him anymore.

It was fine. He was fine, I was sure of it, and we had our own problems to deal with now. "We'll have to move quickly once we're inside," I said.

"Lucky for me, I brought some backup smoke grenades," Felicia replied. "We'll make a hole, then make our cover." She started putting on her mask, but I held up a hand.

"Wait. Bruno?"

"Yeah, Sable?"

"What's the status outside the castle?"

There was a moment's pause, then – "Looking pretty calm. I don't think Tango is putting up enough of a fuss to make 'em start running around scared."

"Let's change that. Send Boris the signal." Felicia had opted to leave him out of the group chat, which I thought was smart – Boris was good at what he did, but he was absolutely unable to keep his mouth shut.

"You got it." There was a faint crackle over the mic as the "party" bombs began to go off, and then – "Yeah, that's got 'em coming out for a look!"

"Party bombs for the win!" Felicia did a little shimmy. "A to Z, baby!" She must have caught my stare, because she grinned at me and bumped my hip. "That's aluminum to zinc. The beginning and the end of the firework maker's ingredient list, and don't get me started on all the great stuff that goes into making glitter. These bombs have *titanium* shavings in them! The street sweepers are going to be picking sparkles up off the ground for weeks!"

"Exactly *who* is the bombmaker in your little group again?" I asked dryly.

"Hey, the best fireworks are illegal in New York. We had to learn to make our own if we were going to throw the most unforgettable rooftop Fourth of July party ever seen. And it was, too." She held up the detonator. "Ready to make our grand entrance?"

I put the mask on that would protect my eyes and airways from the smoke, then nodded. "Ready."

She put her own mask on, then pushed the button. *BOOM!* A shower of dust and gravel fell over our heads as the stone gave way. Light filtered in through the haze – light from the inside of Doom's castle.

It was time to find the Catalyst.

CHAPTER TWENTY-SEVEN

We emerged in the southwest corner of the reception hall to a cacophony of alarms. There were multilingual warnings and orders for evacuation being called out, as well as the buzzing thud of an intruder alert that seemed to come standard for military strongholds and, apparently, Doom's castle. It set my teeth on edge and promised me a headache in short order, but I pushed the discomfort to the side. "We need to get to the robing room." The microphone in my mask carried my words quickly and clearly to Felicia, who nodded.

"That's the plan. Follow me." She headed for the shallow steps at the far side of the reception hall, and I marched briskly behind her, covering her back.

We were on camera right now. Our masks, despite being painted to resemble human features, wouldn't fool anyone for long. Our best hope right now was speed, and that meant avoiding the chance that we might get boxed into an elevator or stairwell and taking the most direct route to the Catalyst possible. I was betting it was being kept in the research and development lab on the third floor – not his private lab, but one where visiting scientists and students might get to look at whatever technological marvel Doom had gotten his hands on recently. After all, technically this item was on loan. He couldn't just lock it away and expect no one to raise a fuss.

Well, no, he *could*, but I was hoping he hadn't. Hope was a fragile thread to hang an entire plan on, but it was all we had right now.

That and our ability to go through anything that got in our way.

I was an expert with many different weapons, but I was also quite good at switching between them rapidly. That was fortunate for Doom's human guards, who probably wouldn't have enjoyed being shot with my high-caliber handguns. They got special Tasers instead, equipped with adamantium needles that could penetrate Kevlar and ceramic armor if needed. Not that it was, because I shot each guard in the neck where their armor was thin, but it was a nice bit of backup.

The Doombots, on the other hand…

There were three of them, two entering from the art gallery and another coming from the hallway behind the reception area. That was where the guards had come from as well – likely mobilized from their checkpoint, which was just down the hall. I needed to block that door. I switched over to my righthand gun, which held explosive rounds, and shot the 'bot just as it cleared the door. It exploded backward, filling the singed doorframe with its smoldering body.

By the time I'd covered that entrance, the other two 'bots were almost to me. They looked less like Doom than I remembered – perhaps he'd grown wary of having robot versions of himself that were so good they could even fool his staff. These ones moved fluidly, but behind the mask I could tell that their eyes weren't real. They glowed with battery power, not Doom's own willpower.

One of them shot lightning at me through its palms, and I leapt out of the way, leaving the carpet where I'd just been standing singed. Yeesh. They might not be Doom, but they were still dangerous.

"You have one chance to grovel before the authority of Doom, insect," the 'bot bellowed. "Or face the conseque – err – klik-whirrrrrrr–"

A katana through the throat could shut anyone up, even a Doombot. People assumed they couldn't be thrown with any accuracy. People were fools. I launched myself into a front flip, landing on the hilt of the katana and using my weight to slice its brutally sharp edge down into the Doombot's chest as I threw a handful of chais at the other Doombot. It blasted them out of the air with disdainful ease but wasn't quite fast enough to do the same with my follow-up bullet, which penetrated straight into its head.

It didn't fall, though. Good. It wasn't supposed to.

My team had developed this bullet after our last big battle in Symkaria. It was designed to penetrate a mechanical device but not destroy its control system completely – rather, it injected a very simple virus into its command program instead. To make it work with a lot of different potential targets, we had to keep the command we gave it simple. So we did.

Shoot everything on sight. Priorities were internal reinforcing structures and lower limbs – we weren't out to indiscriminately kill people, whether they deserved it or not.

Unfortunately, this simple command structure also made me as much of a target as anything else. I jumped down from the Doombot that I'd impaled with my sword and dashed forward, kicking this one hard in the shoulder to spin it around before it could lock onto me. It turned... and laid eyes on another of its kind flying in over the rubble of the one I'd blown up.

"All will face the righteous punishment of Doom!" it bellowed, and sent its lightning bolts blazing toward the new 'bot, which laughed hollowly and responded in kind. I took advantage of the turmoil to grab my sword and run into the robing room.

It was like a giant walk-in closet in here, full of ceremonial garb for a whole host of different Latverian officials. In fact, Felicia looked to be wearing the sacred golden crown of the Master of Ceremonies as she carefully finished cutting her way through the small window that would let us outside.

The windows were electrified – caution was definitely called for. Stealing, however, wasn't. I snatched the crown off her head and put it back on the only empty pedestal in the room.

"Hey!" Felicia complained as she eased a portion of the window out of the frame. "I like that one!"

"We're not tourists shopping for souvenirs," I pointed out. "Do you have the angle for the shot?"

"*Not tourists, blah blah wah wah, ruin my fun* – yes, of course I've got an angle," she snarked as she leaned backward out the window, extending her grapplers up. *Ka-chunk.* "You probably can't take more than two steps along the roof without tripping over one of the gargoyles or flying buttresses. Come here." I came over, and she attached one of her grapplers to my belt. "Ready to go up?"

Noise was building out in the reception hall, zaps and shouts and the occasional "Flee from the wrath of Doom, peasants!" One Doombot wasn't going to hold everyone off for long, though. "Ready."

"Good!" She shimmied out the hole and zipped upward a second later. I followed her, keeping my guns out – there was no telling what we might end up facing out here.

Actually… it looked like her bombs really had done the trick. None of the cameras seemed to be tracking us, and all of the armaments were pointed firmly away from the castle itself, tracking things I couldn't see. The night still flickered with hundreds of sparks, blinking on and off like a swarm of fireflies. I wasn't sure how Boris made them linger like that, but the effect was both beautiful *and* a little creepy. Occasionally one of them drifted close enough for a gun mounted on the castle to take a shot at it, but for the most part they just floated and sparkled menacingly.

"And you doubted me," she scoffed as she took in my expression.

"I didn't expect your bombs to hold everything's attention so well."

"Party bombs – good fun *and* good business," Felicia said with satisfaction as the grapplers pulled us up to be level with the second floor. "They should keep all external eyes nicely distracted for another fifteen minutes or so. By then we'll have the Catalyst and be out of here." From here we could look into Doom's ornate throne room. It had an extra-high ceiling which connected to one of the walls of Doom's personal laboratory. That was our final destination.

"Now, to get us in here – yowch!" She pulled her hand back

from the tall, vaulted window with a hiss. "You've got to be kidding me."

"You knew they were electrified," I reminded her.

"Yeah, but I cut the power to them in the robing room!"

"Clearly you didn't."

"How about you let *me* figure out how to get us in here instead of arguing with me?" she snapped back. Her brow furrowed, usually a sign that she was using her probability generator. I heard a sharp, rising hum followed by silence. "There, that ought to – ouch!"

"Or not," I said.

"How was *I* supposed to know he'd have backups for his backups?"

"I'm sorry, are we talking about the same paranoid genius mastermind here?" I demanded. "Doom isn't a naïve little puppy like the kind of person you try to rob in New York City, he's a bloodthirsty, vindictive wolf! Of course he's going to have backups!"

Felicia scowled at me. "You're not helping. Let me try again." She concentrated, and a second later–

All the lights on this side of the castle went out. "There, maybe that – ow!"

"Well, at least the darkness will provide us with some sort of camouflage," I said.

"I AM DOOM, DESTROYER OF WORLDS!"

Oh, crap. We had another Doombot on our tails – and this one had what looked like an electrified shield up in front of itself as it flew up to our level. These things might not sound like him, but they *did* come prepared.

"Your weapons cannot penetrate my brilliant defenses,"

the 'bot sneered hollowly. "Surrender or be destroyed." Destroying us would be extra easy from this high up – all it had to do was cut the grappling lines. Falling fifty feet down onto solid stone would do the rest.

There was no time to hesitate. I grabbed on to Felicia, retracted the grapple holding me up, jerked it off my belt, and fired it high over the head of the Doombot.

"*Fool!*" it laughed. "You cannot even–"

I waited until the trajectory was just right, then retracted the grapple so that as it arced back toward me, its claws ripped straight into the Doombot's back. The 'bot bent forward, one hand dropping its shield in an effort to reach behind itself and remove the claw. That's when I jerked the cord as hard as I could. The Doombot lost its equilibrium and came flying toward us, its hands still sparking with electricity.

"Up!" I shouted, and Felicia took us up just in time to keep the Doombot from careening straight into us.

It ran into the window instead, crashing right through it in a shower of sparks that seemed to do bad things to the 'bot's control system. It plummeted down directly onto Doom's throne, crushing it, and didn't get up again.

"That," Felicia said, looking from the Doombot to me and back, "was the coolest thing I've seen all day."

I snorted. "Just all day? Come on." I pointed to the arched stone ceiling. "Let's go climbing."

Compared to getting into the room, crawling upside down across the vaulted ceiling was easy. We moved quietly, and not even the guards pouring out onto the second-story balcony or the Doombots patrolling the grounds noticed us. We reached the wall that *should* lead us into Doom's R&D lab in under a minute.

Felicia attached a device to the wall that penetrated straight through it and gave us a look into the room. "No major structural supports in the way, not a lot of electrical work, and no life signs," she confirmed. "All right, then, time to fire up the cutter."

Internal walls were always easier to cut than external, as long as you weren't trying to break into a vault. Three minutes later, she'd cut a path through the sheetrock, insulation, and wiring, and a few seconds later we emerged into the laboratory.

Felicia brushed plaster dust from her hair, then looked around in satisfaction. "Nice." She pulled the mask off her face. "No cameras."

"That you can see," I said, but I went ahead and pulled my mask off, too. At this point the masks were immaterial – Doom would know it was us who broke in, and we weren't about to shoot anything up in a research lab and spread who knew what into the air. All the same, I shot out the controls for the door to give us a bit of a head start. "All right. The Catalyst should be here somewhere."

"In its tiny version, clearly," Felicia said. "Which is convenient. Gotta love those Pym particles Jamie was messing with back in the day."

Of course Tolentino had screwed around with Pym particles. Of course he had. Why do something dangerous when you could do *ten* dangerous things instead? People thought *I* liked to court danger, but I had nothing on most of the scientists I knew.

Felicia went left, I went right, and we began to circle

the room. The lab was enormous, with workstations for a dozen different scientists if needed. It was also a museum of sorts, with glass cases showing off some of Doom's prized possessions here and there. Some of them he'd made himself, others were spoils of war, and a few even looked like they originated on another planet altogether.

"I'm not seeing the Catalyst," I said tensely.

"Me neither, but it has to be – ah!" Felicia beamed as she stopped in front of a small, tiered glass case with a tiny black rectangle sitting at the top of it. "Here we go! Aw, he made it its own little throne. So cute." She glanced back at me. "I'm going to do this the fast way, so get ready to run as soon as I grab it."

Oh, I was. "Got it." Beneath our jackets were sets of extremely thin, strong glider wings, which could be extended in under a second once you were airborne. We'd leave this room the way we came in, sail over the throne room and through the window, and ideally touch down somewhere beyond the castle's outer wall.

"OK." She extended her suit's claws, scratched a circle in the glass, and punched it through. Then she grabbed the Catalyst, and a second later – "Whoa!" She leapt into the air, hanging onto the nearest light fixture for dear life.

I followed suit immediately as I watched the floor beneath us – solid, unremarkable, industrially carpeted flooring – turn into a glowing red river of lava.

"Oh *come on*," Felicia shouted. "Lava? Really? What is this, a video game?"

The heat of it was intense; it felt like all my exposed skin was burning. "We have to get out of here!" I shouted.

"No cr – *aah!*" The light Felicia was holding onto suddenly drooped as two of its rivets fell out. She swung her legs in a wide arc and managed to catch the next one over just before the first one fell apart completely. It sank into the lava with a hiss.

"We won't be able to crawl through the hole I made!" she pointed out.

"The main door won't open for us either," I said. Not after I shot it, it wouldn't, at least.

"Then what are we supposed to do, hang around trying not to burn to death until we're captured?" There was a hint of shrillness to her voice that I'd never heard before – Felicia was genuinely scared. So was I.

I cast my eyes around the room, looking for something – anything – that could help us. Maybe there was another door somewhere, maybe one of the cases had something useful, maybe–

Ah, there. That was just the thing. "Hang on!" I shouted to Felicia, then climbed across the ceiling hand-over-hand until I reached the case I wanted. My shoulders were killing me – I'd pushed them to their limits getting in here – but I could be strong just a little longer. I smashed my heel against the case, and the tiny, sharpened steel spike at the back of my boot did its job. Case broken, I twisted and used my feet to grip the light fixture so that I could reach down, head-first, to grab what was in the case. Loose strands of my hair crisped in front of my eyes, curling up by my face. It was *so hot,* and I was about to burn my hands grabbing this thing, I knew it, but it was our only hope. I snatched up the weapon, pointed it at the floor, and pulled the trigger.

A blast of cold burst from the barrel of the alien gun,

hardening the lava beneath my head and dissipating the awful heat. I kept firing, pointing it in a steady line until the section beneath Felicia was cool as well. I fired until the gun hissed warningly, the back section of it popping open in the universal gesture for "reload."

I didn't have any idea what kind of ammo this thing took. Best to run while we could. I let myself fall to the ground – not as elegantly as I would have liked – and was helped to my feet by Felicia, whose eyes were wide.

"What the heck is that?" she asked, pointing at the gun.

"It's a Skrull freeze ray," I said. "They used it very successfully against Johnny Storm once, I think. No wonder Doom decided to get himself one."

"Wow." She smiled at me. "You know all sorts of useful trivia. I'm going to tease Johnny about this for weeks once this is all over."

"If we survive it," I muttered, turning toward the door. "Now, let's–"

It was like watching the world blink. In a second, the ruined, smoking lab that we'd been standing in was gone, replaced by the original again. No frozen floor, no broken light fixture, no smashed cases. The gun vanished from my hand, and the Catalyst vanished from Felicia's as well. My skin felt normal again, my hair un-crisped. Even the control panel by the door was whole.

"What the…"

The door opened, and a familiar person walked in. Shoulders back, head high, she looked like she was on parade march. She was flanked by half a dozen guards, all with weapons pointed straight at us.

"I see you got to experience Doctor Doom's magical defense system," Kariana Verlak said, a suspiciously affable expression on her face. "The lava is a nice touch, isn't it? It feels so real. Yet everything you just went through was merely projected into your mind."

A magical projection? I'd been worried about burning to death, and the whole time it was actually a spell? Projected directly into my *mind*? That sounded like replacing one sort of danger with another. I wanted to protest, but now perhaps was not the time for protestations.

It was the time for truth.

CHAPTER TWENTY-EIGHT

"So." Captain Verlak folded her arms across her chest. "Tell me what was worth spending every last cent of the meager goodwill you managed to amass with Doom by breaking into his castle."

"Mind control," Felicia said instantly, slightly teary-eyed, her voice trembling. "We were mind-controlled. There was a stage performer in Las Vegas who found out we had the Clairvoyant and they managed to–"

I cut her off. "We needed to steal the Catalyst for the Foreigner."

Felicia turned a fierce glare on me. I knew that she wanted me to follow her cues, but I just couldn't do it. I wasn't going to lie about this. If I was going down – and at this point there was no other foreseeable option – then I was going to do it with my integrity intact.

"The Foreigner blackmailed two of the Wild Pack into stealing the Clairvoyant from us after we finally got it off Tolentino in Vegas," I went on. "They delivered it to him in exchange for the life of a young child. The Foreigner kidnapped the three of them and told us that if we didn't get him the Catalyst to power the Clairvoyant with, he would kill them."

"It sounds to me as though you placed your faith in the wrong people, Silvija Sablinova," Verlak said, her voice frosty.

"I might have," I acknowledged. "I certainly didn't do as good a job as I should have covering their weak spots. I should have known more about them and done more to protect them from scenarios like this." The cold truth of it lodged right next to my heart, making my chest ache. I had failed on so many levels, as both a leader and a friend. "But I didn't, and what's done is done. I *did* try to reach out and inform you of what had happened, but you weren't answering your phone, and I don't exactly have Doom on speed dial." I held my head high. "I won't apologize for trying to save them. I *do* apologize for not fulfilling my end of our bargain, though. If my words carry any weight at all with you, then let my people and Black Cat go. They acted on my orders. I accept full responsibility."

Captain Verlak stared at me for a long moment in total silence before uncrossing her arms. "Don't go anywhere." Then she turned around and walked away from us, toward the doorway of the laboratory, pulling a communicator out of her pocket. There were still guards with guns pointed at us, but it felt almost friendly compared to the atmosphere from a moment ago.

"What was *that*?" Felicia demanded under her breath as we stood there, waiting. "I could have gotten us out of this! I am *good* at getting out of things, I was ready to hand over an airtight story that *still* would have laid the responsibility at the Foreigner's feet, and then you had to go and mess everything up!"

I smiled at her. She looked dumbfounded in return. "If it helps, I'm pretty sure you won't be blamed for my mistakes."

"No, it doesn't help!" she practically screeched. "Your only mistake was being *human*, you don't deserve to get punished for that!"

I shook my head. "Maybe so, but if I had lied about it, that mistake would have been compounded."

"I *told* you, the story would have been airtight! There's no chance that–"

Whatever Felicia was saying was pushed abruptly aside as, with all the suddenness and subtlety of a thunderclap, Victor von Doom himself strode into the room. It was amazing, how dramatically the feeling of a place could change depending on who was in it. With Doom stalking toward us, the laboratory had transformed into a formal audience chamber.

The trappings didn't matter. The *emotion* evoked was everything. I could practically feel Felicia taking mental notes as he approached.

He stopped five feet away. That was plenty close enough. "Silver Sable."

I inclined my head. "Doctor Doom."

"I see that since we last met you have floundered your way around the globe, wasted valuable resources, drawn undue attention to yourself, been fooled by your own ex-husband, and broken into my private domain with the intent of robbing me."

That was a singular and rather unflattering interpretation

of everything that had happened since we made our bargain. Still… "Yes."

"Are you prepared to beg for my forgiveness?"

I would rather die. "No."

"Do you have the Clairvoyant?"

"I have the man who knows its location," I said, not willing to *completely* throw myself in front of the train.

"No," Doom replied. "You don't. *I* do."

I frowned. "What?"

"I have been watching you over the course of your entire operation," he replied evenly. "I observed you every step of the way and have known about the Foreigner's plans for the Clairvoyant since before you even realized he was involved. He was taken into custody by Captain Verlak half an hour ago."

Half an hour… Felicia and I were still in the tunnels half an hour ago. If Doom had already had Basil in custody… "And the Clairvoyant? Did he give you its location?"

Doom chuckled. "He was most eager to use it as a bargaining chip. It is unfortunate that I do not care to do business with liars and thieves. Make no mistake, Silver Sable. If you had tried to dissemble in the face of your betrayal, you wouldn't have enjoyed the consequences."

He didn't even have to try to be menacing. He *exuded* menace with every inch of his body. If I could see into another spectrum, even his aura would probably have been menacing. As it was, though… "What does that mean for us, then?"

"It means that I consider that you have fulfilled your end of the bargain. Your actions were sufficient to deliver the Clairvoyant into my hands."

Wait. This couldn't be right. "But I didn't personally hand it to you."

"Nor should you have. Delivery is the work of foot soldiers, not commanders."

"But…" I gestured around at the chaos we'd had a part in creating. "We broke into your castle!"

"So you did," Captain Verlak interjected, her mouth pinched, eyebrows lowered. "And it shouldn't have been so bloody easy for you, after all the work we did on this place after the *last* invasion. Even with the anarchists helping you."

"You… you knew about the–" Of course they did. Why was I even asking? "So, what you're saying is that you were a step ahead of us practically the whole time, you had the Clairvoyant in your control before we even *began* the infiltration of the castle, yet you still let us go through with it." And do probably hundreds of thousands of dollars of damage in the process. "*Why?*"

Captain Verlak shrugged. "I'm sure you understand the value of having someone pressure-test your defenses. You found holes we thought we had covered." She looked at Felicia. "Those bombs of yours actually did more to blind us than real bombs would have. We have anti-missile armaments in place around the castle that home in on certain chemical combinations, and they didn't even blink even as every camera along the exterior wall was blinded. We have your chemist, by the way."

Felicia stiffened. "I trust he's all right."

"He's fine. He'll be released shortly."

Oh, that was a relief. "So now you've got everything you need to make the Clairvoyant work," I said. Slowly, the relief I felt at the prospect of not being thrown in prison or, knowing Doom, some hellish alternate dimension began to fade.

Soon the world would have next to no defense from a man who had proven himself to be, alternately, a brilliant mastermind and a narcissistic madman. Which way would he tip now?

"Indeed." He reached into his cloak – did the thing have pockets or was this just another bit of magic? – and retrieved a very familiar-looking set of glasses. "The Clairvoyant in my hand, and the Catalyst to power it in my home. I believe I possess more potential in this moment than I have before in my entire life." His eyes burned brightly, fanatically. "The chance to reach heights of greatness that my mind doesn't even know to imagine yet. The world, the universe, more – this device could show me how to make it *all mine.*"

I swallowed hard. It could, and that was a lot more frightening right now, in the moment, than it had been when our bargain was nothing more than words on paper. Was it too late for me to try to get it from him? Had I made a deal with the devil?

"And yet…" He shifted his gaze to the device in his hand. "As powerful as this could make me, there is an even potential to be led down a path of darkness. It is hard not to know what the future holds, but I believe it would be even harder *to* know what could be, and be tempted into something that might undo everything I've fought so hard for." He looked at me again. "You have shown me that even the slenderest of possibilities could be the one that triumphs in the end. If I tried to guard myself against everything, I would end up capable of nothing.

"Better that I choose my own path without knowing what else could be. What I will, is." With that, he clenched down on the Clairvoyant with his gauntleted fist and crushed it, squeezing so tightly that shattered pieces of metal practically oozed from the spaces between his fingers. When he dropped it onto the ground, it was completely unrecognizable. "Have it taken to the incinerator," he told Captain Verlak, who nodded briskly and gestured to one of her subordinates.

I felt Felicia's hand creep into the pocket of my elbow. "Now would be a good time for us to *leave*," she said, tugging slightly. And she wasn't wrong, but…

"What are you going to do with the Foreigner?" I asked just as Doom began to turn away. I couldn't *not* ask. He had hurt me, he had threatened my people and potentially sent me to my death by putting me up against Doctor Doom, but… he was also dying of an incurable disease. Was Doom going to hasten his death?

"I am going to deal with him," he replied. "I haven't yet decided how. If he can be of enough use to me, perhaps I will even solve his problem… but that isn't for you to concern yourself with, Silver Sable."

"He kidnapped three of my people," I persisted. "At the very least, I need to get their locations from him so that I can–"

"You don't need him to locate them," Doom interrupted. "They have already been found."

Oh, thank you. I closed my eyes as a fresh wave of relief swept through me.

"I consider your end of our bargain fulfilled," he continued, removing my last hint of discomfort. Doom had orchestrated this entire final act, but if he had wanted to make trouble for me by saying I hadn't stuck to the exact terms of our original agreement, he could have. "And I will fulfil my end in turn. Now leave."

"Leaving now! Got it! Thanks so much!" Felicia pulled again, and this time I let her lead me away.

A few steps into our march to freedom Captain Verlak fell in step beside us. "I will accompany you to the east gate," she said, staring straight forward. "I wouldn't want you to get lost, after all."

"No, that wouldn't be good," I agreed. Felicia, perhaps for the first time in her life, decided keeping quiet was the thing to do. I agreed with her. I was petrified by how close we had come to failure, and elated to have carried the day despite that. It all added up to an exhaustion best served by staying silent. None of us spoke again until I saw Tango standing between two of Doom's guards, his hands and ankles bound but looking whole and healthy otherwise. His eyes lit up when he saw us, and I smiled.

"Sable, Black Cat! You're all right!"

"We are," I assured him, picking up the pace a bit to reach him. The sooner we were reunited, the sooner we could all get out of here. "What about you?"

"Oh, I'm fine," he said, shrugging as best he could with people holding tight to both of his arms. "It could have gone a little better, but…" As I got close, I could see his makeup was smeared in places, new bruises and swelling distorting the lines of his disguise. He'd definitely taken a few good punches to the face. "At least I didn't lose any teeth."

I laughed. "That's the spirit."

"You tough guys are so ridiculous sometimes." Felicia rolled her eyes. "Hooray, we're all fine, and justice is being served *cold* to the person who inspired our little misdemeanors, so let's get out of here already."

Captain Verlak undid Tango's restraints herself after giving her people a nod that apparently meant, "I've got this." "You would make a decent spy," she told him. "If you ever want to change your allegiance, you could find a place here. I assure you our terms are competitive."

I barely managed to keep my jaw from dropping, or my fist from lashing out. Trying to poach one of my people right in front of me, how *dare* she? It was very soothing for him to immediately reply, "I'm afraid my heart belongs to Symkaria," while glancing in my direction.

Captain Verlak actually *smirked*. "Just something to consider," she said. "The outer gate is open."

"Thank you." I led the way out, Felicia and Tango falling in behind me. As we emerged, the sun was just beginning to rise over Doomstadt, turning the sky purple as the stars began to fade. It was a new day, and we were free to do whatever we wished to with it.

We were free, and it felt good.

CHAPTER TWENTY-NINE

The cleanup after a job was oftentimes almost as hard as the job itself. There were so many things to sort out – locating all the extant equipment, tallying the expenses that had simply been charged while you were working, figuring out repair times, how long you'd need to regroup before the next job, and in this case: where the rest of your people were. Honestly, that was the only thing I cared about as we walked away from Castle Doom.

Boris and Bruno seemed to melt out of the shadows of a nearby alley. "Boss!" Boris called out, rubbing his hands together with glee. "How did they enjoy the show?"

"Your efforts were stunning, as always," Felicia replied with a grin. "The captain of Doom's guard was especially complimentary of your glitter formulations."

"Ha!" Boris turned and poked Bruno in the side. "I *told* you the titanium was worth it!"

Bruno rolled his eyes. "Yeah, sure, but did you have to melt down the valves in my Ferrari to get it?"

"You hate the Ferrari, don't pretend. It's not long enough for you to sit in the front seat without looking like your spine has been compacted like a crushed can, why would you–"

"That don't mean you get to pick through its parts for scrap that you can shove into your toy explosives when–"

"Boys!" Felicia let go of my arm and clapped her hands. "Argue later, focus now. Firstly, where are we staying?"

"Oh, you'll like it," Bruno said, sounding pleased as he led the way down a familiar street. "I took over the Foreigner's room after he got nabbed."

Wait, what? "You saw it happen?"

"Oh yeah. And with communication to you two cut, I needed something to do with my time." He shrugged. "So I took his room. It's prepaid through tomorrow, too."

"Didn't the LMD give you problems?"

Bruno chuckled. "Wasn't much of an LMD left after Doom's people got done with it."

The room he led us to was surprisingly charming, although I suppose it wasn't *that* surprising, considering all the doilies in Basil's New Jersey home. It also bore no signs that he, or his LMDs, had ever been ensconced here, although I could smell a fresh application of paint in some places, and some of the furniture seemed a bit scuffed.

"The people here are real fast when it comes to tidying up after a fight," Bruno said with an air of appreciation. "I moved our bags here from the plane."

"You're very confident that we were going to get out of infiltrating Doom's castle intact," Tango commented.

Bruno shrugged. "Boss has seen herself outta worse scenarios."

I had, too, but that was only evident to me in hindsight. It was a lot easier to fight terrorists on my own soil than it was to sneak into someone else's. I…

I was mentally rambling. "Let's get in touch with the rest of the Wild Pack," I said.

It only took a few minutes to get Juliet on the line, and when I did she had good news to report. "Sable!" she said as she looked up at me out of the screen, pushing a lock of purple hair back from her face. "We got them! We had to move early, the LMDs had become actively threatening, but we rescued X-Ray and Romeo and Ana! They're all OK."

I let myself slump onto the foot of the bed. It was one thing to be told by an outsider that my people were OK, but it really sank in when Juliet said it. "Thank god. You didn't have any issues getting to them?"

"A minor firefight, no injuries sustained, no civilians any the wiser," she affirmed. "Actually, hang on–" Juliet's face disappeared, replaced with Romeo's. He looked bushed – even his head appeared tired – but he also looked… peaceful.

"Sable." He cleared his throat. "Ah… listen, I'm – *we're* – so sorry about what happened in Vegas. We should have come to you, but…" He turned the phone, and I caught a quick glance of X-Ray lying on a bed with a little brown-haired girl in her arms, both of them sleeping soundly. The screen reoriented to Romeo. "It just seemed like too big of a risk, you know? Ana means everything to X-Ray, and–"

I held up a hand. "I understand. We'll discuss this when I get back to the embassy, all right?"

He blinked once, slowly. "You're not… firing us?"

"Well, not immediately." Perhaps not at all, but I wasn't sure of that yet. They had breached my trust, left me floundering when I needed to be strong, damaged my faith in them. I wasn't inclined to forgive that sort of treatment. On the other hand, Romeo was right when he pointed out that saving a child was about as good a reason as you could have for that kind of behavior.

"Just rest and recuperate. I'll be back soon."

Juliet took the phone back. "Where are you headed next, Sable?" she asked.

"To Symkaria, of course." I had a map to retrieve, after all.

"But – *oohhh,* right," she said in sudden understanding. "Got it. Foxtrot and I can handle cleanup stateside, don't worry about a thing."

That was unexpected. "You don't have to do that," I told her. "This probably won't take me all that long, and–"

"Actually," Felicia cut in as she shoved her face next to mine so Juliet could hear her, "it *is* going to take a while, because I've got to get back to the States and grab the book that'll crack the cipher in her map. So, you should feel free to wrap things up and then schedule yourself a little vacation, because I'm going to be keeping Silver busy for a while."

"Deal," Juliet said immediately. "As long as you make 'a while' into 'at least two weeks' so she takes a real vacation of her own for the first time in her adult life."

"I'm right here!" I snapped, offended at being ignored… and maybe a little touched. But that didn't matter. "And I have responsibilities to my people, and–"

"Oh no, our connection is breaking up, sorry!" Felicia ended the call before I could stop her, then dodged my subsequent backhand. "You need this break," she said from a few feet away. "You know you do. Stop punishing yourself and indulge for once."

"I agree," Tango said, looking at me intently. "You worked your butt off on this job."

"We all did," I said, and he shook his head.

"I'm not trying to downplay the roles the rest of us played in making it work, but this was your baby from start to finish. You made it real. You made it a success," he said. "Give yourself a chance to enjoy a job well done, Silver."

Well, when he put it that way... "I'll try," I said at last. "But no promises. And I still need to get to Symkaria."

"I'll join you there in a couple of days," Felicia promised me, looking pleased with herself. "And we'll finally get to the *fun* part of this escapade – the treasure hunt!"

CHAPTER THIRTY

I met Felicia coming off the plane, carrying a bag in one hand and a phone in the other. She was wearing a black minidress and super high heels, and I gave a silent sigh of relief as I squeezed my toes together in the ends of my combat boots. "Welcome to Aniara," I said.

"It looks surprisingly put-together from above," she told me, pushing her sunglasses up onto the top of her head as she joined me.

"Reconstruction efforts are ongoing, but we're doing fairly well." She didn't have Boris or Bruno with her, which seemed odd. "No henchmen today?" I asked as I led her toward my car, an ancient Peugeot that still ran as well as the day it was sold to my father.

Yes, I was allowed to bring a car onto the airport grounds. No, not a lot of other people could do that. Yes, I was willing to admit that I was spoiled in some ways by my homeland, but you couldn't say I hadn't earned it.

"Why, do you miss them?" she retorted with a smile.

Weeeell… "Maybe a little," I said, then opened the trunk

and motioned for her to throw her bag in the back. "Unless you'd rather keep it with you, or take the book you need out of it first."

"Oh!" Felicia actually broke into a genuine peal of laughter. "Ha, no, I didn't actually bring the book for the cipher *with* me! I just went home to get it out of storage!"

What? "Why not?" I demanded, putting my hands on my hips.

"Because you don't just walk around the streets holding a copy of the Gutenberg Bible in your hands," she replied, and my brain simply ground to a halt for a moment.

"You have… a copy of…"

"Yeah."

"But it's…"

"One of the rarest and most expensive books in the world?" She tossed her hair over her shoulder. Smugly. Everything she did was smug. "I know. That's why I left it with someone I trust. I'll relay the information from the map to her, and she'll help decode the cipher."

"*She*?" I didn't know that Black Cat's regular crew extended beyond Boris and Bruno, and I couldn't think of anyone else she trusted that much. Perhaps this was the mysterious Casey she'd mentioned before.

"You'll see," Felicia said, getting into the passenger seat and immediately putting it back as far as it would go. She was still a bit cramped, and it was my turn to smirk as she grudgingly kicked her heels off to the side. "So. Where do we start?"

"In the middle of downtown." I drove along the airport's service road, past a checkpoint where the guard had already raised the gate for me, and onto the roads of Aniara.

Symkaria's capital had been destroyed and rebuilt so many times since the Great War there was hardly any of the old architecture left. Most of it was a mix of styles and influences, with Latverian spires, German A-frames, Russian concrete, and even some Romanian Revival here and there. Occasionally something made of ancient, carved stone popped up, but most of the granite had been repurposed into gravel decades ago. Now the streets were made of cheap, easily pitted asphalt that was in a constant state of disrepair, slowing traffic to a crawl in the summer as roads were diverted again and again while potholes got patched up.

Felicia fanned herself with one hand as she stared out the window. "So. Everybody still on vacation?"

I made a slow left turn, gradually getting us closer to the central market plaza. "Yes. I figured they deserve it."

"Did you give X-Ray and Romeo the boot?"

"I gave them the option of leaving with a full severance package," I said, keeping my eyes on the road. "They both declined."

"Oh, *did* they now?" I felt her attention redirect to me, her gaze practically burning the side of my face. "And you let them do that? You didn't insist? After all that talk about divided loyalties and the fact that they could have gotten the rest of you killed and, oh yeah, the part where we had to break into *Doom's own house* to save their butts?"

I shrugged. "I'm giving them the opportunity to prove themselves. And," I added, "I put them in touch with someone who can guide them toward a safer situation for Ana. I can't tell my people not to have a life or a family, but I *can* help them keep their loved ones safer." It was a shift in my modus operandi, a major one, but I felt better for making it. I couldn't protect everyone no matter how much I wanted to, but my people weren't everyone. They were *mine*.

Felicia made a hmm-ing noise. "That's very accommodating of you. I've got to say, I'm surprised. You have a reputation for being such a taskmaster, and here you are giving away second chances."

"Even the thorniest rose still blooms."

"And you're the thorniest little rose I know," she cooed, then shrieked as I made a sharp right turn that almost smashed the side of her head into the window. "Hey!"

"Whoops."

I drove down the alley until we got to the edge of the plaza, Aniara's central market that stretched for five blocks along the city's original road, widened to make space for street vendors, box stores, and restaurants. At the very far side of it was the castle, a graceful and blood-drenched old abattoir that I had no intention of ever stepping foot in again. Luckily, that wasn't our starting place. There were several buildings in here that had been around when Black Fox was active in Symkaria, and our location of interest was actually not a building at all, but the bridge it was located next to.

"Here we go," I said, pulling the real map out of the inside of my jacket and handing it to Felicia as we approached the bridge. It was an elegant old thing, too small and fragile for cars, but perfect for a pair of pedestrians out for a stroll on a sunny day. The smell of roasting meat and hot flatbread from one of the nearby vendors wafted through the air to us, overpowering the sawdust and cement odor that was otherwise so prevalent.

"Thanks so much!" Felicia took the map out of my hand and peered at the page. "You're sure it starts here? This 'map' could start almost anywhere, given that it has nothing to do with normal geography."

"That's the one spot I could identify because of the bridge," I said. "He wrote down 'Sighs' here, and there's a homophone in Hungarian that means the same thing in Symkarian as—"

"All right, all right, no need to get all polyglot on me, I'm already impressed." She pulled out her phone and took a picture, zoomed way in, of that section of the map, then texted it to someone. Her co-conspirator, no doubt. Felicia pulled up a contact and pressed *send*, then put the phone on speaker. "That way you don't have to lean in and pretend you're not eavesdropping," she told me with a wink.

"I wouldn't have," I replied, knowing it for a complete lie.

"Yeah, right. You – hi, Mom!"

"Hi, honey!"

Wait. Mom? *Mom*? I mean, I knew that Felicia had a mother, I knew the lady lived in New York City, but... her *mother* was the woman she'd entrusted the Gutenberg Bible to? A book worth so many millions of dollars it would fund my team's operations for a decade, and she was letting her mother handle it? Hadn't the woman been a homemaker? What if someone found out she had it? What if they tried to rob her? What if—

"Mom, will you say hello to Silver before she has an aneurysm over here?"

"Oh, of course." Felicia tilted the phone toward me, and I saw a late-middle-aged woman with close-trimmed white hair, a soft, round face, and a beautiful smile looking out of it at me.

She looked ... well, she looked nothing like I remembered my own mother looking, but there was something about her, some aura or essence, that was quintessentially maternal. She was the dream of a mother turned to life, right there on the phone.

"You must be Silver! I'm Lydia, it's nice to meet you. Felicia's told me almost nothing about you."

"Mom!"

"It's just the truth, honey, get over it," her mother said tartly, and I laughed. It sounded a little wet, but nobody called me on it.

"It's very nice to meet you as well, Mrs Hardy."

"Just Lydia is fine," she said. "Now, if you girls will give me a moment to turn to the right page ..." A white-gloved hand rose briefly into view before Lydia turned to look at the book, which was just out of sight of the screen. "Let see, I've got to cross-reference it with the King James version, give me a moment ... ah, here we go. Hmm." She looked back at us. "It's about the Temple of Dagon."

"What's Dagon?" Felicia asked

"An ancient god," I replied.

She immediately started shaking her head. "OK, I love a treasure hunt as much as the next girl, but I absolutely draw the line at summoning ancient gods. I have *nothing* but trouble with them. I'm lucky I got away from the *last* supernatural pact Black Fox tried to drag me into, so–"

"He what?" her mother asked sharply.

Felicia mouthed a silent "oops." "Oh, you know him, always trying to make the next big score. It was nothing, just–"

"And how did he drag you into this 'nothing'?" Lydia

pressed. "Because I don't care what pocket of Hell that man is lodging in right now, I will grab him by the ear and pull him out, kick his butt, and throw him back in there for messing with my daughter like that."

"*Mom!*"

Aw, it was so sweet. But in this case… "Dagon is also the name of a town," I said, interrupting their budding argument. "It's about two hours from here. There's a famous medieval church there that might be the reference he's getting at."

"Only if it's a wealthy medieval church," Felicia said. "The Fox didn't have much use for religion, otherwise."

"It isn't wealthy *now*, but it once housed a statue of the Madonna made out of solid go– Oh." Oh, wait. I saw the pattern emerging here now. It was one I should have seen from the start. "It was stolen around the time the Black Fox was active here in Symkaria, but before I went after him," I continued. "I didn't really make headway with catching him until he went to New York to try to fence some of the things he'd stolen."

At which point Spider-Man, of all people, had helped that old fox escape justice. I'd gotten back some of the treasure he'd stolen, but it was clear he'd disposed of a lot of it before leaving the country. The Madonna, for instance, hadn't been in the loot recovered in New York.

Felicia looked thoughtful. "So, is he sending us to relive his greatest hits, or is there something more to this treasure hunt than meets the eye?"

"You knew him far better than me," I said. "And you and your mother are the only people capable of deciphering this map. What's his game?"

Felicia chewed on her bottom lip for a moment before glancing at the phone. "Mom?" This wasn't the voice of the supremely confident master thief I'd worked so much with over the past few weeks. This was a daughter, talking to her mother about someone they'd both cared very much for, once upon a time.

"I think you should see this through to the end," Lydia said pensively. "I'm honestly just as curious as you are to see what this might lead to, and even if it goes nowhere in particular, you'll still get to have a nice, relaxing trip with your friend."

I thought about correcting the misrepresentation of our relationship, but the words stuck in my throat. Felicia, after a glance at me, said, "Yeah, that's true. It's been a while since I've had a vacation myself."

"Well, there you go!" Lydia smiled, then said, "I'm not carrying this thing around with me, honey, so if you need something deciphered, be sure to text me with plenty of lead-time, all right? Otherwise I'll be at the farmers market for the rest of the morning."

"OK, Mom. Will you get me some–"

"Yes."

"And a, oh, you know what they're called, the ones with the pink and–"

"I will."

"You're the best. Love you, bye!"

"Love you, too, Felicia. Goodbye, Silver!" The call ended, and for a second it felt like my airway had been cut off.

I had rarely been jealous of Black Cat for anything before this. Not for her closer relationship with Spider-Man, not for her unending poise, not for her ability to brush off hardship like it meant nothing to her. Certainly not for her lifestyle – we were both jetsetters who sold our skills for money. I did feel a pang over her closeness with her crew, but I knew that I was on my way to developing that with my own people.

But right now? Seeing her sign off with her mother, watching the effortless ease with which she took for granted the woman's presence in her life, her love and assistance, I just had to wonder… what would my life have been like if my mother had lived? Would I even be able to recognize myself anymore? Would I have gone in a totally different direction, become a different person? It was too late for regrets, but a part of me still wondered.

"So." Felicia broke the silence. "Shall we go to church in the city named after a pagan god and hope for the best?"

I cleared my throat. "Sure. Why not."

The ride was pleasant, and very quiet once you got out of the city. So much of the working population of Symkaria had been drawn to the capital, first by the promise of work in the factories – which Countess Karkov and Norman Osborne had converted from farming supplies to weapons manufacturing – and then by the work rebuilding Aniara. The only people who remained in the country were either families who could sustain themselves, or older people whose children and grandchildren sent them money. So much of the landscape had been devastated by industry, but here and there a home or, in some cases, an entire village reflected the Symkaria that once was.

Or maybe I was deluding myself, and the peaceful nation

I envisioned had never existed at all. All I knew, all so many people knew within our own borders was constant struggle – against our neighbors, against foreign invaders who wanted to subjugate our people, against international corporation bent on subjugating our economy. It was all just so–

"It's pretty here," Felicia commented as she looked out at the sun, which was now close to setting over the Carpathian Mountains.

"It has a long way to go," I said, but a bit of pride resurfaced. Symkaria was small, but she was strong. "We should be at Dagon soon."

"Great. I'll look up a place to stay the night."

I jerked my thumb toward the boot. "I have a tent in the back."

"Does it come with running water?" she asked.

"Of course not."

"Then we're getting a hotel."

So prissy. Never mind that it had been a hot day and I wasn't exactly *bothered* by the thought of washing the dust of travel off in a real shower that night.

We got to the church just as the sun finished setting. It wasn't anywhere near as grand as the cathedrals of Paris or the temples of Srirangam, but the stonework was decidedly Gothic, the stones themselves hewn from black basalt. The small side entrance next to the three-meter-tall front doors was locked, but a minute of work with her sunglasses – which apparently broke down into lockpicks, I'd have to remember that trick – and we were inside a moment later.

It was far darker inside than it ought to be, even after sunset. I turned on my flashlight and illuminated where the windows should be. "Ah." They were boarded up in an effort to preserve the stained glass beneath them, which had worked... at least in a few cases. I shook my head, then turned toward the sanctuary at the far end of the church. "That's where the Madonna would have been."

We walked past the silent pews, wood stained dark in places from hundreds of years of humanity sitting and holding it, then past the altar and up to the wall where a small stone shelf sat, empty. It must have been gorgeous, gold bright against the black of the walls. So striking. Now gone, stolen to feed a thief's ego.

"These scratches in the stone..." Felicia leaned in closer. "Hand me your flashlight." I gave it to her. "Huh. I think they're..." She suddenly leaned back and laughed. "That old–I'm amazed he lived as long as he did without being struck down by some higher power. He carved a note into the wall."

"Of course he did." As I looked closer myself, I could see the lines she was talking about. They looked vaguely familiar. "Runes?"

"A variant. He made me learn all sorts of stuff when I was in training. I thought so much of it was useless." She shook her head. "And most of the time it is, but I guess it's coming in handy now. This says 'Find.' Which... OK, not very helpful."

"It's pretty on the nose for what we're already doing," I agreed. "Perhaps it's just one word in a sentence."

"Let's hope so. Otherwise it's just casual tagging, which – in a church?" She rolled her eyes. "And he was always so uptight about being 'classy.' How is this classy?"

It wasn't, but I didn't need to belabor the point anymore. "Let's go find a place to stay."

"Oh, I've got one booked!" Felicia spun on her heel and headed for the door. "Then we can call Mom and figure out the next clue."

We ended up in a converted barn, rather nice even with the pervasive smell of hay. After a quick shower and a meal with the family who'd listed the lodging, we ended up in a pair of twin beds, relaxing in pajamas while Felicia talked to her mother again.

"It's got to be this one… right? If we're correlating this to real locations in Symkaria, then–"

"Hold your horses, honey. Let me give you the actual verse first." Her mother turned some pages. "Hmm, looks like something in Isaiah. 'And I will give thee the treasures of darkness, and hidden riches of secret places–'"

"The mine!" I exclaimed. "The gemstone mine, on our eastern border. The Black Fox stole over a thousand carats in emeralds on his way through here, and plenty of diamonds, too. I got them back, but half of the stones reported missing never made it to New York." I had never trusted the manifest I got from the mine's owner – it had seemed ridiculously inflated, something I thought he was doing for insurance money, but perhaps he really *had* lost all those gemstones. "The mine has been shut down for over a decade," I added. Yet another loss to Symkaria. I wondered if it could be revived. Symkaria deserved to keep *some* of its treasures, even if we had to mine them all over again.

"Sounds like the perfect place for us to head to next," Felicia said. "Thanks, Mom!"

"Have fun, girls."

CHAPTER THIRTY-ONE

To my infinite surprise, the next few days actually *were* fun. Felicia was amusing company, and as we wound around the country from the emerald mine to an abandoned manor house to an industrial manufacturing facility, I actually learned some interesting tips on breaking and entering that might come in useful someday. Not that I wanted to be a thief, but you never knew when you were going to have to bluff your way through someone's first line of defense, and Felicia was excellent at bluffing. She also didn't dig into my soft spots the way I'd worried she might, limiting her personal questions to, "So, where's Tango? I wasn't sure we'd be able to pry him away from you at the end there."

"He's also on vacation," I said primly as I took a left turn. We were heading for the final spot on the map, which was a set of coordinates instead of a literary clue like the others were. I hadn't been back here since I was a child. I didn't even remember where my old house was – all I recalled of it was fire, but vague, misty recollections of the rest of the place filtered through my mind every once in a while. A tremendous apple tree in the town square, a single cobblestone street, the scent of fresh szarlotka in the air…

"Waiting for you?" Felicia pressed.

Yes. "Maybe," I said.

"Ha, I knew it!"

Time to change the subject. "What *I* want to know is what that message Black Fox left you really means," I said as I turned again. We were only a few minutes' drive from our destination, and I needed to focus to keep my mind from floating away with me. "*Find Your True Legacy*? What's that all about?" If she tried to sell me a line about this referring to *things*, I was going to smack her. Not hard, though.

Felicia smiled faintly. "It's something he used to say when he was feeling philosophical. The things we steal, the money and the gems and the tech – those are nice, but when it comes right down to it, what do we want to remember? What's our personal legacy? It's in the *doing*, not the having. The experience, the job itself and what you learn from it – *that's* the legacy for people like us. Money comes and goes, but I'll never have another chance to be with–" She cut herself off, then restarted a moment later. "I think this map is meant to show me the experience he had on one of his most epic jobs ever."

"So it's a brag in the form of a treasure hunt." How was I still propping up that old thief's ego after all these years?

"Hey," Felicia joked as I made my final turn, "at least there's treasure involved."

"Probably not, though," I said as my phone beeped. I parked the car and got out. "He probably cleaned out the cache here years ago, and we're just… just…" As my eyes adjusted to where we were, the breath abandoned my lungs.

I knew this place. I knew it. This wasn't just my old village, this was the place that had been my home. This was the place where my mother had died, where the entire arc of my life had changed. This should be a burned out, blasted wreck… or after all this time, at least retaken by the wilderness. Instead… there was a house here.

It was a little thing, more of a cabin than an actual house. It looked nothing like the place I had once lived, and yet seeing it made me flinch all the same. There was a building where my heart had once stood, and I was dizzied by its very existence. "What… what…"

"Let's go take a look, huh?" Felicia took my hand and led me down the overgrown path to the cabin's front door. "Hmm." She touched the doorknob. "An Integrator 5000 lock. Pretty good, even though they haven't been commercially available for years. I learned on one of these – I can get us through it." She pulled her sunglasses off her head, then looked at me. "That is, if you *want* me to open it."

"As if you would abandon the hunt now," I said hoarsely.

"I could at least do it sometime when you're not around," she replied with too much kindness. It made me uncomfortable to hear it.

I stiffened my spine. "Do it now." I would go into this place, I would face my old demons, and soon it would all be over. Felicia could go back to New York, I could fly to Mallorca where Tango was waiting for me – the next step in my first romance in a long time – and we could put this whole ridiculous mess behind us.

The lock was a good one. It took her almost a minute to break in, but when she did and the door opened with a little click, we both exhaled with satisfaction. Felicia opened the door, but I was the first one to step inside.

It was a single room, as I'd suspected. There was a table, a few shelves on the wall, and a basic kitchenette in one corner. There was no bed, and only one chair. Clearly not a place where Black Fox had intended to spend much time. It looked nothing like my old home, and I found myself relaxing a bit.

"Macabre of him to build a hidey-hole here," Felicia observed, swiping a finger through the dust on the tabletop. She walked around slowly, the space lit by a single window in the far wall.

"What did he want you to find here?" I asked, looking around. The walls were painted plain white and were bare except for one with a single photo in a round frame. "Was he a religious man?"

"No," Felicia said, joining me by the wall. "I mean, not seriously. He pretended to be one sometimes, to get close to a mark."

"Then why did he put a photo of a cross up on this wall?" It was a Greek cross, its arms all equal length.

Felicia stared for a moment, then grinned. "He didn't. The picture slipped. That's an X."

My jaw dropped. "You can't be serious."

"Even the Black Fox could give in to juvenile humor sometimes." She knocked on the wall. "Yeah, this is hollow. Let me go get the tire iron out of your car and we can–"

I leaned back, then lifted my foot up and kicked right

through the wall. *Smash!* I did it again, and again, until the hole was big enough for us to see into… and for the light to catch the gleam of gold glimmering on a statuesque head.

My breath caught again, this time for an entirely different reason. "The Madonna," I whispered, reaching into the ruins of the wall and pulling it out. The statue was dusty from being locked away, but it was nothing a bit of time wouldn't solve. I stared into the silent mother's face, her eyes downcast toward her child, and felt a wall inside my mind crumble.

"My little Silvinka." Warm lips press against my forehead. "People like your papa fight for the soul of our country, but it's our children who are the heart of our world. You are my heart, my whole world. I would do anything, give anything to make sure you're safe. Do you understand?"

"Yes, Mama." I reach up and touch her face with my tiny hands, and for the first time in years I can actually see her face. I can see the furrow between her eyebrows, and the tiny scar at the corner of her lip. I can see her bright eyes, full of tenderness as she looks at me, and trace the dimples that appear in her cheeks. I see the love she feels, and I feel it right back. "I love you."

"I love you, too, my darling."

"–kay, let's just sit down, hmm?" Careful hands guided me into the only chair, undoubtedly leaving my rear covered with more dust, but I couldn't bring myself to mind right now, not when my lungs were shuddering and my eyes were streaming tears I hadn't even felt come into existence. "I didn't know you felt so strongly about statuary," Felicia joked as she patted my shoulder.

"I usually don't," I said with a faint laugh, still staring at the

Madonna. "But this – for some reason, I got a flashback of my mother when I looked at it. I thought I had forgotten her face. But… I haven't." I looked around and, for the first time, wished I could see my childhood home again.

Perhaps that memory would return someday, too, if I stopped fighting so hard.

"Why do you think Black Fox built this here?" I asked as the image of my mother faded from my mind. I let it go, content in the knowledge that I could call it back whenever I wanted to. I wouldn't shove her away into a lockbox again. "Of all the places he could have picked…,"

"Oh, I'm sure it was deliberate," Felicia replied. "I mean, he had to know about your reluctance to have anything to do with your old digs. Of all the places in Symkaria, this is probably one of the best for evading the notice of the great Silver Sable."

I rolled my eyes at her. "Don't patronize me."

"I'm not!" she insisted. "And, ah, I think you should come over and look in the wall with me again. The Madonna isn't the only thing he left in there."

"What are you talking about?" I set the statue down on the table – it creaked with the added weight of the solid gold work of art – and went back over to the broken wall. Beneath the shattered pieces at the bottom of it were a series of burlap bags. We hauled them out into the main room, opened them up, and–

Emeralds, both polished and rough, emerged from over a decade of darkness. Diamonds, high-quality ones that the manufacturing facility we'd visited had listed as "industrial grade" in the exact amount that they claimed had gone missing during Black Fox's stealing spree. A collection of Scythian art and antiques that had been taken from the now-dilapidated manor house. And *gold*: gold coins, bars, jewelry, even a few gold bricks. I didn't know where it all came from, but Black Fox had clearly decided that this was the place to stash it for a later date.

"Incredible," I breathed. "There's so much history here, pieces of our cultural heritage I thought were lost."

"Not to mention another source of cash for Symkaria, if you want to go in that direction with it," Felicia said.

I looked at her. "Are you saying you're giving up all claim to this treasure?" It hurt, but… "I would never have found it if it weren't for you. It might have stayed hidden until the walls fell down around it, if your map hadn't brought us here."

"True, but remember what I said about legacies?" Felicia patted the pile of gold. "This horde is *your* legacy. Finding it? That was mine. Besides, half of this stuff will need to be repatriated to the original victims or their descendants anyway."

She was right. Not all of it belonged to Symkaria. Some of it Black Fox had taken from Nazis, who in turn had stolen it from its rightful owners during the Second World War. I wasn't even surprised that she brought it up – Felicia had a complicated but very strong sense of right and wrong, I had learned.

"Although," she added, picking up a golden choker set with emeralds and lapis lazuli from the pile, "I wouldn't say no to a finder's fee."

"I think we can do that," I said with a grin. "Still… that's a pretty small fee given all the work you put into tracking down

Tolentino in the first place. Are you sure there's nothing more I can give you?"

"Funny thing about catching Mr Tolentino," Felicia drawled as she stood up and held the choker up to the light. "It turns out the Clairvoyant *did* retain a little bit of juice for a few seconds after you took it off the guy. Not enough to get a real clear look, but I'd be lying if I said this wasn't one of the futures I'd caught a glimpse of. And as for the rest of it?" She winked at me. "I've gotta say, things are looking *real* bright.

"Now, I'm going to go move the car closer, so we don't have to haul a bunch of heavy metals farther than we have to!" She practically bounced out the door, leaving me surrounded with enough treasure that my poor little Peugeot was going to scrape the pavement every time we went over a bump. Cataloguing this find would take days, but I couldn't bear to just shove it into storage again while I swanned off to a tropical island vacation.

Perhaps...

Slowly, I reached into my pocket and took out my phone. I turned it on, called the first number in there, then held it up to my ear. Two rings later, the call picked up.

"Hey, Silvija." Tango's voice was warm, and slightly concerned. "Everything all right?"

"Everything is fine, just... how do you feel about meeting me in Symkaria instead of me coming to you?" I blurted out.

"I can do that, but... this isn't for work, is it?" I had promised I'd take a break from work, and he was holding me to it like I'd asked him to. Honesty between us was important, more important than ever given how many dishonest relationships

I had endured. I wasn't going to abuse his trust in me any more than he would abuse mine.

"No," I said, my eyes lingering on the Madonna again. "It's not. Something... good, but unexpected, kind of fell into my lap, and–" I swallowed and forced the next words out. "I want to share it with you."

"I'll be on the next flight."

I closed my eyes and let myself, for the first time in a long time, simply enjoy being happy. "I'll see you soon."

ABOUT THE AUTHOR

CATH LAURIA is a Colorado girl who loves snow and sunshine. She prefers books to TV shows, has a vast collection of beautiful edged weapons, and could totally survive in the wild without electricity or running water, but would really prefer not to. She loves writing speculative fiction of all genres, and has a long list of publications under her belt as romance author Cari Z.

authorcariz.com // twitter/author_cariz